THE BIG BUBBLE

BY THEODORE PRATT

Florida Novels

THE BIG BUBBLE

THE FLAME TREE

THE BAREFOOT MAILMAN

BIG BLOW

MERCY ISLAND

HANDSOME

MURDER GOES FISHING

MURDER GOES IN A TRAILER

MURDER GOES TO THE DOGS

General Novels

MR. WINKLE GOES TO WAR

MISS DILLY SAYS NO

VALLEY BOY

THUNDER MOUNTAIN

THE TORMENTED

COCOTTE

MR. LIMPET

MR. THURTLE'S TROLLEY

NOT WITHOUT THE WEDDING

SPRING FROM DOWNWARD

MURDER GOES TO THE WORLD'S FAIR

Short Stories

PERILS IN PROVENCE

THE
BIG BUBBLE

A Novel of the Florida Boom

Theodore Pratt

DUELL, SLOAN AND PEARCE
New York

AUTHOR'S NOTE

This novel is the third in a panel of books, each of which can be read as an independent unit, depicting the development of the southeast Florida coast. The first novel is *The Barefoot Mailman*, which tells of the initial event of significance that took place in the section following the Seminole and Civil Wars. This was the arrival, in the Eighties, of a substantial number of settlers. They made it necessary for mail to be delivered between Palm Beach and Miami, which was done by a carrier walking barefoot along the only road between the two points, the beach.

The second book, *The Flame Tree*, takes up the story a few years after *The Barefoot Mailman* leaves off. The next important thing to occur along the coast was the arrival of Henry M. Flagler with his railroad and string of grand hotels, particularly the immense Royal Poinciana at Palm Beach, the largest wooden building ever erected anywhere. Flagler established an era and a place for millionaires that has passed forever from the American scene.

Not many years after *The Flame Tree* closes came the first intimations of the Florida boom, the greatest land bubble in history. This was the fantastic acme of what started with the first settlers, making for the third book, *The Big Bubble*. A real-estate boom is a period of building, so this part of the story of the Florida coast is told largely in terms of an architect who influenced the country in an unexcelled manner. Except for the brief appearance of William Jennings Bryan, at this time a barker for the developing city of Coral Gables, there is no intention to represent any actual person, living or dead.

My Florida historical trilogy is now complete. In it my main purpose has been to try to present, with candid interest and deep affection, the spirit of an exciting and colorful period in what is perhaps the most unique section of our country. That time, from 1887 to 1926, a mere forty years, saw the section grow from a wild frontier to a luxurious civilization. My three stories are of its intense growing pains.

THE BIG BUBBLE

ADAM PAINE STOOD

on the sidewalk of the private drive in the inner court of the New Rochelle Arms apartment house and called up to the third story of the immense building. He didn't have to cup his hands around his mouth to make himself heard. His normal voice, raised only a little, boomed like a foghorn. "Eve!" he called. "Eve! Stick your head out!"

One of the windows on the third floor was raised. A handsome woman of perhaps twenty-five appeared, to lean out and look down with alert interest. She was dark-haired, with a clear white skin, big black eyes, and a full mouth. Pleasantly she inquired, "Why are you hollering out there like a fishwife, Tiny?"

She called him Tiny because he was so huge. A little more and he would have been abnormal, a giant. He stood six feet three in his socks. Almost everything about him was enormous, from his great torso to his head, which was covered with sandy hair usually uncut. His slightly florid face was heavy, with lines in it that made him look older than nearly thirty. Only his hands and feet were small. His hands were delicate and fine, with slender, pointed fingers. His feet did not seem large enough to hold up his hulk of two hundred and fifty pounds. He appeared to balance precariously on his undersized feet.

"I've just been paid my fee for the Wright building!" he roared. "I want you to see it."

"See it?" Eve demanded. "How can I read a check from up here?"

"It isn't a check!" he shouted.

"Then what is it?"

"I thought you'd notice."

9

Puzzled, she looked down at him. "I don't see anything. Except you should wear a hat, in winter at least."

"Look over my head, in back of me, at the curb," he advised.

She stared. On the drive stood a black Rolls-Royce phaeton. Its broad flat German-silver radiator gleamed in the bright, crisp January morning. Silver studs ran along the edges of the long hood. The large drum headlights were made of solid white metal. A glimpse could be seen of black leather seats within the custom-made body.

In a voice that expressed she was no longer amazed at much he did, Eve asked, "That's your fee?"

"Best one I ever had!" he boomed. "Come down and see it."

Eve closed the window and in a moment she came out of the building. She had thrown a gray herring-bone coat over her shoulders against the chill. Standing alone, she looked tall, and was, being nearly six feet. She carried her height well, with grace. As she went forward and joined Adam she seemed to shrink in contrast with his size, and by illusion she became only medium height.

Gazing at the car, she said, "I should have known that you and a Rolls would come together some day."

Adam chuckled. He sounded like a gurgling waterfall. "After Frank Wright's company went into bankruptcy he told me he'd pay my architect's fee if he had to do it out of his own pocket. I accepted, and this morning he paid off. He's liquidating, a tycoon being shrunk down to size, though he says he'll come back some day. He asked me if I'd take his Rolls instead of money. You can see what I told him." Adam's blue eyes gleamed with satisfaction; he was vastly pleased with his transaction.

"What did you do with the Buick?" Eve asked.

"Well, I'll tell you: I let Wright have that—for being an honest man—not many about these days. And he needed something to get around in."

"You mean," observed Eve, "you didn't want to be bothered with it. It would have interfered with the little boy's fun in his new toy."

"Look at it," he exulted. He took her by the arm and pulled her around the car, pointing out its smart wire wheels, with two extra, complete with tires, one mounted on each side forward of the front door. He opened the door and exhibited the luxurious interior, dwelling upon the right-hand drive with its four speeds forward.

Hardly letting her see the inside, he dragged her to the front of the car where he said, "I want you to meet the Lady."

A six-inch-high figure of a woman, made of German silver, was mounted on the radiator cap. The Lady's long skirts blew back against her shapely little legs, and from her shoulders sprouted graceful silver wings.

"How do you do?" Eve told her, bowing.

"They call the whole car the Silver Ghost," Adam explained. "We'll call it the Ghost." He paused, then said, "Eve."

She turned to him, at the new tone he used. His voice became low. He sounded serious, always slightly unusual in him. She acknowledged her recognition of the fact that he had something important to say by asking quietly, "What is it, Tiny?"

He waved at the New Rochelle Arms. "Let's get out of this rat trap."

"You mean the most expensive apartment house in Westchester County?"

"Look," he said, "they won't let me build what I want to around here. Spanish stuff doesn't fit the landscape or climate, anyway."

"Well," she said, "congratulations."

"I know I've been stubborn about that. But now I can see I was wrong. I want to go to some place where my ideas will fit."

"For instance?"

"Florida. Probably Palm Beach. They say you don't have to wear a hat there at any time. It came over me suddenly that that's where I belong. The war's over, or at least Wilson says he got himself an Armistice last November. People haven't been able to go to Europe. They've been going to Florida and they like it. From what I've heard things are going to happen there."

"But you've never been there," Eve protested. "How can you be so sure so quickly?"

A slight impatience came to his deep voice. "I've got imagination, haven't I?"

"Lots of that, Tiny." She studied him candidly, and inquired softly, "When do you propose leaving the rat trap for Palm Beach?"

"Now. Today," he said without hesitation. "If I had my way we wouldn't even go in the apartment for our clothes, but just board the Ghost and start out."

11

She didn't protest again, but merely reminded, "We're playing auction with the Dunhams tonight."

"Eve, don't be funny." He was annoyed with such a small consideration.

She searched his face. The crinkles around his mouth and eyes had flattened out. Most evidences of his great enjoyment of life had disappeared. A slight desperation had taken their place.

She stated, "Adam, you want this."

"I need a change. A big one."

"All your changes are big." She looked away, to consider.

It began to snow. The large flakes dropped lazily on the canvas top of the Rolls and melted almost as soon as they fell. On Eve's dark hair they stayed, powdering it. She turned and left the Ghost, going into the apartment house, followed by Adam. "This change is pretty impulsive, Tiny."

"Do you remember the first impulsive thing we did?" he reminded. "I've never regretted it, and I don't think you have, either."

She didn't speak as they entered the automatic elevator, closed the door, and he punched at the button for the third floor. As they got out and entered their apartment she said, "Somebody's got to think a little about this."

"You go ahead and think," he said. "But don't take too long or we won't get very far today. To save time I'd better pack."

"What if I decide against it?"

"All I ask," he growled, "is that when you come with your husband, you do it without telling the Dunhams or the management of the rat trap. We just walk out."

He went into their bedroom and closed the door. She could hear him moving about. She caught the sound of a suitcase clasp unsnapping, then another.

She had an instant of rebellion against his high-handed tactics. Then she thought of what he had said about the first impulsive thing they had done together.

That had been the night they met, at a party in Pelham Manor. For nearly a year she had been hearing about Adam Paine. People told her, "You ought to meet him." When she asked why, they said, "For one thing, he's Adam and you're Eve."

"Cute," she replied without enthusiasm. "Why else?"

12

They looked at her height, then, and hesitantly suggested, "Well, he's over six feet. He'd . . ."

"Fit me?"

"You can't say you're a midget."

She had always been annoyed when urged to meet someone and being assured that she would be crazy about him. Every time that happened it turned out that she took an instant, and often violent, dislike to the person. She was sure it would be the same with Adam Paine, and therefore avoided rather than sought a chance to meet him. She knew that he was a stage designer and an architect of sorts. She had seen his photograph in the papers; she wasn't sure she liked his looks. He appeared to be gross and dissipated.

At the Pelham Manor party she was dragged to meet him. People clustered about to witness the meeting of Adam and Eve. She was fully prepared to loath him. In the face of the big man, whom she recognized immediately, she saw the same expectancy.

They had exactly the opposite effect on each other. They went still, and stared. They were both surprised. They paid no attention to people shouting at them. They didn't hear them, but only each other.

"Hello, Eve."

"Hello, Adam."

He held out his arms in an invitation to dance. She went into them. In spite of his size, he was graceful and light on his tiny feet. She couldn't get over his height. All her life she had been made to feel ungainly and too long because most other people were so short. She knew how to stoop to get down to their level. She was practiced at sitting as often as she could instead of standing. This man made her feel small. He made her feel fine.

She had glanced at his face. It was intent on her. It didn't look gross or dissipated. His expression was that of a man who had found something he had long sought.

They danced three consecutive dances without saying much. Once in a while they looked at each other. By now he had a silly grin on his face which he didn't try to hide. She was smiling and couldn't close her lips. She was glad she had on her wine-red evening gown cut low to show a little more than a hint of her breasts.

He took her out in the garden. There was no question about her

13

going. He had her arm firmly in his and she went. She wanted to go. They stood, close, in the soft, dimly lit night, and he said, "You first."

She knew what he meant. She told him, "I commute to New York to work at textile designing. I do the patterns, draw them, for various fabrics. That is, I originate the designs. It sounds important. It isn't. I make a little money and am a small cog in a large organization. I like it. I like design. I once had a potter's wheel and made bowls and vases which I decorated. I enjoy working with my hands. That's why I'm happy in what I'm doing." She hesitated, then gave him the essential fact he wanted, "I'm all alone. I haven't even any family."

His question was a demand. "Ever been in love?"

She looked straight at him and told him seriously, "Not the way I've wanted to be." She tried to keep any meaning from her voice that now, here, perhaps she was.

"That all you got to say for yourself?"

"It's enough."

He shook his large head. She noticed that he needed a haircut. "It will take me a lot longer," he said.

"Go ahead."

"I'm out of Texas," he rumbled. "I guess that accounts for my size; a lot of things are pretty big down there. I've got family somewhere—I don't mean a wife—but we broke up, and I couldn't tell you where they are or what they're doing. As a kid I saw the Alamo. Usually that makes a Texan boy decide to be a soldier. It made me want to be an architect. I got to New York and went through Columbia while I worked as a draftsman. I saved enough to get to Paris and take the examination for the Beaux Arts. That's the Holy Grail for architects. You need that to be thought really good —even if you aren't. Nearly five hundred take the entrance exam and only about fifty or sixty are taken. I was taken. I stood their damn academic traditions for two years, mostly because Paris was —well, fun. Then I tried to be original. They don't want that. You've got to conform. That isn't in me. I rebelled. I told them to go to hell. I told them to stick it. They'll say I was kicked out of the holy Beaux Arts, but I got out under my own steam. I barged around Europe, doing anything, bartender, guide, spieler on rub-

14

berneck wagons, sketch artist, photographer, snooper on confidential matters—meaning getting the goods on people for divorces, both male and female. I was a prizefighter in Rome. I designed a night club in Madrid. Mostly it was in Spain. That's where there's architecture. Buildings, doorways, towers, inns, monasteries, cloisters, woodcarving, ironwork, tile—God! I'll tell you sometime, maybe show you. I spent a couple of years in Spain just looking, sketching, and collecting drawings and pictures. Then I came back to New York. Without the damn Beaux Arts official stamp, I didn't get far. I could work as a draftsman. I worked in the theater, designing sets. That got me to know people with money, some of them important. They let me do some houses for them, not many, but some. They're good houses. But the careful people, the conservative people, still fight shy of me. They say I'm not solid. Who the hell wants to be solid? I'm a Maverick. You know what a Maverick is? An unbranded steer, not of the herd. I go my own way. I want you to know that, because I've never been in love, either—until now."

"Now?" she asked.

"You know what I mean. Don't pretend you don't. Forget all the stuff that leads up to what we both want. We don't need to waste time on it."

"No," she whispered, "I guess we don't."

He kissed her, then. She had been kissed by other men, but never stirred like this. She was lost in his huge arms. She felt giddy. Her head whirled. She began, instinctively defensive, to suspect him. She stopped almost immediately when she felt his heart beating against her, racing so fast that it shook her. It was like a big, rapidly working, excited pump.

Their lips parted, though they still held on to each other, almost desperately. They stared. It was hard to believe. They hadn't known each other a full hour.

"We'll get married tonight," he declared.

"Oh, no! We don't know each other at all."

"We know enough."

"I've got to think."

"How long do you have to think?"

"Several months—a few weeks, at least—a couple of days, cer-

15

tainly—why," she pleaded lamely, "I shouldn't be saying I'm even considering marrying you at all."

They were married at five o'clock the next morning by a sleepy Justice of the Peace in Greenwich, Connecticut. The friends from the party who went with them said they weren't sober, but that was only because these people failed to be. Adam and Eve were completely in control of all their faculties. Each knew fully what he was doing and by then was sure of himself. After congratulating them, their friends told each other privately it wouldn't last six months.

It had lasted three and one half years. And Adam's status as a married man with an attractive wife made him seem solid enough so that he could give up theatrical work entirely and live well off doing houses and business buildings. He made money and a certain reputation. He had an office and a regular staff.

Eve, sitting on the couch of their living room in the New Rochelle Arms, thought back fondly on their first impulse. As Adam said, she never regretted it, even during his rages, which she had come to understand and accept as a part of him. Not even his body was massive enough to contain all his feelings. Sometimes they effervesced and overflowed onto those about him. That wasn't always pleasant. But he got over his quick tantrums. Occasionally he apologized.

The door of the bedroom opened. Adam appeared, carrying several suitcases. He dumped them on the floor and went back for two more. He returned a third time to drag out a small steamer trunk. Neither of them kept possession of many clothes; she had more than he; it was rare when he had three great baggy suits.

"Well," he demanded, "done all that thinking you do? Are you ready?"

Eve stood up. "Tiny, I don't care about the Dunhams or the rat trap. But you've forgotten something else."

He scowled. "What?"

"Your office."

"I'm closing it."

"Aubrey Sheppard has been your chief draftsman for a long time."

"I'll send for him later."

"And meanwhile keep paying him and give the others two weeks' salary."

"All right on the first. I suppose so on the last."

"Then, as soon as I look in the drawers and closets to see what you've left behind, I'm ready."

He hadn't been entirely sure until now that she would agree. His face lighted. The crinkles came back to the corners of his eyes and mouth. He strode to her and put his arms about her and picked her up and kissed her, roaring, "Good girl!"

"Put me down!" she cried. "Put me down, you big lug!"

It always made her feel small when he did that. She loved it.

ADAM DROVE THE

Ghost on a narrow red-brick road. The car sagged slightly on the right-hand side because of his weight, far from evenly balanced by that of Eve beside him. Close on their left was the Indian River. The Dixie Highway skirted the broad, long lagoon for miles. On either side grew palms, hibiscus, and sometimes orange groves hacked out of the dense growth; here golden fruit hung heavily from bending, laden branches. The top of the phaeton was folded back and the sun was warm, the sky as blue as Adam's eyes.

Eve, pleased herself with Florida, asked, "Is it what you expected?"

Adam had kept looking first to the right, and then to the left as he drove. Once he nearly ran off the road. Eve had never seen him so entranced. "It's like Spain," he muttered. "At least, the sun and some of the vegetation. It's much more lush here. I wish it wasn't so flat. But I can take care of that by giving different levels to the houses themselves."

Already he was seeing houses he would design for the landscape and terrain.

The whirring, muddied wheels of the Rolls had passed many hitchhikers. At the sight of the first ones Adam wanted to pick them up. "Might be some good characters to talk to," he said. Eve, more cautious and practical, objected, recalling stories in the newspapers about motorists who had picked up hitchhikers only to be robbed and sometimes murdered.

Now ahead they saw another man standing on the side of the road waiting to be picked up. A hard straw hat was placed at a jaunty angle on his shapely head. He looked well dressed and dapper. He had no luggage. As they approached he grinned, show-

18

ing dazzling white teeth in a winning smile. At the same time he lifted one hand and then the other, thumbs held up and gesturing in the direction they were going.

"How about him?" Adam asked.

Eve shook her head.

They passed the man who, instead of scowling at them as had most of the others, clasped his hands, held them high, and shook them. Eve, looking back, saw the man unclasp his hands and wave gaily to her. Suddenly she felt sorry for him.

"Let's stop," she told Adam.

He glanced at her and then pressed both foot pedals while he took the Ghost out of fourth gear and brought it to a stop. The car had only begun to slow down when the man started running toward them.

Adam didn't have to reach around and open the rear door. Breezily, the man did it himself and climbed in quickly, shoving a suitcase to one side to make room for himself on the back seat. At the same time, before they could say anything, he announced, "I knew you'd stop for me. I could see you're my kind of people. The car, you know. A Rolls means something." He settled back comfortably.

As he started the car forward again, Adam asked, "What does it mean?"

"Why, people who travel in a Rolls aren't clods," was the glib reply. "They've got money. This job cost you from eight to ten thousand dollars. Usually they're society, too."

"Tell him," Adam instructed Eve.

Eve began to explain who they were, wondering a little crazily why she did so to this self-assured total stranger they had picked up.

He interrupted her. "Of course! I thought there was something familiar about you. So you're Adam Paine. I've seen your stage sets and admired them—they're very dramatic and effective. And I've been in some of your houses. You have great talent, Mr. Paine."

Dryly, Eve asked, "You don't mind that we're not wealthy society?"

He forgave them magnanimously. "It doesn't matter in the least."

He grabbed at his straw hat as the car gathered speed. One side of the brim gave way, parting from the crown. The man didn't regard this ruefully. Cheerfully he said, "It has done its good duty, seen its day," and then he tossed it out. The wind ruffled his sleekly parted brown hair. His suit, seen closer, was neat and clean, but threadbare; his white shirt was frayed at collar and cuffs.

Without looking around, Adam requested, "Let's have you."

Eve could detect no hesitancy in the man's voice when he said, "My name is Gerry Vance," but Adam must have noticed something, for he asked, "Is that your real one?"

He wasn't offended at all when he answered, "Yes, indeed."

Adam chuckled.

Eve observed, "My husband doesn't seem to believe you."

"Oh, I'm sure he does, Mrs. Paine," he replied smoothly. "I'm certain it isn't in Mr. Paine's nature to be skeptical of such matters."

This time Adam laughed outright. "More," he said. "And as right as you can make it."

"As right as rain," Gerry promised. "I'm a salesman, really a promoter, mostly of real estate. I've been in some pretty big things, in California, on the Jersey shore, Long Island, many places. I can sell anything, as long as it can be made to sound big, even if it isn't." He lowered his voice, taking them into his confidence. "Right now I'm between things. I've been in New York for the past year selling oil stocks."

"Were they any good?" asked Adam.

"Not very." Both he and Adam seemed to find this amusing.

"Do you mean," Eve asked, "they were fake?"

"Of course I didn't know that at the time," Gerry assured her. "Not until recently, when I was asked to desist from selling them."

"Talk your way out of it?" asked Adam.

"It left me hoarse," admitted Gerry. "And without funds." He and Adam laughed.

Eve twisted about in her seat and inquired accusingly, "You were told to get out of New York or be arrested?"

"Oh, nothing like that, Mrs. Paine," he assured her. "There was nothing really wrong, simply a misunderstanding. It was merely suggested that I spend the winter in Florida."

Eve now was sorry that she had taken pity on him. She wished they could get rid of him.

"I can't see you from up here," Adam said, "but from the way you talk it sounds as if it's a little out of the side of your mouth. I'll bet you've worked carnivals."

"Specialized in barking cootch shows," Gerry admitted readily. "I spent most of my boyhood on midways. It was my schooling. It prepared me well for the higher and better things of life."

"What's on your mind now?" Adam inquired.

"I smell things in Florida. It's a coming country here, for it has an incomparable climate. Up to now it's been mostly a place for millionaires. That's the way it was first promoted, by Flagler and Plant. But now there's such a thing as the automobile, to bring the common man. There's more general wealth, too, after the war, more people with money and leisure. They're going to come here. The land will become valuable. I wouldn't be surprised if it is subdivided many times, with large profit for all."

Adam and Eve looked at each other. He nodded to remind her that he had told her something like this himself. He asked Gerry where he was going.

"I thought first of Miami," Gerry said. "And undoubtedly things will be big down there. But I like class. I think I'll make the Palm Beaches my headquarters." When Adam said that was where they were going, Gerry exclaimed, "Excellent! That's exactly where you belong, too, Adam." The familiarity slipped easily off his tongue. "You'll do big things here; you'll fit the country. We need people like you in Florida."

"Mr. Vance," Eve asked, "have you ever been to Florida before?"

"Not physically," he said, "but spiritually Florida and I can be said to be identical twins."

"Wonderful!" cried Adam. "Gerry," he said, "do many think and plan as we do?"

"Only a few," Gerry told him, "here and there. It takes a keen sense for these things. You have to feel it in your bones. It isn't going to come right away, and I shall have to wait patiently, until the clods catch up. But when it does come, mark me that it will be big, perhaps the biggest thing ever."

"I hadn't thought of it exactly as you do," Adam told him. "As a matter of fact, I was thinking more along the lines of millionaires. I'm planning on mansions, not houses for the masses."

"Oh, there will be room for you, Adam," Gerry assured him. "Plenty of room. It will be just as big for you in your way as it will be for me in mine."

"Thanks," said Adam. "You're very kind."

"Not at all," Gerry said.

They both roared with laughter. Eve wasn't altogether sure what they were laughing at. She was certain that she did not like the slick man they had picked up.

They stopped at a restaurant in Stuart for lunch, but when the Paines got out of the car, Gerry stayed where he was. "Actually," he said, "I don't believe I'm hungry."

Adam regarded him. "I didn't realize you were that flat."

"Pancake flat."

"Get the hell out of there and come in and have some lunch," Adam ordered him gruffly.

Gerry asked, "Mrs. Paine doesn't mind?" By his question he acknowledged her disapproval of him.

Eve felt a momentary compassion that didn't last long. "Of course not," she said.

Gerry got out of the car and went around to the front, where he unscrewed the radiator cap with the figure of the Lady on it.

"What's the idea?" Adam demanded.

Gerry slipped it into Adam's capacious pocket. "You'll have it stolen on you if you don't do that. I'm surprised you haven't had it taken before. People think the figures are made out of solid silver."

"I expect you know a lot of useful things like that."

"Honest men," Gerry replied, "must know a little more than dishonest, so as to keep ahead of them."

Adam clapped him on the back, nearly knocking him down.

After lunch, on the way again, Gerry wanted to know where they were staying. "Of course, wherever it is, it's in Palm Beach, not West Palm Beach where the plebeian people live."

"You're a snob," Adam accused.

"One of the best."

"We're going to the Royal Poinciana," Eve said.

Gerry nodded his handsome head. "Very proper."

"You'd better stay a few days with us there," invited Adam, "until you can make some connections."

Gerry glanced at Eve, who looked straight forward and didn't say anything. "Most kind of you," Gerry murmured.

"And you won't make any connections in that down-at-the-heels outfit you've got on," said Adam. "In fact, I won't take you to the Poinciana that way. We need some summer clothes ourselves, so we'll stop in West Palm Beach and we'll all get some."

"You are my benefactor," Gerry acknowledged, "my dear and valued Maecenas."

"A sideshow barker talking about the patron of Horace and Vergil?"

"I read a book once."

In West Palm Beach, on the narrow busy main street where they parked, they entered a small department store. While Eve searched for light dresses, the two men looked over and chose white flannels and jackets. Gerry, accoutered and looking smart, fingered a new hard straw hat, looking beseechingly at Adam. "Put it on," he was told, and Gerry clapped it on his head. It fitted, a precaution about which he had already seen.

"I think," he said, "it will be best for me not to accompany you to the Poinciana. My place, at least for the moment, is over here."

Adam regarded him. "You sure about that?"

Gerry glanced swiftly toward the door and then back again. "I hope you don't mind if I thank you quickly and tell you that some day the bread you have cast upon my waters will be returned many fold."

Adam looked at the door in time to see a woman turning away and then walking out slowly; she wasn't at all pretty, but she was very well dressed.

Gerry put his hand on Adam's arm. "Please say goodbye to Mrs. Paine."

Adam watched him go and disappear into the crowd as Eve joined him, carrying several packages. "Where's the big promoter?" she asked.

"He decided to stay here."

"Tiny, if you wanted him I hope my attitude didn't stop you. Or discourage him."

"It wasn't that."

"What did he touch you for?"

"Only the clothes."

Eve stared. "What will he do?"

"Oh, he'll sell somebody something."

"He hasn't anything to sell."

"He'll find something."

"But what?"

Adam did not answer directly, or right away, as they made their way out of the store. Then he said, "Good-looking fellow, isn't he?"

Eve was startled and a little shocked. "You mean he'll sell himself to a woman?"

"Fetch a good price, too, with his looks."

They got in the Rolls. "Adam," she said, "before we met—those years you spent in Europe—did you ever do that?"

"On a few extremely rare occasions," he answered, "when no other financial opportunities presented themselves, and to keep body and soul together I—"

"Don't say any more."

"I was going to say I contemplated the proposition, but finally turned it down."

"I'll bet Mr. Gerry Vance likes to do that."

"I don't think so," Adam rumbled. "I believe, speaking from the limited experience of my temptations, that it is done only in desperation when he is really on his uppers. Something tells me he'd rather sell real estate than anything else."

"Or fake stock to innocent people."

"I know it's hard to believe," Adam said, "but the Gerry Vances have their place in this life, if only because they often have vision to the future."

Eve shivered. "Let's go, Tiny. Let's see this Palm Beach."

WEST PALM BEACH

was a small commercial city. It serviced, across Lake Worth, which was a quarter-mile wide continuation of the Indian River, a community more purely resort than any other in the world. Created by the multimillionaire Henry Flagler, once no automobile was allowed to smell up its expensive air, vehicles being limited to bicycles and wheelchairs. Palm Beach was like a place near the United States, an exclusive foreign colony, a desired spot created not for people merely to exist but devoted entirely to pleasure. To partake of its delights you had to be either a near or actual millionaire, or a bonafide member of society, preferably both. There had never been anything even remotely like this.

Adam and Eve crossed to it on a wooden bridge whose one side was occupied by railroad tracks leading to the great hotels in the resort. As the Rolls passed over the water they saw, directly to the south on the lake shore, an immense wooden building painted lemon yellow with a white trim. It was the largest wooden building ever built anywhere, so long and extended that it was nearly unbelievable. Looking at it you were sure that a person at one end viewed from the other would appear to be slightly over the horizon, his feet invisible behind the curvature of the earth. It was six stories high, set in extensive gardens in which grew many kinds of palms.

"Good God!" exclaimed Adam. "What's that?"

"I'm sure it's the Royal Poinciana," said Eve.

"I don't believe it. I don't believe what I'm seeing," Adam declared. "Nothing can be that monstrous."

"It looks sweet."

"Sweet! That yellow wooden Victorianism! Maybe in its day it was wonderful stuff, and probably was. But that wasn't less than a quarter of a century ago, something over from the looks of that useless ornamental gable. Look at that steep roof! Do they think it snows here to need that pitch to run it off? A Northern architect did that, you can be sure, and didn't even look at his country here while he did it. They ought to put a match to the place. It offends the eye and the landscape."

"It must be awful to be ahead of your time," Eve said.

"Painful, when I have to look at a thing like that." A thought struck Adam. "And live in it! Can't we go some place else? I think I'd get sick to my stomach there."

As they drove off the bridge into Palm Beach, Eve saw a white building on their left. She began to recognize distinctive landmarks from pictures. "That must be Bradley's, or the Beach Club, the famous gambling place. It's beautiful, Tiny."

Adam examined Bradley's swiftly. "No, it isn't. Not that. It looks like a couple of barns brought together and mated in the hope they would give birth to a few outhouses, and did. Not any of these buildings are beautiful, Eve. I speak with simple good taste."

"I mean Palm Beach."

Adam didn't turn into the driveway leading to the Royal Poinciana, but kept on toward the ocean. To the right, across a golf course, was another hotel. "I think that's the Breakers," said Eve. "It wouldn't be any better staying there, because that's wood and painted yellow, too."

"Flagler must have owned a paint factory that made nothing except yellow paint."

They drove to the beach, which they saw was magnificent. Adam couldn't say the same of a line of frame shingle cottages built along the shore. Disgustedly, his judgment was, "Practically Eighteen Ninety stuff. And I've read that these right here are occupied by the very best people. I always knew the rich are soft in the head."

He left the cottages hurriedly, as though not wanting to stay in their proximity longer than necessary. They drove about Palm Beach, taking it in, looking and gawking, rubbernecking unashamedly.

"You've got to admit," Eve pointed out, "that the vegetation is wonderful."

Adam's eyes were darting to right and left. Sometimes he glanced back, as if to see something he had missed. Now he glared at the carefully nurtered bushes, hedges, lawns, and palms they were passing. Grudgingly, he conceded, "In a certain manicured way. But why does everything have to be so perfect, so clipped? So neat and subdued? Can't they let a bush have its own way a little? Can't they leave one blade of grass to grow the way it wants to? Don't they know there's beauty in naturalness? Can't they understand this is artificial and unreal?"

"Do you want answers to those few questions?" Eve asked.

"I don't want answers," he replied testily. "Because we already know them. And I've got another question that answers itself. Why is everything made of wood? Don't they realize this is stone country? Any hot or even continually warm place should be, for coolness. Houses here should be built of stone or at least hollow tile."

He had turned off the main road and gone back in the direction of the lake on a street north of where they entered. On the lake shore they now came upon a large, low, square building occupied entirely by smart shops. In the center, on the second floor, was a small movie theater which advertised Eva Tanguay in *The Wild Girl*. Eve exclaimed at seeing Bonwit Teller, De Pinna, and Arnold Constable. The place was called the Fashion Beaux Arts. They circled it.

"At least that's stucco," Adam grumbled. "Terrible, but not wood." He drove away from the Beaux Arts as though it reminded him of the institution of the same name in Paris. "As far as I can see," he raged, "Palm Beach has no architectural viewpoint or integrity at all. Nothing in the place has been built for the country or the climate. They've used Northern models, importing them and inflicting them where they don't belong. It's crazy and insane and awful. It makes me want to spit."

He let go over the side of the Rolls-Royce. His plentiful liquid ammunition narrowly missed a beautifully groomed and aristocratic-looking couple seated in a wheelchair being pedaled by a Negro in knickerbockers. The couple looked shocked; the Negro rolled his eyes.

Eve said, "I hope they aren't prospective house clients."

It was Adam Paine's first contact with the people of Palm Beach.

"You really like it, don't you?" asked Eve.

"Like it?" he demanded. "I abominate it! I have never seen such senseless bad taste in my life. Cupolas went out with bustles! This turning-lathe ornamentation! This fricassee Queen Anne! This— this . . ." He couldn't find another word to castigate it.

Eve giggled. "You wouldn't be so excited if you weren't crazy about Palm Beach, if it weren't everything you wanted it to be and even more. I've never seen you like anything so much, Tiny."

He began, "I don't—"

She turned to him on the seat of the car and stated, "You can't fool me, little boy."

"I—" He stopped and shot her a look. "How do you know me so well?"

"Call it love."

"Damn you, woman, I'm not sure I want anybody knowing me that much. Sometimes I think you know me better than I know myself."

"Who knows himself?"

"Are you going to be a philosopher on me?"

"Only a wife."

"That's better. You won't ever get smarter than I am, will you?"

"I won't show it."

"Evie, if I ever want to give you up, will you shoot me?"

"I'd be glad to. Thanks for the invitation."

He waved one of his small, graceful hands at Palm Beach. "You're right. Outside of the houses, which are so bad they offer a great chance for something better, this place has got everything." As he drove the Ghost erratically, the words tumbled out of him in a near shout; he seemed to crackle uproariously with them.

"Listen, Eve, this is the damnedest place ever for what I want to do. More than everything is right—that lake on one side, the ocean on the other, making this a reef, little different from those of the South Seas. That ocean out there, with the Gulf Stream so near you can see it bucking the waves—why, damn it, I want to build houses on it, right down to the surf line; I've got an idea how to break the force of it in storms so it won't eat away what I build."

He thought about that for an instant, then rushed on:

"Even the air is right. Feel it." He reached out and grabbed a handful of it. "Breathe it!" He took several deep breaths. "You

28

don't get air like that everywhere. It's soft, warm, it's right. Look at that sky and see a Spanish tower thrown against it. Let that sun touch you and know you can shut it out inside a high dim room with a tile floor—then you've got the sun and escape from it, both, by walking a few feet. Can't you see a barrel-tile roof against coconut palms? It's a combination you can't beat. Put up a high masonry wall and then plant hibiscus along it. And color, color, color, above all, is needed, not that bilious yellow, but pastels, cool stuff that's nice to look at. I'll build pink houses, Evie, pink and blue and green and brown and even white—you can't beat white in a bright dazzling country like this."

He looked across the road they were traversing to an open field where tall, sprawling trees grew. "Those trees!" he yelled. "That's what I need. They've got real height, the only thing here that has. I need them for background." He jammed on the brakes, stopping. "Hey, George!" he called to a Negro pushing an empty wheelchair. "What are those trees over there?"

The Negro looked and asked, "You mean they name?"

"That's it." Impatiently, Adam thrust his hand in his pocket, brought out a quarter, and threw it at the man, who caught it wonderingly, and then said with more alacrity, "They's called Stralian pine."

" 'Stralian pine?' " Adam repeated. "What the hell are you talking about?"

The Negro looked slightly frightened of Adam now, and repeated, "Stralian pine, they called." The man started to pedal away.

"Wait a minute!" called Adam. "Do you mean Australian pine?"

"Stralian pine, that right," the Negro called back agreeably. He pedaled faster.

Adam laughed uproariously, happy with the man. "Damned old bastard!" he cried fondly.

Adam drove on, still more wildly. "Why people go to the French Riviera instead of here," he proclaimed, "I don't know." He nearly ran into another car.

"Why we aren't getting in a wreck," observed Eve, "I hope to know."

"Look at that royal palm!" Adam exulted, paying no attention.

29

"A row of them, a double row, two double rows leading up to a Spanish Renaissance entrance, and you can look right through the whole house to a patio with a swimming pool and the ocean beyond that. And look at that banana plant! It's got bananas on it, real bananas!" He stopped the Ghost again with a jerk and started to get out.

Eve grabbed him by the arm. He nearly pulled her out of the car before he sat back again. "Now wait a minute," she soothed. "I think it's wonderful you've found what you want, Tiny. But no matter what you think of the Royal Poinciana, I'd rather sleep there than in jail, which is where we'll spend our first night if you pick somebody else's bananas."

Adam stared longingly at the bananas. "Oh," he said. "Yes, I suppose so."

"So calm down, little boy."

"Calm down? Nothing doing! We're going to celebrate. We'll have champagne with our dinner. Where is that monstrosity?" He looked about and saw the rearing form of the Royal Poinciana; it was virtually impossible not to see it in Palm Beach.

He started the Ghost toward it.

EVE SAT ROCKING

in a green chair on the main piazza of the Royal Poinciana. The Ponce, they called the hotel. Up and down the wide veranda others rocked. A broad striped canvas awning shaded them from the burning afternoon sun. From the Coconut Grove, faintly, came the sound of the orchestra playing for tea dancing. On the broad walk at the bottom of the steep steps, wheelchair men pedaled their vehicles soundlessly. Out on the lake gleaming white yachts rode serenely, while others were tied up in the boat basin directly in front of the great hotel.

A slight frown was on Eve's forehead. Her black eyes were troubled. She was worried about Adam. They had been here two weeks now and no one liked his ideas for changing the architectual landscape. Fury was mounting in him that would explode at any moment.

Eve glanced about at the other people on the porch of the hotel. From most of them exuded an air of quiet good breeding, of money long in the family, of knowing and feeling their special position in life. Others might show evidences of being ill bred, but for the most part they, too, had that air of a background of wealth. Those who had long had it wore it easily; those who had recently acquired their money wore it with a slight defiance.

She and Adam knew none of them. They had a formal nodding acquaintance with a few, engendered by unavoidable proximity. They had made no friends, for these people rarely became intimate through casual hotel meetings. They had been treated coolly, with that unique coolness Palm Beach people were practiced at showing. They had even been cut once or twice when they presumed to speak to some who did not wish to be spoken to.

Adam wasn't bothered by this. He laughed at it. He had little respect for anything except architecture. He claimed he had none for social position or wealth; the first was a silly sham, he held, the second something convenient for paying for a building.

Eve was disturbed. In spite of his saying he didn't care about these people, their indifference to what he wanted to do was touching him. It made Eve feel like an outsider, as though she and Adam both did not belong here. She thought their impulsive move was turning out to be a mistake.

She looked up as the large top half of Adam appeared on the steps. As more of him came into sight he glanced down the line of chairs. He saw Eve, and then all of him appeared as he climbed the rest of the way and gained the piazza floor.

Eve made the crease on her forehead leave it, and forced the trouble to depart from her eyes.

Adam looked discouraged and down in the mouth. His full lower lip sagged. His eyelids looked heavy and drooped. His hands hung limply at his side. His big frame seemed to drag itself as he let it fall like a sack of potatoes into the empty chair at the side of Eve.

She didn't speak, knowing there was nothing to say to fit the moment, even though she yearned to soothe him.

He didn't say anything for some time. He stared morosely at the bright scene in front of them.

When he did speak it was suddenly and harshly. "They won't listen to me, nobody will listen to me!" Adam spoke so loudly that people nearby were startled. They stared. Eve noticed that the man on the other side of her was caught with attention, for he stopped rocking.

Adam went on, not caring who heard. "I've talked myself blue in the face. I've talked with the architects, or the creatures here who call themselves architects. I've talked with the town officials, with builders, contractors, with the editors of the newspapers, with large landholders, and with some people who have big building investments here. I've told them what this place could be like, should be like, what I'd like to do here. I've told the same thing to people who want new houses. And what have I got? Nothing!

None of them, not a single one of them knows what the hell I'm talking about. It's the same as back in Westchester."

Eve knew how some of them had been told. By now Adam had lost his temper, and was reviling them. Probably he called some of them names. It wasn't quite the way to sell a new architectural plan to exclusive, careful Palm Beach. Even though additional people were staring, Eve advised, "Blow off some more steam."

"They don't want good taste!" Adam bellowed. "They don't want anything beautiful. They want this." He indicated the hotel. "They want to stay in their own sticky little safe rut." He glared at some of those so openly listening to him, as if blaming them personally. They turned away.

Adam fell silent, working his lower lip against his upper. He was pouting. He conceded, "The only good thing about the whole business is that right now, even if somebody wanted the kind of thing I'd like to build here, you couldn't build it anyway because the war restrictions are still on."

That gave Eve her opening. She suggested cheerfully, "Then let's just have a winter vacation and enjoy ourselves, Adam."

He shook his large head. He wasn't having any of that. He wanted to build the houses he visualized.

They sat glumly.

When the man sitting on the other side of Eve spoke it was like an intrusion into their dark mood. He said, "I beg your pardon, but what is it you would build?"

They turned to him, and saw a medium-sized man in his thirties. He had a narrow, homely face, topped with closely cropped blond hair. He was quietly dressed in white flannels and buttoned navy blue jacket. He looked contained, yet aware, full of interest and curiosity.

Adam demanded, "Who are you?"

"Adam," Eve scolded, "don't be rude." She turned to the man. "My husband doesn't mean to be. He simply feels strongly about certain things."

"That's what I want to know about," the man said. "May I introduce myself? My name is Sumner, Michael Sumner."

Eve inquired, letting it hang in the air, "Breakfast food . . . ?"

33

Michael Sumner lowered his eyelids and then lifted them again. "Breakfast food," he corroborated.

Eve knew he was the bachelor head of the wealthy Sumner family who appeared at most American breakfast tables. "Our name is Paine," she said. "I'm Eve, and this is Adam."

The millionaire's eyes came to rest on Eve. She saw a veiled, polite, but certain admiration.

"I know the Garden of Eden aspects of your names," he said. "I've seen some of Mr. Paine's work around the New York area."

Adam regarded him suspiciously. "What do you want to know?"

"I'd like to hear your ideas on houses for Palm Beach," Michael Sumner replied.

"What for?"

"I'm interested."

Adam glared at him across Eve. After a moment of inspection, he seemed only slightly mollified. "Well, that's the first time anybody here has used that word."

"For instance," the breakfast-food manufacturer inquired, "generally speaking, if you could do what you wanted here, what would it be?"

"Well, it wouldn't be built of wood," Adam asserted. "And it wouldn't be painted yellow."

"Those are negative statements so far. What would it be?"

Adam examined the other man more thoroughly. He didn't yet fully accept the idea that anyone was sincerely interested. "You ever lived around the Mediterranean?"

"Quite a bit."

"South of France?"

"There, and the Italian Riviera. Even the Spanish coast."

Adam stared. "If you've lived in Spain, then maybe I'll tell you. Can you see that here?"

"I'd like to hear your ideas about using it here."

"Well, I've told everybody else, or tried to. You might as well hear it, too."

Michael Sumner glanced about. A number of people were frankly looking and listening. "Shall we go to my suite?" he suggested.

"Nothing the matter with right here," Adam declared. "I want them all to hear it," he said vindictively. "Now the first thing—"

34

Eve spoke in a low, vibrant voice. "Adam, take the chip off your shoulder. Mr. Sumner didn't put it there. You've been trying to get somebody to listen, and now you've got the chance. But not in public."

Sumner smiled, flicking his gray eyes appreciatively at Eve.

Adam pushed out his lower lip as though he would protest Eve's interruption and brief lecture. Then he grinned and bellowed, "My wife cuts me down to size when I need it. Where's your suite, Sumner?"

They stood up. Though he was not a short man, the top of Michael Sumner's head hardly came to Adam's shoulder. It did not reach to much more than Eve's nose. He led the way into the hotel.

In the rotunda Michael Sumner spoke to the bell captain, asking for ice to be brought to his suite. The hotel service responded so efficiently that a Negro bellman, carrying a silver bowl of ice, rode up with them in the gold metal-strap elevator to the fourth floor.

They entered a sitting room whose floor was covered with green mats and which had green-painted wicker furniture. A soft couch occupied a wall; there was a writing desk and several tables. A bedroom and bath led off to one side. After the bellman left, Sumner indicated a tray of bottles and glasses and inquired, "What will you have, Mrs. Paine?"

"Scotch and soda, please, if you have it."

"We have it. Mr. Paine?"

"The same doubled in spades."

Sumner laughed lightly. "I can see you need a good drink."

Eve sat on the couch. Adam took a wicker chair; it creaked and cracked under his weight as though it would collapse.

Sumner made three highballs and passed two of them to the Paines. With the third he sat on the couch beside Eve and told Adam, "I didn't speak to you or ask you here idly. I've had a plan in mind for some time now. It may fit in with your ideas, or it may not." He waved his hand with expectant invitation, and sat back to listen.

Adam, gulping at his drink, began immediately. "A Spanish house fits this country. That is, the basic make-up of big cool stone rooms, tile floors and roofs, loggias, and courtyards—here they'll be called patios. I don't mean the Spanish house as you know it. That was based on a design of being a fortified castle, with stark outside walls, a few narrow, heavily shuttered windows set high, and a single, barricaded entrance, all put around a protected inner court where the living was done safely. That house was designed for a medieval day of brigands and raiders. You don't need that here, for the pirates here are legalized, taking your money on roulette wheels."

Eve, sipping her highball, relaxed. Adam's eyelids no longer drooped; he spoke with spirit, watching Michael Sumner, who in turn studied him calmly.

"What I want to do," Adam explained, "is to turn the Spanish house inside out like a glove. Use the beauty of its features, but make it more livable on all sides. I'll have plenty of openings on the outside, big ones, letting in the air and sun when you want it. Every room will face at least two ways, sometimes three, and I even have a plan for a house whose living room will have four exposures. I want towers, galleries, outside stairways curving up and around corners, and balconies where you can sit in the moonlight overlooking the water. I want my ceilings beamed or carved in wood, sometimes whole rooms of paneling. I don't want much to be exactly even or regular. For plastering I'll take it Wop-finished, meaning rough, inside a house as well as out. I know how to make roof tiles by shaping them over your thigh, and I'll teach local workmen how to do that—you can get an incomparable effect with them. They don't provide any heat in the houses I've been in down here, and heat is needed at times, such as those few cold days last week. There should be fireplaces, big jobs in ornamental stone, that really work; I want them in most bedrooms, too. Here and there in a few houses I'll spot a small kidney fireplace, waist-high to catch you in the right place."

He stopped and asked Michael Sumner, "Do you know what I'm talking about?"

Sumner didn't reply except for lifting his glass to Adam and drinking.

"By God," said Adam, "maybe you do." He handed his empty glass to his host, who got up and filled it, giving it to Adam and then returning to the couch. Meanwhile Adam rushed on:

"Maybe there will be two or even three patios in a house if it's a big one. And swimming pools—you can build some whole houses around them, running a cloister down one side of the pool. Part of Palm Beach, where it's narrow, invites estates running from ocean to lake; there you'll have the chance to do everything I visualize; you'll have a beach house as well as your main house, and a boathouse on the lake for your boat or boats. The big problem down here is to give a house character without having any ground elevations. You can do it, by using changes of level in the house itself; even a few feet would be effective here. And building terraces and sloping lawns, too. Throw the big houses up as high as you can, giving them a strong skyline. I haven't told you about color. There's got to be lots of that, in many shades, delicate shades to kill the glare and rest the eyes. I want grillwork on windows and doors, ironwork of all sorts, antique, of course, nothing new, or if it has to be new, then battered and aged and rusted until it looks old. There must be pottery, lots of it, both bisque and glazed in color. And always decorative tile in varied design."

He stopped again and looked at Michal Sumner narrowly. "That's only part of it, of course. And don't think I'm held down to the Spanish. Making everything Spanish would be monotonous. I'd like Italian, French, and Moorish, too—of course, in the Spanish you'll find a strong Moorish influence already there. What I want to do is build something in this country that fits it. Nothing here now does. Or don't you agree? I've told you enough so you can see what I mean."

Michael Sumner still didn't reply. Instead of looking at Adam, he stared off into space. His silence was so long that even Eve wondered about his reaction.

"Well," demanded Adam impatiently, "what do you say?"

"I'm thinking," the other man replied.

"That's what my wife does," said Adam. He sighed. "A waste of time."

Sumner turned his gray eyes on Eve, and she looked back. She could see decision in his.

He began, "Mr. Paine—"

"Wait a minute," said Adam. "Do you like what I've said?"

"Very much. Quite definitely."

"Then call me Adam."

"All right, Adam. And I'll be Michael. Especially since—I think —we are going to get to know each other well."

Only with difficulty did Eve keep herself from sitting up straight with acute, anxious interest. This was always the crucial point in getting a commission, the delicate moment before final decision to order a house, the time of commitment. She had been through it a number of times, but this one had taken on an importance far beyond being just another house. It meant the chance for acceptance or rejection of Adam's entire plan for Palm Beach.

Adam attacked it bluntly. "Well, come on, Mike, if you want a house, say so."

Michael was not offended by Adam's tone or manner. Eve's heart dropped when he said, "It isn't a house I'm thinking of," and then rose still higher when he went on, "It's something more than that."

"Hotel?" inquired Adam.

"Not exactly," said Michael. "Though that is closer to it. No, what I have in mind is something perhaps new, certainly for here. I believe that what could be used here is a club of some sort. Right now there is only Bradley's, which isn't a club in the true sense of the word at all. People who don't gamble, and there are many, never go there, or want to. The golf course here for the Flagler hotels has become quite public with the expansion of the hotels."

"A country club," Eve guessed.

"Almost that, but still not quite," said Michael. "Perhaps it is hard to explain. I'll try. I see it as an exclusive club, partially residential for those who don't want to take cottages for the season, with a golf course attached. It will be for people who want more privacy than the big regular hotels offer. For instance, myself here —the thing I have in mind would suit my purposes and needs exactly. In fact, if it is built I mean to have an apartment in it, perhaps designed especially for me. There would not be many of these, perhaps not more than a dozen or so. The rest would be club with lounge, reading, and dining rooms, a library, too." He turned to Adam. "Have I conveyed my meaning to you at all?"

Adam didn't even bother to answer that. "And you think what I told you is what you want in design?"

38

"I believe it would fit it perfectly."

Adam looked around the sitting room, making his chair squeak mightily. "Have you got a piece of paper here?"

"Nothing except writing paper, I fear."

Adam was out of his chair striding to the writing desk. He sat here and pulled out a piece of hotel stationery. He turned it upside down so the letterhead would not take up any room. Out of his pocket he took the stub of a thick-leaded pencil. He began to sketch.

"What are you doing?" asked Michael.

"Drawing you your club," Adam muttered. "At least a rough idea of how I think it should look."

"Don't you need regular drawing paper and some time for that?"

"This will do."

Michael glanced at Eve. She nodded, smiling, and explained, "He likes to do it this way."

It was only a few minutes before Adam, with a flourish, completed his sketch. He brought it over to them on the couch, thrusting it at them and saying, "Here."

On the paper was drawn a building whose plan looked as if it had been worked out carefully for a long time. It had been, for Spanish and Moorish architects hundreds of years ago evolved its general style. Adam simply adapted their work and transferred it to a piece of paper, with certain innovations of his own.

Excitedly, Michael cried, "But this is exactly what I mean! How could you know with so little explanation?"

"Little?" asked Adam. "You gave me a lot. Let's face it, Mike. I'm an architect whose work you like and you're a multimillionaire. I'll furnish the genius and you furnish the money—if you really want to do this."

"I really want to do it. But I'm flabbergasted at your grasp so quickly." He flicked the drawing with one finger. "And shouldn't there be a plan first? This is a rendering."

"I do it backward," said Adam.

"He draws what the house looks like first," said Eve, "and then fits in the rooms."

Contemplatively, Michael murmured, "I really don't suppose

it matters." He glanced sharply at Adam, and ran his hand through his close-cropped hair.

"Wait a minute," said Adam. "It's all very well to say you like this and want to do it. But how are you going to do it when you can't get materials?"

Michael smiled. "There is always more than one way to skin a cat, Adam. I've already thought that out. You can get materials if it is for a purpose such as building a hospital for convalescent soldiers."

Adam laughed. "That's what we say it's going to be?"

"And if necessary," said Michael, "it will be a hospital for convalescent soldiers. But I'm informed from Washington, on quite good authority, that such a thing won't be necessary soon, at least down here."

"Then the hospital is turned into a club?"

"That's it." Michael turned to Eve. "Perhaps this seems a reprehensible thing to do. But as long as it will be such a short time until most things are back to normal, possibly it isn't as bad as it sounds."

Watching Adam, Eve replied, "I don't see anything the matter with it."

"I must warn you, Adam," Michael went on, "I'm not sure how Palm Beach is going to take your building."

"They'll like it when they see the finished job. They've got to."

"But don't you understand? It's more than changing the architectural design of the place. We'll be breaking tradition—the wooden-cottage tradition. The conservative view. It will be disturbing, and the one thing not wanted here is anything seriously disturbing."

"Then we'll disturb them."

Eve inquired of the manufacturer, "Do you mind my asking why you want to build this club? Why should you? I mean, it's more than just your getting the winter living quarters you'd like."

He looked at her, nodding slightly to acknowledge that he appreciated her question. "To tell you the truth, the breakfast foods just about make themselves these days. I'm bored. I don't find it very exciting here, with the same old routine year after year of going through the same moves. In the morning you go to the Breakers Casino and watch everybody while they watch you. In the afternoon you change your clothes and dance in the Coconut Grove or rock on the Ponce veranda. In the evening you change your clothes again and attend the cake walk or go to Bradley's. I'm looking for something new."

"I'm going to ask another question I shouldn't," said Eve. "Have you ever thought of getting married?"

He lowered his eyes, then looked up at her fully. "Right now," he said, "I think the club would be fun."

Adam roared, "Let's have some fun!"

THE FIRST THING

they did was to send a long wire to Aubrey Sheppard in the north instructing him to pack Adam's notebooks and portfolios and all the drafting equipment of the closed office, and bring them and himself to Palm Beach by the next train. In reply they received a telegram reading: CANNOT ARRIVE NEXT TRAIN BUT WILL GET THERE.

Adam said of the Royal Poinciana, "We can't stay here. It would kill me. Besides, I need room, lots of it. I want to stretch and expand. I want space for my drawing boards. I want it near Michael's land where the building will go up."

This site was about a mile south of the hotel on Lake Worth. Here Michael owned nearly a hundred acres. It had been decided that the club would be built on the northwest corner of it, right on the water, with the golf course using up the rest of the land. Adam had spent hours there studying it, and walking over it, and now he was sketching madly, making drawing after drawing, until he had a thick pile to add to the original.

While he worked and waited impatiently for Aubrey to arrive, Eve took the Rolls-Royce and looked for a house. She found one the second day of searching. It was located on a lane only a short distance from the building site. Until a few days before it had been occupied by a family who had to return to Chicago because of acute illness. It was a barn-like place of three stories, covered with green-stained shingles.

"Whoever heard of a three-story 'cottage'!" Adam raved when he examined it. "But it's just what we want. We'll put Aubrey and the drafting room on the third floor. Us on the second with plenty of room for guests. What about servants?"

"No servants," said Eve.

"You've got to have servants if you live in Palm Beach," he pointed out.

"I may live here," Eve said, "but I'm not of Palm Beach. Adam, I've got to have something to do."

"But meals and housekeeping—"

"I'll have somebody in a few times a week to clean up. I'll do the rest and get the meals."

"You'll never be taken up by society."

"From what I've seen of society, that's all right with me."

"You don't care what they think?"

"Only if it would hurt you in some way. Would it?"

"To hell with them."

"You haven't answered my question."

"Eve, I intend to be such a damned success here that nothing can hurt me." He looked at his wrist watch. "You'd better get over to the train to meet Aubrey. Hurry back with my Seville portfolio —I need the detail of the arcade in the Lonja."

"Some day," said Eve, "when somebody asks me to point out my husband, the great architect, I'll show them your Spanish portfolios and say, 'There goes Adam Paine.'"

"You'll be right," he admitted. "All I do is crib and copy."

She became serious. "You know it's more than that."

"I do. You do. A few others may. Most won't. Now beat it."

Eve went to meet Aubrey at the Royal Poinciana depot at the north end of the hotel. It was the last of January and the height of the season. The hotel orchestra played on the second story of the colonnade to greet the train. As the train backed over the lake Eve stood on the platform. A number of private cars passed, which would be detached from the Pullmans before the train went on to Miami. It ground to a stop, and then Eve was searching eagerly in the crowd for a glimpse of a familiar figure.

She saw him, from her height, above the heads of the others, and waved. "Aubrey!" she cried. "This way, Aubrey!"

His pink, serious face beamed. He was a chunky man of thirty-two, always good-natured and faithful. Adam had been attracted to him first because Aubrey was an honor graduate of the Beaux Arts. But Aubrey had no imagination. He could follow and carry out, but he could not create. This made him one of the most

43

exacting draftsmen in the business, but kept him from establishing himself as an architect.

As he came forward and they met, Eve impulsively put her arms about him and kissed him, voicing her welcome.

Aubrey flushed a deep pink. The glass in his steel-rimmed spectacles steamed. "Florida," he stammered, "is hot." He looked about, staring at anything except her. He had to take off his glasses and wipe them clear of steam.

Eve didn't laugh at his shyness, but rescued him from it. "Is the luggage with you?"

"In the baggage car." He indicated his bag at his feet and a bundle of portfolios he carried under his arm. "I've got some with me, the things most valuable to him, that I know he wouldn't trust out of anybody's hands. I haven't let go of them since New York."

"Aubrey!" she thanked him. "Do you think Seville is there?"

"It is."

"Then come on, and check things, and we'll get back to him."

On the way to the cottage Aubrey stared at the Rolls-Royce and at Palm Beach, asking, "How is he?"

"Never better. This is it, Aubrey, what he's always looked for."

"I can see it must be. It doesn't look as if much has been built here since nineteen hundred."

"Not much has, and what was kept strictly to that date."

At the cottage Adam ran out to meet them, making the porch shake under his weight. Aubrey got out of the Ghost and backed away, crying, "Now don't you clap me on the back, Adam! The last time you did you knocked the breath out of me and I wasn't the same for days."

"All right, all right!" yelled Adam. "But it's only because I need you so much." He took one of Aubrey's hands in both of his and shook it vigorously, making the other man nearly drop the portfolios to which he still clung. Adam then saw these and grabbed them. He riffled through them, hollered, "Seville!", thrust the others back at Aubrey, and yanked at the bowknots of the tapes holding the Seville portfolio together. He got it open and flicked through its contents until he came to what he wanted, a print. "That's it! I couldn't remember exactly. Now I've got it." Of Aubrey he demanded, "Can you go to work right away?"

Resignedly, Aubrey answered, "I suppose so."

"Now you look here, Tiny," Eve scolded. "Let him alone until tomorrow."

"I don't mind," said Aubrey.

"Where's the rest of the stuff?" Adam wanted to know.

"It's coming from the station by baggage truck," said Eve, "but can't you wait—"

"I've got board table-tops on horses in there," Adam said, pointing back to the house. "It's rough, but broad and workable. Got you some comfortable padded stools you like and plenty of rolls of paper and everything else."

"Will you let me wash my hands?" asked Aubrey.

Quite seriously, Adam replied, "I guess you can do that."

"Stop it, Adam!" Eve ordered. "Aubrey isn't going to do any work until tomorrow."

"Come on in, Aubrey, and we'll talk about it." Adam picked up his bag and led the way into the house.

Aubrey told Eve, "You know he won't be happy and all he'll do is sulk unless he can at least tell me what we're going to do here."

"Telling you means showing you the drawings, which means you'll both start to figure and work."

"What's so bad about that?" Adam asked. "That's what I'm here for and that's what Aubrey's here for."

"But not today," objected Eve. "Tomorrow."

"That's a mere waste of time. Aubrey doesn't mind. Do you, Aubrey?"

"Of course not."

"What else can he say?" Eve asked. "All right, go ahead, go on up there and I'll have the men bring the things when they come. But you're both coming down to dinner right on time when I call you and there won't be any hurry about eating."

"Yes, dear," Adam replied meekly. He almost pushed Aubrey upstairs.

Adam would have been lost without Aubrey, who was an excellent delineator man. This meant that Aubrey could take Adam's sketches and rough floor plans and carry them out in detail. Adam could do this, too, but it bored him, so he left it up to Aubrey when he could, restricting himself to the elevations and the nature of the rooms.

In the days that followed they both had long conferences with Michael, who told them what he wanted in the line of chambers and apartments, and listened to Adam's suggestions. It was decided to have twenty-four housekeeping apartments. There would be two towers, one very large and utilitarian, which would contain Michael's master apartment, the other purely decorative with a gold Moorish dome. On the ground floor cloisters would entirely surround a large open patio whose columns and walls could be completely covered with purple bougainvillea. The bar would be of Spanish colored tile, the main lounge pure Spanish Gothic with a groin vaulted ceiling supported by stone ribs and a bay of five large ornamental Gothic windows of leaded glass.

The final drawing Adam made of the complete building showed a rambling, picturesque structure exuding an Old World atmosphere, with a hint of Spanish missions thrown in. It might have been a particularly attractive monastery. Michael, looking at it, shook his cropped head in admiration for Adam's skill, and observed, "It's going to make the old shingle and clapboard places much more obsolete than I thought."

Aubrey slaved night and day on the working drawings. Adam helped him, becoming a draftsman himself again. He didn't want to employ any local men because he didn't feel such draftsmen would understand what he was doing. And he didn't want a stranger in the place, perhaps questioning and wondering and probing and carrying wild tales outside.

Michael came to dinner the night the final plans were submitted to him for acceptance. There wasn't any doubt about his decision, for he had spent much time watching the progress of the drawings, approving as they went along. Eve had no anxiety when the three men descended from the third floor following the formal submission of the plans to Michael. She could see in their faces the glow of having something they all liked.

Over highballs in the living room Adam brought up the question discussed many times before. "You've got to get a name for this thing of yours soon," he told Michael. "I'll be showing the plans

46

for a building permit in a few days and I'll have to tell them what it's called."

Aubrey nodded. "The name should go on the blueprints."

Along with Michael, they had all considered many names. Adam wanted to call it the Everglades Club, but that sounded too wild to Michael, who said people would think it was a hunting lodge. He favored Bougainvillea Club, but Eve pointed out that the word was both too hard to spell and pronounce. Aubrey had no ideas.

Tonight it was decided quickly, when Eve said, "I don't know what you'll think of it, but in a shop window today I saw the most beautiful painting of some pink flamingos. You're going to paint the club pink, so I thought—"

"That's it!" cried Michael. "'The Flamingo Club.' Temporarily, of course, 'The Flamingo Hospital For Convalescent Officers.'"

Adam never thought over his decisions. "I'll take it," he said.

"Eve's given it the name." Michael turned to her. "I thank her."

Eve, pleased, asked, "Can I break a bottle of champagne on the doorway opening night?"

"By all means," promised Michael.

"I don't really mean that."

"You do now," he assured her.

"We'll have to have some real flamingos around the place," said Adam.

"Now you're going crazy," observed Aubrey.

"Only exotic," Adam corrected him.

At dinner Michael and Adam had their first and only difference. This came about when the question of furnishings was discussed. "They've got to be genuine Spanish antiques," declared Adam.

"I agree," said Michael.

"Bought in Spain and imported," said Adam.

"Can't we locate enough of them right in this country?" Michael wanted to know.

"It would be a hodgepodge."

"But—"

47

"They've got to be of the same genre, blend with each other, be of the same age, from the same place as much as possible." Adam spoke flatly, as though handing down a judgment. "This means each piece will have to be selected in relation with all the others, so it will fit. And this has got to be done for every apartment as well as the main rooms."

Ordinarily Michael was soft-spoken and rarely raised his voice. He had a habit of considering a problem carefully before giving his opinion or decision. But now, goaded perhaps by Adam's didactic tone, he spoke instantly and rather sharply. "Isn't that carrying things a bit far?"

"No farther than you agreed to," Adam retorted. "You said you'd do it my way."

"Within reason," Michael reminded him. "Is this reasonable?"

"I'll tell you how reasonable it is," Adam declared. "I'm going to make this building perfect in structure. It must be perfection in furnishings as well. If at any time I can see it isn't going to be I'll pull out."

Michael began, "You're being pretty arbitrary—"

"Damn it!" Adam swore. "I think I'd better pull out now! You haven't meant what you said! You're trying to crawfish!"

"Tiny!" cried Eve.

Aubrey looked down at his plate, pushing at his food with his fork, not eating.

Michael regarded Adam evenly across the table. Now he returned to his usual manner of calmly weighing and thinking a thing out. He carried a forkful of food to his mouth, chewed methodically, and swallowed before he observed, "It would seem to me that that hair-trigger temper of yours would get you in a lot of trouble."

"It does," said Adam. He wasn't admitting anything, or expressing any apology, but merely stating a fact.

Quietly, half smiling, Michael inquired, "Aren't you ashamed of what you just said?"

Adam glanced at Eve, who compressed her lips slightly and shook her head. He was like a small boy when he mumbled, "I guess I am. But I wouldn't tell anybody else that except you. I forgot that you're giving me the chance I want."

"I wasn't thinking of that so much," said Michael, "as I was of us gathered in friendship around this table. We've gotten to know, and I hope, like each other, all of us, Eve, Aubrey, you, and myself, during this work. There isn't much call for hard words."

Adam hung his big head. "I'm a heel, a vulcanized, stinking heel." He meant this sincerely, though it didn't seem so when he looked up and said, "But the furniture bought in Spain still goes."

They could only laugh at him, and he wasn't wholly aware of what caused their merriment. "After the building is completed," he persisted, "I'm hoping some time in July, I'm going to Spain to select it myself. Eve's coming with me and you're paying for the trip."

This was the first time Eve knew about any such thing. She glanced at Adam, startled, and then at Michael, to show her wonderment.

Michael, looking at Eve, said, "Have a good time."

"You can come, too," said Adam generously, "if you want to see what you're getting."

"Adam," Michael told him, "you're hopeless. You're a bull in a china shop. You've no tact, no respect for other people. I suppose those qualities, missing in you, go to make up the extra something you have for your work." He glanced about, at Eve and Aubrey. "I expect we've got to accept you on that basis, taking you for what you are."

"Now," said Eve, "you're getting to know the overgrown brat."

"I'll leave the furniture up to you," Michael told Adam. "To you and Eve. I'm not sure I'd leave it with a stubborn egg-head like you alone. If you'll pardon what I'm calling your husband," he apologized to Eve.

"I said you're getting to know him."

Adam joined their laughter. This time he could understand it.

ADAM WALKED UP

to the door of the shack-like office of a building contractor on a fenced-in lot in the south end of West Palm Beach. Above the door a sign read: George Andrews, Builder and Contractor. Adam glanced about the yard at the man's equipment. He had plenty of it, though most of it looked unused for some time.

Unceremoniously, Adam opened the door and strode in.

A barrel-like man, with his shirtsleeves rolled up over his thick hairy black arms, sat at a desk. He was alone in the shack. His broad face looked tough as he glanced up at Adam.

"You George Andrews?"

The man fiddled with a pencil that looked fragile in his big hands. "Yep."

"I'm Adam Paine."

"All right."

"You aren't impressed with me?"

"Should I be impressed?"

"No. But do you know who I am?"

"Yep."

"You asked for a set of plans for the Flamingo Hospital."

"I got them." Andrews pointed his pencil at a pile of plans resting on top of others on a rough table.

"Why didn't you figure it?"

The contractor sat back in his swivel chair, making it creak, and regarded Adam. "Look, Mister, I thought I could build anything, but I don't think I could build that."

"I was told you're the best here."

"Maybe I am. But I don't understand your building."

Adam studied the other man more closely. He invited himself to sit down in a straight-backed chair in front of the desk. It creaked louder than had the other chair. Adam asked, "Will it hold me?"

"I don't know. You're pretty big. You're the biggest guy I ever saw."

They regarded each other. Adam didn't move on the chair, keeping it quiet and not risking anything that would cause it to collapse under him. "The others," he said, "bid without understanding it. Or pretended to. Or only think they do. That's why I've come to see you."

"Give it to one of the others. They'll do your job—if it can be done."

"It can be done. What don't you understand about it? The plans?"

"The plans are all right, if anybody wants something like that."

"Then what's the matter?"

Andrews sat up and pointed his pencil accusingly at Adam. "I'm talking about the materials."

"Talk," said Adam.

"You specify you want to build it out of hollow tile mostly. I've never had any experience with it."

"It's good stuff; the best."

"I haven't got any men who know how to work it."

"They can learn."

"Who'll teach them?"

"I will."

"You?"

"Listen, part of the job of being an architect—or at least the kind I think I am—is being able to do any job any workman can do. That way I know it's being done right. The great builders of the past did that, the master craftsmen. Michelangelo—"

"We aren't talking about Michelangelo," the other interrupted. "We're talking about you."

Adam examined George Andrews still more closely. "You look like the kind of guy who has a bottle in his desk," he suggested.

For answer, Andrews reached down, pulled upon a drawer, and came up with a quart bottle of whiskey. He didn't hand it to Adam, but planked it down on top of his desk. Adam picked it up, extracted the cork, and tilted the neck of the bottle to his lips. He took a deep draught. He wiped the neck with the palm of his hand, said, "Thanks," and handed it to Andrews. The contractor regarded it for a second, accepted it, took a drink, picked up the cork, put it back in the neck, and returned the bottle to its drawer.

"Now," said Adam, "I feel more like telling you that I know how to lay tile and—"

"Have you ever laid it?"

"Don't interrupt. I've laid it, and can go on the scaffold to show your men how to lay it."

"Yeh?"

"Yeh. And if you've got any carpenters that don't know how to saw a board I can do that, too. I'm a pretty good electrician and I can wipe a joint in plumbing as well as the next man. I'm not a bad blacksmith, either, and like to work in wrought iron."

"I suppose you can slap plaster, too?"

"I can slap plaster."

"The hell you say."

"The hell I say. I'm not boasting, I'm just telling you what I can do."

"Maybe you aren't boasting," admitted Andrews. "But you sure sound as if you are."

"You'll get used to that," Adam predicted.

"Who says I'm going to get used to anything?"

"I do. Got any more objections to the materials?"

"Yes. That barrel tile for the roofs. I saw some of that down in Cuba when I was there last summer."

Adam started to sit up with interest, but didn't complete the movement when a cracking sound came from his chair. "Thigh-shaped?"

"I guess so. I brought some back with me thinking I might do something with it here, but—"

Now Adam interrupted. "You've got it here?"

"It's laying out in the yard."

Adam got up. "I want to see it."

Andrews stared at him. "You don't say please, do you?"

"Do you?" Adam countered.

Andrews got up and led the way out into his yard. He took Adam to the side of his board fence where several dozen brown, partially round roof tiles were laid, piled against each other vertically.

Adam stooped and picked one up, then another. Easily he held one heavy tile in each hand. Excitedly he cried, "This will save me a lot of time!" He glanced at Andrews. "Can you get more where this came from?"

"As much as you want."

"I mean to make this myself later on, but I haven't got time now. You were on the right track. Why didn't you use it?"

"It looked fine down in Cuba, but back here—" Andrews spread his hands.

"Just because it hasn't been seen here?"

"Maybe."

"Is that any reason not to use it here?"

"Maybe not."

Adam put down the tile as he saw something else. He straightened to accuse Andrews, "Damn it, man, you've been playing a game with me."

Belligerently, Andrews demanded, "What do you mean?"

Adam pointed to a small pile of hollow tile. "You've got it right there."

"Sure I have," Andrews defended himself. "But not because I asked for it. The manufacturer's agent was through here a while ago and tried to make me take some of it. I wouldn't. He asked me to let him leave some. I let him dump it there."

"Andrews," Adam said, "I'm going to make the rest of this short and sweet: do or don't. I like you and your whole attitude. The best thing I like is your bringing back that tile from Cuba. It shows that down there, for a minute at least, you recognized something good. I know damn well you learned how to lay it while you were there, too."

"What if I did?"

"All right, here's the short and sweet: if your men can be shown how to use hollow tile, you don't care what a building is like, so will you bid this job? You can be generous with yourself. I'm not out for the lowest bid, but the best builder."

"What're you trying to do—flatter me?"

"When you know me you'll find out I never do that."

Andrews looked quizzical, then decided, "I guess you don't."

"Well?"

"Look," said Andrews, "your job can't be bid. You know that as well as I do. If those other guys gave you figures they were so far overboard that they thought they couldn't miss. But they might. That thing you want to build could only be taken on a percentage-above-cost basis."

Adam smiled broadly. "That's all I wanted to hear."

"You mean you'd accept a builder on that basis?" Andrews asked wonderingly. "That could be stiffer than the overboard bids."

"I'll take my chances on that."

"You talk as if expense is no object."

"It's always an object," said Adam. "But in this case not such a big one that it gets in the way of the contractor I want."

Andrews regarded him now from narrowed eyes. He rubbed one hand over a furry arm. Adam saw that he had accepted but didn't want to admit it right away. Andrews asked, "When you planning to start?"

"Tomorrow."

"There's an ordinance in Palm Beach saying you can't do any big noisy construction during the season. It all has to be done in summer when the people aren't here."

"This is a convalescent hospital. An exception is being made."

"I saw that hospital stuff on the blueprints. Some hospital. What's it for—millionaire doughboys?"

"That's about right."

Andrews gave him a last look. Tiny suspicions of respect and excitement were in it. He said gruffly, "Let's go back in the shack and look at those plans."

EVEN BEFORE WORK

started on the building a storm of criticism of it began to be heard. A picture of it had been printed in the newspaper, with a description of what it was to be like. It shocked Palm Beach.

Letters were written to the editor of the newspaper deploring the structure. It was called radical. It was said that it would never fit into Palm Beach and should not be built. It would ruin the resort. One letter writer stated that Henry Flagler must be turning in his grave. The town clerk was called upon to revoke the building permit he had issued. If he didn't, it was threatened that an injunction would be obtained to stop the construction.

Adam was furious. He went into one of his towering rages. "What the hell do they want to do?" he demanded. "Stifle everything that's got any good taste to it? The damned old fogy bastards! All this place needs to make it decent is a couple of hundred funerals! That Old Guard! They're the ones who should go first."

He had calmed down slightly by the time Michael came to the cottage. "Can they do anything?" Adam demanded of him.

"I'm not sure," Michael said. "I'm hoping we're going to be able to go ahead, but we certainly won't be popular. I know they'd stop it if it weren't for the convalescent hospital purpose. Thank God we announced that. It's difficult to argue against. Another thing in our favor is that everybody is taken up right now with preparations for the Washington Birthday Ball at the Ponce. Then, after that, most people leave. Can you postpone breaking ground, put off starting for a while?"

"I can't and won't," Adam said. "It's set for day after tomorrow and it's going ahead."

"I was thinking of that for still another reason," Michael told him. "The breakfast foods need a little attention and I've got to leave for the North tonight. I thought if you could put off things for a few weeks I could be back and help you take some of the criticism."

Adam looked down at the millionaire manufacturer. "Mike, why do you always make me feel like a rat?"

"Perhaps," said Michael, "because you are one a little."

"By God!" Adam roared. "I stuck out my jaw that time and you landed on it."

"The thing is," Michael said, "what are you going to do?"

"I'll take back the won't and leave it only can't," said Adam. "Everything is set to go. George Andrews has ordered materials to be dumped on a schedule that can't be stopped now; some of them are on the site already. Besides, if we did stop it we might be prevented from getting it going again."

"Then go about it quietly," advised Michael. "If you get into real trouble, wire me. The town clerk won't take any action; I've seen him. And an injunction won't stick, I'm advised, and therefore won't be tried. But you'll have public opinion to contend with, not only among people here, but the regular local year-round people of both the Palm Beaches. Don't forget they make their bread and butter from Palm Beach and will be against anything they believe might hurt it."

"To hell with them."

Michael sighed. "I don't suppose you could ever learn something we know in the breakfast-food business."

"What's that?"

"We show a profit only as long as every one is pleased with what we serve him for breakfast. And because he allows us to tell him it's good."

Adam tossed this off. "That's big-corporation stuff, production-line business you do on the billboards. A building like this is an individual thing. It isn't another machine-made package of breakfast food."

"Possibly you're right, Adam. At any rate, I've become convinced that this thing has got to be done your way or not at all."

"Mike, I love you." Adam put his arms about him and hugged him tightly.

Michael gasped, "Well don't kill the goose that's laying your golden eggs."

The next day, when George Andrews measured his ground with transit and steel tape, he growled at Adam, "I don't know what you got me into. I've been threatened if I go ahead with this job."

"You don't threaten well, George."

"You damn right I don't." He directed a workman to drive short, pointed two-by-fours at a corner, to which were nailed batterboards. "But just the same we may get trouble."

"What kind of trouble?"

Movable lines were tied to the batterboards, by which the corners could be found, and George manipulated one of these. "I don't know. Just maybe trouble."

Adam was on hand the following morning when George started to work his men. The men themselves, arriving in battered cars, mostly Model T Fords they called Flivvers, were an odd assortment. Some of them looked about the site with intense curiosity. One grinned and said something to a companion, who cackled. Others were sullen. It was evident that they all knew about the building and had feelings in regard to it. They stared at Adam in wonderment, not understanding his size or what he represented, and therefore resenting both.

Adam eagerly accepted when George made a small ceremony of turning the first shovelful of dirt, asking, "You want to do it?"

Adam seized a spade and plunged its blade deep into the sand. It slicked in exuberantly with his weight behind it, and he came up with a great gout of earth. This he threw over his shoulder as if it were a handful of dust. Instinctively, he kept on digging, thumping the spade in again. George stopped him by putting out a hand and taking it, saying:

"Wait a minute—you're the architect, I'm the builder." He handed the spade to a tall, lean Cracker, telling him, "You take it, Orey." Orey took it, but he glared at Adam from dark, deeply set eyes. He had a mean expression of one who enjoys hating for its pure satisfaction. There was a moment while Adam glared back at him. Gruffly, George broke the tension by ordering, "You men dig along this line first. You others, over here."

The men gazed wonderingly while they dug for the foundations, erected forms, and poured concrete. Some of them, particularly Orey, worked bitterly. Others snickered occasionally. George didn't say any more about trouble, but Adam knew that was what he meant when it came time to show the men how to lay the hollow tile and George advised, "Now take it easy. Most of them aren't too bright, don't want to be, and don't like anybody who is."

"I'll be good," Adam promised. "It's too important to me to have anything happen now."

The men gathered around in a group near one of the footings. Concrete had been mixed and Adam handed a trowel. "Mr. Paine," George told the men, "is going to show you how to work this."

The men turned expressionless faces from him to Adam.

Picking up a hollow tile from the pile brought to the place for work to begin, Adam asked, "Will each of you men pick up a tile?"

They did so, slowly, passing the tiles among them.

"I'd like to explain exactly what it is and how it works," said Adam. He went on, to tell them the purpose of the shape of the tile, how the air-space acted as insulation. He listed the advantages of strength and prevention of sweating walls.

The men kept turning the tiles over in their hands. They looked skeptical. When Adam was through, Orey cackled, "Looks like some new kind of skunk trap to me."

The other men guffawed.

Adam kept his temper. He grinned broadly and told Orey good-naturedly, "Look out you don't get caught in it."

Orey scowled. The men didn't smile. None of them chose to take Adam's remark as kidding. They decided that he had called Orey a skunk.

George motioned for Adam to get on with it.

"I'll lay a few," Adam went on, "to show you." He gave a practical demonstration with a number. The men watched diffidently. Most had put down their tiles. To win him, Adam picked Orey for the first man to try, handing him the trowel.

Orey asked George, "Am I working under him or you?"

George gave the Cracker short shrift. "You're working under me and Mr. Paine is trying to teach you something you'll find valuable if you want to learn it."

Without smiling, resentment written all over him, Orey followed instructions, at least partially. Adam was patient when he advised, "More mud; you aren't using enough to set it properly." Orey jabbed viciously at the concrete and carried a large gob of it to his task. "That's too much," Adam said. With a grimace, Orey discarded some. That job done, Orey picked up another tile and prepared to set it in place. Adam, watching, cried, "You've got it sideways! Good God, man, haven't you got eyes?"

There was silence.

Adam realized his patience hadn't lasted long, and spread his hands at George.

Orey muttered, "I got maybe as good eyes as anybody else around here. And what I see with them is I got enough of this job." He flung down the trowel. Deliberately he let the tile drop on the footing, where it broke into several pieces.

The other men murmured.

George began, "Now look here, Orey—"

"We don't work on no job for him," Orey stated, jerking his thumb at Adam. "Particular on account of there being no call to put it up in the first place."

"Let's walk off it," another man suggested.

"You walk this job—" George began again.

"It ain't a popular thing," a third man pointed out.

"I'm telling you," George threatened, "you walk this job and none of you will ever work for me again."

Hesitation appeared on a few faces. It disappeared when Orey muttered, "That being all right with us."

The men, led by Orey, turned and strode to their cars. They got in them, started, and drove off.

George spat and observed to Adam, "You sure showed them how to lay hollow tile. You sure fixed it fine so we can go ahead. Did you have to yell at that crazy Cracker?"

"Does he have to be a half-wit?" Adam inquired. He had picked up the trowel, brushed away the pieces of broken tile, and taken up another to lay.

George glared after the men. "I'll be damned. That's the first time that ever happened to me."

"Go get yourself some more men."

"Fat chance. They're going to spread the word so fast you won't

59

get any white man to come to this job. You don't know how sore people are about this. The rich over here don't like it so much they've got them all stirred up. That's mostly why those damn fools walked."

"What are you going to do?" Adam knocked the edge of his trowel on his work to shake excess concrete from it, and laid another tile.

George demanded, "What do you think *you're* doing?"

Adam said calmly, "I like to work this way sometimes. You ought to learn how to do this yourself, George. It's the coming thing."

George looked at him. "All right, Michelangelo, we'll build it ourselves. Just the two of us."

George took up a trowel. He watched Adam for a minute and then tried a tile himself. He did a second, and said, "They go together nice."

They worked together in the hot sun, which soon had perspiration dripping down their faces. The wall grew only gradually. They looked at the outlines of the large building and Adam inquired, "Why not Negro labor?"

"Black men can't do this kind of work."

Adam didn't pursue it. At noon he took George back to the cottage for lunch. Eve was aghast to hear the news, and glanced with accusation at Adam.

"It wasn't him so much," George defended him. "It's just that word is around against the building."

Aubrey took the situation solemnly. He changed his clothes to go back with them that afternoon to work. Eve cried, "You three don't think you're going to build it yourselves?"

"We'll work while we keep figuring what to do," said Adam.

In the afternoon the three men looked up from their work at the sound of a Model T coming down the lane. Adam recognized Gerry. He hadn't seen or heard of him since the day they met. On Gerry's handsome head, instead of his straw hat, was a cap which read, "Jitney." He got out with his usual aplomb and Adam greeted him, "When does the boom start?"

"Patience, friend," advised Gerry. "It has already started for you and it will be here for me in all good due time. I got to Florida a little sooner than I expected."

"The leading promoter of the state," Adam introduced him.

"I hear you got trouble," Gerry said.

"Your ears are bigger than they look."

"You hear a lot when you run a jitney. That's the way I'm marking time until things really start," Gerry explained.

"Do you own that thing?"

"At the moment it belongs to a friend of mine, but I expect to own it quite soon."

He gazed at the work they were doing. He shuddered. "Well, much as it's against my principles to do physical labor, I've come to return some of the bread you cast upon my waters."

Delighted, Adam hollered, "Grab yourself a trowel!"

Gerry changed his cap for his straw, which he kept in the jitney. They worked through the afternoon. The sweat poured off them. Gerry complained, but kept on working. They laid a portion of one wall. "Now that it's become work," Adam asked George, "why can't black labor do this?"

"They're too ignorant."

"I can't see how they'd beat Orey at that," Adam persisted. "At least they'd take orders and not talk back. Don't you know a couple of bright ones we could start with?"

George thought. "I know a couple of Bahamans. They're smarter than those here. If they could learn it they could teach others and act as foremen. That's what you need most; you've got to work black men with a foreman of their own; he's the only one who can really drive them."

"Bring on your Bahamans tomorrow morning," Adam promised, "and I'll be the politest I can be to them."

"I'll bring them," countered George, "but you'll stay out of it. I know how to lay your damn tile now. I can show them. If we're going to work together on this we'd better start off on the right foot from now on. You keep to being an architect. I'll be the builder. If you want anything you do it through me. You keep away from the men. That's the way it will have to be, Michelangelo."

61

Adam regarded him evenly. "It's good enough."

The only difficulty that came up about this plan was the transportation of the Negro workers from West Palm Beach to Palm Beach. None of them had cars. Gerry was hired to bring them in batches in the morning and to return the batches at night. George offered him a job during the day, but Gerry shied from it as though it might bite him.

The walls of the building rose steadily. An army of black men swarmed over it. Soon the roof was on and it had been dried in. Meanwhile the Palm Beach season had long closed. Active criticism of the building no longer came from those who guarded their domain so jealously; they were not on hand to voice it. With their departure work for many in West Palm Beach ceased. The long summer doldrums, with little income, set in. When it came time to hire plumbers, electricians, and others, these men, though not approving, quietly accepted the work and kept their opinions to themselves.

Adam was at the site every day, staying all day. No move escaped his eye. He criticized. He changed. He worried. Once in a while he approved. When men said something couldn't be done, he showed them, by showing George, that it could. He swore and raged and stomped and lost weight. He slapped at insects and cursed the burning summer heat when it came. But he kept to his word with George. Anything he had to say was said through him.

In July, the time Adam anticipated, the main shell of the Flamingo Club was finished. There was no longer any necessity to pretend that it was to be a hospital. It lacked tile floors that were to come later, along with paneling, fixtures, ironwork, and the furnishings, but the building itself now rose exquisitely from the shore of Lake Worth.

Michael came down to see it. When they met him in the Ghost at the station, he first asked Eve, "Has he done it?"

"Michael, it's beautiful."

"Come and see for yourself," Adam told him.

Michael walked with them through the big empty rooms. He said nothing at all on the tour, not even when they mounted to his special apartment in the tower. He asked only a few questions here, in the large bathroom inquiring, "The blue and yellow tile there?" He had only a brief glance for the golf course being laid out on the grounds to the south.

Downstairs again, he stood silently looking along the cloisters with their rows of delicate columns. In the patio he saw that the bougainvillea had already been planted, so that it would grow and be in bloom next winter for the opening of the Club. Fully grown orange and coconut trees had also been transported and planted close to the walls. Michael stared at them and Adam said, "They told me it couldn't be done."

"All I can say," Michael gave as his judgment, "is that I'm glad I was sitting next to you that day on the Ponce veranda. You've done something here, Adam. We know it's good, wonderful. Others don't. Not yet. When the season opens next year there is going to be a moment when it can go either way. Acceptance of anything here is a very tender thing, not being based upon worth by any means, but usually on pure whim. I know that because I'm a part of it. They are my people who make these decisions. I've gone against them in this. They will sit in judgment on me as well as you."

"Michael," said Eve with discovery in her voice, "you sound frightened."

"I am. Frightened that they won't see how fine this is. They may not, you know. The building is done, outside of what you will bring back for it from Spain. But it hasn't been accepted yet."

"It will be," Adam predicted.

"I wish I had your damn-fool confidence," said Michael. "You don't yet understand what you're bucking. I may not even be able to get them to come and look at it."

"I WANT YOU

to see all of Spain," Adam told Eve, "but mostly we'll spend our time in Andalusia, the southern part of the country, and there, it's Seville for me. That's where I lived; it was my headquarters." The very name of the place seemed to excite him. "That's where Columbus was received after he discovered America."

"Do you think you'll get the same kind of reception?" asked Eve.

"Well," he pointed out, "I'm bringing what Columbus went for and didn't get—gold."

Eve complained that the Spanish ship they took to Cadiz was dirty and Adam defended it, "Only by comparison with our fetish for being clean. We spend far too much effort at it. Like thinking over something before doing it, being too clean is a waste of time."

The closer the small, tossing ship got to Spain the more excited Adam became. Eve had never seen him like that before. He was like a man going back, after long absence, to a desired mistress. When they landed at Cadiz and the question came up of how they should make the short trip to Seville, he cried enthusiastically, "We're in luck. One of the river steamers is about to leave."

Eve looked about the port. "Do they have trains, too?"

"Yes, but—"

"Adam, I'm not a wife who asks much, am I?"

"What do you mean?"

"No more Spanish boats, please. I've got visitors. They've been biting me."

"Fleas already?" Adam asked. "Now you know you're in Spain."

She itched. "What's the best thing to do for them?"

"Let them bite you until you build up an immunity."

"Do you mind if I try the railway variety?"

"All right, the train it is."

On the way, looking at the thin, serious faces of the people on the train and in their carriage, Eve inquired, "Why is everybody so sad?"

"They aren't sad exactly," Adam explained. "They're sort of morose—in a way they enjoy."

"You can enjoy being unhappy?"

"You'll never understand the Spanish people unless you can see that," he told her. "Look at their country. Maybe that will show you."

Eve watched the landscape as the train crawled through Andalusia. The bare, dry brown land was desolate. Even the foothills in the distance looked arid and unproductive. A bullock cart making its way along a road raised a cloud of dust.

Adam was nearly shaking with excitement when they arrived at the station in Seville. Outside, while their luggage was loaded onto a carriage—Adam spurned one of the few taxicabs about— he stood for a long moment looking at the city. With reverence, his voice softer than Eve had ever heard it, he said, "I can hardly believe I'm back. It makes me want to stay here for the rest of my life. This is age, stone that means something. This has been good enough to pass through the fire of centuries. It's what I hope to do back in Florida."

That was the nearest Eve ever heard her husband come to prayer.

He bustled her into the open carriage and they started out. Though it was early evening, the beginning of twilight, it was very hot, yet so dry a heat that it caused little or no perspiration. Eve was charmed with patches of gay awnings stretched all the way across narrow streets to keep the sun from beating down into them. She noticed palm trees, different in variety from those in Florida, but reminiscent of them.

Adam cleared his throat. He sounded a little like a foghorn. Eve recognized this as announcement of telling her something she might not like. "Eve," he said, "instead of going to one of the big hotels where the service will be good, and there won't be any fleas, I'd like to stay where I lived when I was here. I've told

65

you about it, the rooming house in the old part of the city—
you'll like that part—but there'll be only a bedroom for us to
live in. And no private bath."

She put a hand on his huge knee. "Do what you want, Tiny;
you don't arrive home every day."

He put an arm about her, nearly squeezing the breath out of
her, and yelled to the driver in Spanish.

The carriage rolled through ancient streets where there was
barely room to pass. People withdrew into doorways and narrow
alleys to let it by. The sheer white walls of the buildings rose
blankly except for sparse windows on the ground floor heavily
barred and closed even in the heat. Sometimes the walls were
thick at the base, thinning as they rose. Few buildings were as
much as four stories.

Eve stared. "It's like a hundred years ago."

"Five hundred," Adam corrected. "It's just the same as it
was then."

The driver brought his horses to a stop in front of a building
that looked like all the others. A large arched doorway led into
it. Adam descended from the carriage, letting it spring back into
the air from his weight, and in one stride crossed the narrow sidewalk, to stand in the open arch and bellow:

"Maria! Maria!"

In a moment, waddling into sight as though coming to see
something she could not believe, there appeared in the archway
the broadest woman Eve had ever seen. She had heard people
described as being nearly as wide as they were tall, but Maria
illustrated this almost literally. Black hair parted in the middle
and slicked back, voluminous dark dress dropping to the ground,
her bright eyes stared at Adam incredulously and then she cried
shrilly, "Señor Paine! Señor!"

When they embraced, the sight was so grotesque, with Adam
stooping low enough, almost crouching, to make it possible, that
Eve nearly laughed. She couldn't understand the excited Spanish
that followed, but afterward Adam told her what was said:

"It is you!"

"So it is you!"

"You are bigger!"

"You are broader!"

"You are here!"

"I told you I would come back some day."

"You have kept your word."

"You are crying!"

"A speck of dust . . ."

"Spain weeps for me."

"A few tears, that is all."

"Spain welcomes me back."

"Always she misses you."

"You are still alive; how can this be?"

"My heart kept beating for you."

"It beat for others, too."

"No, only you. Even if you never wrote a letter."

"What is writing? It is not living."

Maria, touching a knuckle to her eyes, looked beyond Adam and saw Eve in the carriage. "What is this?"

"That is my woman."

"It is not true. No good woman would have you."

"It is my woman, and she is good."

"There are little ones?"

"None yet."

"God does not like that."

"Some day he will help us to gain his favor."

Eve stepped out of the carriage when she saw them looking at her and obviously discussing her. Adam introduced Maria in Spanish and Eve received a flood of welcome, none of which she understood. She replied with the only words she could bring to her command, knowing they were not right, "Buenas noches, Señora." What she said meant, "Good evening."

Maria stared, momentarily shocked, until Adam explained, "She has none of our language, Broad One. If she had, she would say that she is happy and proud to make your gracious acquaintance."

"She is the right size for you."

"I searched long and far."

67

"She is good to you?"

"Better than I deserve. It is strange to hear you ask that, making me realize I am home again more than anything else, for in the United States you would ask if I am good to her."

"Are you, then?"

"I am wonderful to her."

"One cannot believe everything he hears."

"Let me hear that you have a chamber for us."

"A marriage chamber, yes."

"Not a marriage chamber."

"What is this? With your woman you do not wish a marriage chamber?"

"What I mean to say is we would like a chamber with two beds in it."

"You do not sleep with your woman?"

"I sleep with my woman, but also we wish to rest apart. That is the reason for two beds."

"I do not believe it. It is not a true marriage you have if you do not sleep with your woman."

"I tell you I sleep with my woman."

"Then you wish only one bed."

"We wish two beds."

"You cannot sleep with your woman in two beds."

"I sleep with her in one bed."

"As I said, another bed is not needed."

"Do not be as thick in the head as you are in the body. The other bed is needed for resting."

"One bed is enough to rest in. Now I am sure you do not sleep with your woman."

"I—"

"I do not think I want in my house a marriage that is not a marriage."

"I say again it is a true marriage."

"Is this an American custom, not sleeping with your woman? That is the reason there are no little ones. Why did you marry her? Is it she who does not accept you? I do not believe that, for she looks like a woman of feeling. Then it is you. You spurn her. You must change your ways. Here is the place to change them.

68

You must prove to me that you have a true marriage by taking a room with but one bed."

"I begin to see, Broad One. It is so long since I have been here and heard your way of thinking, I had forgotten. The only room you have free has but one bed."

"It is truly long since you have been here, Big One."

Their room was a large, square, high chamber with a bed in it so immense that it could nearly be regarded as two. It faced the street and had, in addition to long glass doors, thick heavy wooden shutters. Both, Adam explained, were tightly closed at sundown to keep out the bad night air and robbers who would climb in your window if left open.

He was impatient to get out into the city again, to see it anew. He pulled Eve along on foot through streets which were beginning to be crowded after nightfall. "Now the life of Seville starts," Adam explained. "The shops are open in the morning and then close in the afternoon. They open again at night when it's cooler."

Adam rushed along so fast that Eve could hardly keep up. "What's the hurry?" she asked.

"I've got to see it," he said.

"See what?"

He stopped, grabbing her by the arm. "There! This is where I wanted to get to, where you can see it from a block away. That's the most beautiful tower in the world."

Lighted faintly by a new moon, the square Giralda rose like a lovely ghost, its tiers of decorated panels and balconied windows set one upon another in unrivaled, delicate symmetry. It was topped by a belfry with a graceful turning female figure, acting as a weathervane, at the peak.

Eve looked for some moments and then said, "I don't blame you for wanting to get to that."

"It's a building. Those old Moors had an eye for using the sky as a backdrop. They were as good as the Greeks in architecture, and of course far more subtle. It was a big mistake to kick them out of Spain. The Church never touched them, the best thing it did being to let some of their buildings stand."

As they left the Giralda, Eve said she was hungry and Adam

69

informed her, "You'll get hungrier. Restaurants aren't open here until nine or ten o'clock at night."

"Nine or ten!"

"We'll go to a nine o'clock one. Right now we'll promenade on the Sierpes and look about and get a drink and maybe a pastry for you."

They entered a narrow, winding street with shops like bazaars on either side. Open-air cafes and restaurants were here, together with theaters and dance halls. There was no vehicular traffic. Everyone was on foot. Men called out lottery numbers they were offering for sale. Bullfight posters looked down from the walls. There was the smell of freshly roasting coffee.

Eve was fascinated, but asked, "Where are the women? There are hardly any."

"You'll see a few more at dinner time," Adam explained, "but most women at night are kept home behind thick walls. The Moors left more than their buildings behind."

Men sitting at the cafe tables or standing in groups near the white walls looked openly at Eve. They stared and some of them spoke. Their words were soft and casual, their eyes darkly luminous.

"Adam! Are they talking about me?"

"You know they are. It's a custom."

"What are they saying?"

"Are you sure you want to know?"

"I—yes."

"One said, 'The tall one is beautiful.' Another said, 'It would be good to embrace her.' "

Eve laughed uncertainly. "I don't know whether to be flattered or furious."

"You'd better hear some more before you decide."

They passed three men, all of whom stared at her frankly and made remarks.

"What did they say?"

"One said you have a lovely, tall body. Another thinks your legs are long and gracious. The third is of the opinion that he is in all ways, except height and weight, as large as your husband."

"I've never heard of such a thing!"

A lone man leaning against a white wall offered his grave

comment. When Eve asked Adam to translate, he said, "You'd better let that one go."

"Tell me."

"He said, 'My eggs are for you.'"

"What? Oh!"

"I gave you a broad version. If you had the literal you'd go back and slap his face."

"I think I will, anyway."

"They all mean what they say as compliments. You're getting as much and as good as any I've ever heard."

"I don't think I appreciate them."

"I do; it's a compliment to me, too."

"To have men on the street make insulting and dirty remarks about your wife?"

"They aren't insulting and they aren't dirty. You're in Spain, Evie, where people aren't afraid of the facts of life and treat them naturally. They don't make them shameful or label them sins."

"I won't argue it, Tiny, since it's your pet country and I've only been here a few hours. But you'd better make it produce that drink and pastry before I faint."

"We'll get it here." Adam sat her down at an open-air marble-top table. "I think we'll dine here, too, inside; I used to come here when I was in the chips."

It was eleven o'clock by the time they completed their dinner. Adam led Eve off the Sierpes to another street where they could get a carriage, and said, "Now we'll call on Don Fadrique."

"At this hour?"

"Oh, it's just the shank of the evening. And he'll be expecting me about this time."

"I didn't see you sneak off and make a phone call."

"I wrote to him when I was sailing. He'll know the rest. In this country there is subtlety and intuition to life."

He hailed a carriage, they got in, and he gave the driver the address. "You'll find that when we arrive he will have sent his family inside. Women don't associate with strangers, especially foreigners. He'll be surprised that I bring you, but he won't show it. Now you'll see the private life of Seville. You'll see something

71

superior, something I'd like to have in all the houses I'm going to build, but won't be there. Still, the opportunity for it is a part of what I'll build into those houses."

Eve marveled that he made no question of the Flamingo Club being accepted and his going on from there. He wasn't being optimistic; he believed in himself thoroughly. She remembered Michael's warning and was frightened for Adam.

They came, after a few minutes' drive through somewhat broader streets, to the entrance of a large two-story house. The street-front side had no windows at all on the ground floor, and presented a drab and uninviting appearance. The house had the usual wide arched entrance; barring it were heavy wrought-iron gates. Behind its bars sat a manservant who rose, after Adam spoke to him, and opened one side to let them enter.

They were ushered into a big courtyard paved with marble. Arcades entirely surrounded it. In one corner a staircase led to the second floor. Here a glassed-in gallery surrounded the court. A movable awning, which could cover the entire courtyard, was now pulled back. In the center a fountain played softly, dropping its thin stream of water back into a dark pool. The space about it was furnished as though it were inside a dwelling. Rugs lay on the ground, while there were sofas, tables, chairs, and even a piano. Lamps and colored lights shed a glow upon the scene. From somewhere came a woman's voice singing what sounded like a dirge.

The single occupant of the courtyard was a lean, spare man with a goat-like gray beard. He had a sharply pointed, arched nose and deep-set, piercing eyes. As the servant brought Adam and Eve to him he rose from the chair he occupied and stood waiting to greet them. His welcome to Adam was quiet and modulated, almost hushed. It was so casual that they might have parted only yesterday instead of some years ago. It was also warm; Eve, even though she didn't understand the language, thought its tone was actually affectionate.

This was Don Fadrique de Rioja, Spanish aristocrat.

Adam adjusted himself to the mood of his host. Eve had never seen him so subdued. He presented her to Don Fadrique as though to royalty. Eve, feeling inadequate again, got off her

"*Buenas noches*" once more. Don Fadrique did not stare, but bowed low, murmuring graciously to her.

"He says," Adam translated, "that you do him honor by coming to his poor house, which is yours even though it is not worthy of you."

Don Fadrique spoke again to Eve, making his meaning clear by gesturing with quick, bird-like movements of his hands, at the chairs. He waited for her to seat herself, and then sat down again himself. Adam took a chair, waiting for it to creak and crack under him. It didn't. There wasn't a sound. He told Don Fadrique, "It is good to sit again in a chair that does not threaten to fall apart under me. Later, may I study its construction?"

"It is yours, my friend."

Eve, glancing at the open sky above their heads, could not resist asking, "What happens when it rains?"

Adam translated this for their host, who smiled while Adam explained to Eve, "It rarely rains here in summer. If it does, the awning is pulled over to catch it as it is during the day to keep out the sun. Even if it rained hard Don Fadrique has so many servants they could put all the furniture here back under the arcades in a few minutes. This is sort of a summer parlor; in winter the furniture is taken in."

While Eve looked about, watching the fountain and listening to the unseen singer, Adam and Don Fadrique spoke together. She thought they spoke of the business they were to conduct with each other. Don Fadrique was to act as Adam's agent in Spain for the purchase of all the articles he needed.

In the middle of their talk Don Fadrique turned to Eve and asked her something she didn't understand until Adam explained, "He wants to know if you will do him the favor of accepting a glass of wine or if you will take coffee."

Eve essayed, "*Vino, muchas gracias, Señor Don Fadrique.*"

Their host bowed his head and called softly. A servant appeared almost instantly with wine.

"Not bad," Adam told Eve, "except you were far too familiar. You should have used his full name; the way you put it was like calling somebody 'George' the first time you met him."

73

Eve put her hand to her mouth and looked contritely at Don Fadrique. "I'd better keep quiet."

"It's all right," Adam assured her. "He understands foreigners."

The two men spoke again, earnestly discussing something. Eve sipped her wine, sweet but delicious. To the sounds of the fountain and the singing now was added the odor of orange blossoms, as if to go with them. For the first time she saw the orange trees standing about the courtyard.

Adam rose and turned upside down the chair in which he had been sitting. He examined the way it was made, nodding his heavy head with approval. He did not sit down again, but prepared to leave, and Don Fadrique also rose.

Eve, getting up, said, "I expect you finished your business."

" 'Business?' " Adam repeated. He spoke to Don Fadrique, explaining what Eve had said, and then turned back to her, speaking again in English, "We haven't been talking about business beyond setting a date to meet tomorrow morning at ten. You don't do things that way here. We've been discussing the development of civilization up to the point of his courtyard here. I've been claiming that man need go no further. He differs with me in saying that, no matter how unfortunate, it is always necessary for man to change his ways, for stability that lasts too long becomes stagnant and weak. He says that is the condition of Spain now. On another thing we agreed. This is an old German saying that goes like this: 'He whom God loves has a house in Seville.' "

DON FADRIQUE CALLED

for them the next morning in a wheezing Spanish automobile driven by the servant who had admitted them to his house the night before. Don Fadrique sat with him in the front, while Eve and Adam occupied the rear seat. The corner of the car occupied by Adam sank sadly, throwing the whole thing off balance. As if protesting this the car coughed, spat, and bucked before starting off.

They drove to the Rio Guadalquivir, crossing the river over a stone bridge, and then came to a factory section where also were the houses of workingmen. In a moment they pulled up before a sizable one-story warehouse. Entering this, they came into the presence of about an acre of Spanish antique furniture. In places it was piled to the ceiling. Eve gasped at the sight. "Is Don Fadrique the head of the company that owns this?"

"He is the company," Adam explained. "This is just one of his warehouses. He has them in Cordoba and Granada, and another here, a smaller one where he has—well, selected things. He'll probably take us there later. Right now you'd better keep track for me of what I'll buy here. And the prices."

Don Fadrique, who had left them for a moment, returned with a clerk who carried several pads of paper and pencils. At Adam's request the clerk gave one set to Eve, while he retained the other, using it to make his own notations as they proceeded to examine the furniture.

Adam knew exactly what he wanted. He had been in this warehouse before; some articles here then were still here, and he greeted them like friends. Now he was excited again. He ran his hands over the scarred, worm-eaten surface of tables and chests which were hundreds of years old. He patted them lovingly, sometimes slapping them with the palm of his hand, and called upon Eve to appreciate their beauty.

She could not deny that they were beautiful, but she cautioned, "The way you're acting you won't get any bargains."

"I know what they're worth," he replied, "and Don Fadrique knows I know."

Followed by the others, he walked down the aisles all through the warehouse once before he decided on anything. Then the transactions began to take place. He pointed to a high, ancient chest of drawers and asked, "How much for that?"

Don Fadrique named a price.

"I want twenty-four," Adam told him, "like that in size and period, but none exactly like the other. Can you get them?"

"I have them already," replied Don Fadrique.

Adam glanced about. "I see but half a dozen."

"I have them," Don Fadrique assured him.

"And the price each, when ordering so many?"

Don Fadrique mentioned a lower figure than the one he had already quoted. To this Adam agreed and gave Eve the notation; she wrote it as Don Fadrique listed it for his clerk.

Adam bought mirrors to go with the chests, not perfect in their glass, but exquisite in the decorations of their heavy gold frames. He went on to tables upheld by long, graceful arms of iron beneath them. He chose smaller tables inlaid with decorated tiles. He selected tremendous bedsteads, great low chests, and tall, capacious armoires. He wouldn't buy a chair if it made a cracking sound when he sat in it, but he bought several hundred that did not; he was partial to those with rawhide seats, and tireless in trying them out. Additionally, he chose a number of praying chairs with low seats and high backs.

The morning was spent on heavy furniture, and before he was through Adam had nearly cleaned out that section of the warehouse. Eve's hand was tired from writing. After lunch, with wine, served in a corner of the warehouse, most of the afternoon was taken up with the selection of rugs, silks, hangings, and tapestries, many of them ecclesiastical. Candelabra, both for tables and floors, together with wrought-iron fixtures that could be converted to electricity, were studied, chosen, and ordered in quantity that made Don Fadrique's clerk stare with surprise.

Adam and the aristocratic Spaniard rarely haggled. Adam wanted a lower price on all articles he bought in numbers, and never failed to get it. Don Fadrique's quoted price on single articles was usually accepted. When Adam occasionally requested a lower figure it was given. Only once, as if it might be a subtle warning, did Adam refuse an article because of its price. Eve was amazed at the lowness of most of the figures, whispering to Adam, "They're ridiculous," to have Adam reply, "Not to him. He's become a rich man selling to foreigners, and he'll be richer than ever when I'm through."

That evening, back in their rooming house, Eve asked, "But what about the other warehouse? Why did you stop in the middle of the afternoon and we didn't go there?"

"We'll see that some other day."

"Tell me, Tiny."

"Well, there he has some things he doesn't trust showing to everybody."

"You mean they were stolen?"

Adam rumbled, "That's a word never used in Spain, Evie. Things are never stolen. They are not even taken. Sometimes they wander, that's the way to put it."

Suspiciously, she demanded, "And what has wandered to Don Fadrique's other warehouse?"

"It isn't the way you think," Adam explained. "It isn't stolen goods in our sense and Don Fadrique isn't a fence as he would be called in our country. Everything he has or gets is paid for. Usually he doesn't even know where it comes from. The main part of the difficulty is that most of it is—well, it comes from public buildings or is even a state art treasure."

"Then," Eve accused, "this aristocratic Don Fadrique I've been admiring so much is nothing but a thief who hires men to steal—"

"No, no," Adam cut her short. "You're thinking of it in American terms. You can't do that. In every country there are different sets of values, various forms of honesty and dishonesty. Don Fadrique doesn't hire anybody to do what you say. Certain articles happen to get on the market and he doesn't question their source when he acquires them. He can't help it if people want to sell them. Any more than I can help it if I want to buy them from him. In fact, tomorrow we'll start visiting places where some of these articles may be available at the source."

Dubiously, Eve asked, "Why don't we go to the other warehouse tomorrow? Doesn't he trust you?"

"It isn't that. I didn't ask to go there right away because he'll run the price up on those special goods. I didn't want to appear anxious to see it."

Eve thought. "Wait a minute, Tiny. On the things you bought today you're going to get papers to show they're authentic. What about—well, the other things?"

Adam shrugged his big shoulders. "On those you've got to take your chance."

"One more thing," Eve persisted. "On the regulation things, with papers on them, you'll declare them and pay American custom duties. What about the others? How are you going to get them into the United States in the first place? If some of them are actually Spanish state art treasures it will be found out and somebody will get into trouble."

"Oh," said Adam, "Don Fadrique will take care of that. He's been doing it for years."

"How?"

"I don't know how he does it, Eve. All I know is that it works all right."

"I think you do know, Tiny."

"Even if I do," he asked, "you wouldn't want to know, would you?"

"I guess I wouldn't. But I'm not sure I like it."

"Don't be naive, tall one."

"I never knew I married a pirate."

"It's the only way I can get some pieces I want. It has to be done this way."

Eve said little during the following days when Don Fadrique drove them out of Seville into the surrounding countryside to visit small villages and several monasteries. In one town they entered a large building which had no name on it. Deserted, it was completely furnished. Adam indicated certain pieces he wanted. The

78

walls of one room were covered with carved woods in wonderfully worked linenfold panels. The words went swiftly between Adam and the Spaniard, and then they left the building.

"Did you buy that whole room?" Eve asked.

Adam nodded.

"What was that place?"

"Oh, the building of a man who needs money."

"A public building?"

"Nothing like that."

"Tell me."

"Don Fadrique is waiting for us. He's going to take us to another monastery."

The group of ecclesiastical buildings they visited deep in the countryside was in a bad state of repair. Only a few monks in ragged habits were about. One of them, the bearded abbot himself, took the party to a room which had a highly decorated beamed ceiling. The three men spoke long of this. Adam paced it off and seemed dubious, though Eve saw he was not. Finally he agreed to something. They went into the chapel where Adam examined stone statues; he bought all that were for sale. In the sacristy he purchased a tapestry hanging on the wall.

Outside again, Eve protested, "Adam, not religious things!"

"You don't understand. This monastery is in a state of disintegration. The order is falling apart. It needs money. What I'm paying will bring it together again."

"But their ceiling, their statues, and—"

"They'll make others—perhaps better, though I doubt it. But make no mistake about it that I am doing a good thing here; the abbot is grateful and gave me his blessing, you saw that."

They went to other towns and Adam bought more entire rooms and ceilings. He purchased staircases, doorways, and doors by the dozen, some of them great double high affairs with a wicket gate cut into one of their sides. He bought fountains, great jars, entablatures, fire screens, coats of arms, lanterns, and handbasins set upon the most delicate of ironwork. Once he bought a chimney that caught his fancy and even Don Fadrique shook his head at that. Sometimes he only arranged to procure certain articles, with the definite order to be given in the future.

On other days he and Eve went alone to tile and pottery factories. After their many purchases they were allowed to watch the operations. Eve admired the pottery work and the designs in some of the tiles; the first reminded her of the potter's wheel she once had, the second of her work on fabrics. She murmured that she would like to make both pottery and tile.

"Then watch closely," Adam advised.

"You're going to make this back in Florida?"

"If you mean what you say, *you* are."

She watched, catching his enthusiasm, but still disturbed by some of the circumstances of his purchases, and horrified at the amount he was acquiring. "You've already got far more than enough for the Club," she pointed out. "What are you going to do with all the rest of it?"

"I'm buying for myself now."

"But why one of everything you see that you like?"

"Eve, if the Club goes over, I'm going to go over—in a big way. It would take half of Spain to provide everything I'll need. The rest I'm going to make. I'm going to reproduce things. Clean up both ways, by selling my clients my products."

"What if—Adam—what if the Club isn't accepted?"

"Then I've lost the gamble of being here now and getting what I want while I'm here."

On days they weren't with Don Fadrique they haunted bookshops, publishing houses, and places that dealt in prints, engravings, pamphlets, and printed matter of all description. Adam purchased every book he saw that had pictures of Spanish buildings in it. Some were tremendous tomes a yard high and two feet wide, heavily bound in thick leather. He purchased whole portfolios of prints and sometimes of photographs. He ordered all the publications of a publishing house that issued only books on architecture.

During this time nothing more was said about visiting the second and smaller warehouse of Don Fadrique. Finally, when there seemed nothing left for Adam to buy anywhere else, it was arranged that they visit this building. Don Fadrique drove them himself this time, and at the warehouse there was no clerk, but only an aged watchman who lived there.

Eve could barely believe her eyes at the sight within. She heard

Adam involuntarily suck in his breath. This warehouse was only about a third as large as the other. Nothing here was piled on top of anything else. Each piece stood by itself, with plenty of room left about it so that its charms could be seen readily. It looked as if the furnishings of some rich castle had been removed and placed here. The pieces were all fine enough to be in a museum, and they were of every kind.

Don Fadrique's deep-set eyes burned as he led them to the very center of the warehouse. Here, in a cleared space larger than any other, stood a bed so immense that it made the one in their rooming house seem small by comparison. It was a four-poster, wondrously carved and fashioned, with decorated head and foot-boards. Don Fadrique had rarely spoken in praise or explanation of any of his wares, but of this he did at some length.

"He says," Adam told Eve, "that it was the bed of Queen Isabella of Spain."

"Adam! Do you think it is?"

"It could be, and probably is. It's the right period. God knows. All I know is that I want it for us. I want to sleep in Queen Isabella's bed with you. I want everything in here, too, the whole damn place. I've got to have it."

The courtly manner of dealing that had gone on between him and Don Fadrique now was deserted. As soon as the Spaniard saw that Adam was enamored of every piece in the warehouse, his thin, high-arched nose smelled gold in quantity. He named a figure at which Adam merely bellowed and turned away. Don Fadrique named another price. Adam held his nose. Don Fadrique demanded to know what Adam felt he might be able to afford to pay. Adam told him. Don Fadrique was so cruelly affronted by it that pain came to his eyes and he did not deign to reply. Adam added a sum to what he had mentioned. Don Fadrique stated that he was sure they could not agree and had better drop the matter. Adam added more. Don Fadrique claimed it was impossible. Adam added a little more, inquiring if this were possible. Don Fadrique said it was not. Adam shouted that the whole thing, then, was off, and he didn't want the fake, broken-down excuses for good furniture that stood before them at any price. He took Eve by the arm, as if to leave. Don Fadrique mentioned certain things about Americans being robbers who wanted only to despoil his fine country and strip it of its greatest treasures, including the bed of a queen, paying nothing for them. Adam then leaned down to him and stuck his face into that of the Spaniard and said fiercely that he would pay the exact figure between the generous sum he had offered and the exhorbitant robber's amount Don Fadrique was trying to extort, but that he would pay nothing more, not one centimo above it.

With a sigh of resignation, Don Fadrique said that they had done business.

They shook hands, friends again. It was arranged that the articles here would be held until Adam wanted them in the United States. None of them could be shipped legally, for they were all state art treasures. The large number of them made Don Fadrique question, "They are to go to Florida? A whole shipload, perhaps more. It will be difficult to get so much in. I will guarantee only to the Bahama Islands; once I landed something there. There is too much for your authorities not to see."

Adam thought he could arrange matters from the Bahamas, just over the horizon from the Florida shore. He was more interested in the bed at the moment than this. "How did it find its way here?" he asked.

"Who knows?" countered Don Fadrique.

"You can produce no proof even for my eyes?"

"It is too far a day for that."

"Is there anything in a book?"

The Spaniard shrugged. "I have seen nothing."

"I am to understand that you believe this bed is what you say it is but that you make no claim to it?"

"Think," Don Fadrique reminded him. "The bed of the great queen. I would not dare."

On that tantalizing note Adam's business with Don Fadrique was completed. It left Eve more disquieted than ever. "It makes me feel guilty," she told Adam.

"You'll get over it," he predicted.

That evening they attended, late, flamenco dancing at a cafe-restaurant in the Sierpes. It was nearly three o'clock in the morning when they emerged into the street. A full moon hung directly above Seville, bathing the quiet city with bright light. When Adam spoke of obtaining a carriage, Eve suggested that they walk. He hesitated while she said, "The old quarter will be beautiful and we'll see it better on foot." His agreement was reluctant.

White and gleaming in the strong glow of the moon, the narrow, winding streets of the old part of the city were deserted and had the aspect and quiet of a tomb. Only a solid face of barred and shuttered windows appeared in their walls.

The three men, walking silently on rope-soled shoes, were upon them before they fully realized they were being attacked. Eve found herself pushed tightly back up against the wall by a man standing close in front of her who pressed the point of a knife at her stomach. Adam had two men at him, both with knives. The men were dressed from head to foot in dark clothes. They wore large broad-brimmed hats that threw their faces into shadow.

"*Fantamas!*" Adam exclaimed.

The man holding the knife at Eve spoke to Adam sharply, spitting out one word, "*Cayase!*"

Adam whispered to him, asking a question. In her terror Eve noticed that he asked it politely. Eve's man, who was evidently the leader, gave a hissing consent, "*Si!*" At the same time, with his free hand, he stripped her of her pearl necklace and then plucked the pin from her dress.

The other two men went through Adam's pockets while he spoke to her, advising in a serious whisper, "Don't try to do anything. These men would just as soon use their knives as not. If we give them what they want they won't harm us. For your life, don't try to resist. Now listen to me: no matter what they do, you do nothing. No matter what. Do you understand?"

"I—I—yes."

"*Cayase en Inglés!*" The leader, keeping the sharp point of his knife firmly pressed against Eve's stomach, making her quail, grabbed her hand and snatched off her rings, then her watch from her wrist.

Adam began speaking to them in a low voice in Spanish. They didn't seem to mind that, and even replied. Incredulously, Eve, though not comprehending the words, caught the light note of banter. Adam was kidding them while they threatened his life and took his money, watch, and other valuables. One asked a question of the leader and he replied, "*Si.*" Adam whispered, "*Gracias, Señores,*" thanking them respectfully for something.

The men were finished. Eve's pocketbook and all her jewelry were gone. It was over, or nearly so. The leader, with the knife still pressed against her, stood on his tiptoes. As if in a crazy dream, Eve saw his face coming close to her and she remembered Adam's strict instructions not to mind what the men did, and then the robber was kissing her, fully and firmly on the lips. He murmured, "*Por favor, muy simpático señora.*"

The knife was withdrawn from her stomach. The men ran away without sound, black shadows lost around a curve in the street as Adam called after them, laughingly, "*Hasta la vista!*"

The most amazing part was that Adam failed to be aroused. In a shaky voice Eve called this to his attention and he said, "Be glad you're alive."

Eve wiped her lips with the back of her hand, having been left with no handkerchief. "Did you know he would do that? Is that why you told me not to resist, no matter what?"

"I knew they'd do anything."

Indignantly, she resolved, "We'll tell the police."

"A waste of time. I managed to talk them into not taking our passport and letter of credit, useless to them anyway."

Eve more fully realized what had happened. "Their knives! I don't know whether to be sick or mad."

"Be mad," Adam advised.

That was what she felt most, she found. She raged against the unfair procedure of being held up. "My wedding ring!" she cried.

"I'll get you another. Besides the rest," he said, "they took around two hundred dollars' worth of pesetas from me. With our watches and other things they got away with well over a thousand dollars. How does the whole thing make you feel about my robbing Spain?"

"Better," she declared. "Much better. What did he say?"

"Who?"

"The other robber, when he kissed me."

"That's a woman for you. He said, 'By your favor, very sympathetic lady."

She mused, "Do you suppose he was one of those who have seen me on the street and made comments?"

"I'm sure he was and that he's your devoted admirer."

"And yet he would have stuck his knife in me?"

"Oh, yes."

"I'll never understand Spain, Tiny; never."

MICHAEL MOVED INTO

his tower apartment in the Flamingo Club in December. It was the last to be finished, because of the erratic shipments from Don Fadrique of articles Adam wanted especially to put into it. The rest of the Club was now complete down to the final glazed tile in the floors.

Michael decided to open it on January seventh. This would be right between New Year's Eve and the beginning of prohibition, which had been voted to take effect at midnight on the sixteenth. He didn't want the opening connected with either of these events because the excessive drinking associated with both would detract from the Club.

"I'm going to accept what you said about it," he told Adam. "It's an individual thing that can't be sold to people by the breakfast-food method, by persuasion. Memberships won't be offered and no effort will be made to rent the apartments. I'm going to try to make people ask for both, by letting them sell themselves on it."

He planned an invitation charity dinner as the opening-night event. It would be for the benefit of the hospital in West Palm Beach. That tied in neatly with the first announced purpose of the Club.

"It will get the people here," Michael explained, "because the one thing they can't turn down or resist is an expensive, exclusive charity affair. Best of all, it leaves the way open for those to come who have criticized most. They'll come to find fault and remain to cheer—I hope."

Adam's work was done. Michael handled his own hiring of a manager and staff for the Club. There was nothing for Adam to do except mark time. He found a small task that amused him, the importing of half a dozen pink flamingos from Cuba. These arrived the day before the opening and were placed in a corner of the patio, caged behind high chicken wire. The ungainly birds, on their high, spindly legs, gazed unhappily at the sky but did not take off as Adam half expected.

Michael invited only four of his intimate friends to be at his table along with Adam and Eve. He asked Aubrey to come, but the shy draftsman refused, saying he had work to do on prospective buildings Adam had put him at since last summer. Michael told the Paines, "What my friends say won't mean much. They'll like the Club because it's mine. It's the others, and especially one of them, we want to approve."

"The Bradburys?" Eve asked.

"Mrs. Bradbury. She's our social leader, you know. If she thinks something is smart, it becomes smart, and the others follow. If she likes our Club, we're a success; if she likes your work, you'll be taken up. If she doesn't—well, let's not think of that."

"It's a hell of a thing," Adam raged, "when one damn woman can turn thumbs up or down on you. Does this battle ax know something good when she sees it?"

"She knows," Michael said, "the difference between what she likes and doesn't like."

Adam and Eve dressed for the great event in their bedroom in the cottage. She had seen to it that he had a haircut. He looked as neat in his Tuxedo as any man his size could look. He was silent. It wasn't like him to be saying nothing for as long as five consecutive minutes. Eve glanced at him worriedly and asked, "What's the matter?"

He turned to her. His face was almost stricken. Woefully, he asked, "Do you think they'll like it?" All his cocky assurance was gone. He was like a frightened little boy. He pleaded miserably, "Do you think that old bitch will see it's good?"

"Well, look at him!" Eve exclaimed. "There's a human being in that hulk somewhere."

Irritably, he said, "You couldn't give me any sympathy, could you?"

Eve came, in her shimmering evening gown, to stand right in

87

front of him. "No, I couldn't, you big lug, because you'd eat it up and start feeling sorry for yourself. All you've got is stage fright, and from the looks of you a severe attack of that."

"I can't go over there, Eve."

She stared at him. This was a new facet in the man she had married. Suddenly she loved him for having a weakness; it made him seem closer to her, and more dear. She would have liked to express this, but she knew that what she had said before was true, and she could not.

"What if they don't like it?" Adam wanted to know. "What do I do then? What do I say?"

"You know what you'll say," she told him. "I shiver at how you'll tell them what you think of them."

"And then what?" he inquired anxiously.

"Then we'll get in the Ghost and drive to greener pastures."

He shook his head and repeated, "I can't go over there."

She didn't press this, but treated it lightly. "Well, come on over and watch me give a name to the ugly thing, anyway. Nobody will be there yet."

Glumly, dragging his feet, Adam accompanied her to the Flamingo Club. Michael hadn't forgotten his promise to have Eve break a bottle of champagne on the doorway of the Club on opening night. He was there, with the manager, the maître d'hôtel, and part of the staff, readying the ceremony. A bottle of imported champagne had been strung by a strong red ribbon from the railing of the balcony over the arched entrance.

Michael gave Eve the bottle, instructing her how to hold it by the end of the neck and watch out for flying glass. "All right," he said.

Eve glanced at Adam. "I won't knock the building down," she promised.

She lifted the bottle. "I christen thee," she announced, "the Flamingo Club!" She swung with the bottle on the edge of the stone-carved Moorish entrance arch, closing her eyes at the last second.

The bottle broke with a crack and a rush and sizzle of champagne. There was a small cheer. Eve stood away from the dripping, shattered remains of the bottle, holding it out in front of her,

88

and opened her eyes to look at the spot where she struck. She told Adam, "It didn't even nick."

While the manager took the bottle neck from her and the maître d'hôtel instructed his men to sweep and clean up the entrance steps, Eve told Michael, indicating Adam, "He's scared."

Michael laughed. He took up Adam's limp hand and shook it. "Glad to know you, brother. I'm just not showing it."

Adam turned to go, but Michael caught his arm. "Wait a minute, wait a minute! If you aren't here, no matter what happens, you'll kick yourself for the rest of your life."

"I can't stand it, I tell you," Adam moaned. "I can't sit there with people while they decide."

Michael looked at Eve, his glance conferring with her about what to do. She suggested to Adam, "Why don't you sit somewhere so you can listen without being seen, until you know how things are going?"

A faint gleam of interest showed in Adam's tensely worried face.

"That's it," said Michael. "We'll have them fix you up with a chair behind palms, if we can find enough to hide you."

Adam inquired, "You think—?"

Eve put her arm in his and pulled him into the building, saying, "Come on."

They placed him, surrounded by potted palms, in a corner of the cloisters that was near the entrance hall and stairway to the upper floors. People coming in would pass within earshot, and from the spot, also, Adam could catch a glimpse of the patio with all the tables set and ready for their parties. The small terrazo dance floor gleamed in the middle of the tables under the colored lights.

"Don't laugh," he pleaded to them.

"I'm laughing," Michael said, even though he didn't.

"It will be all right," Eve assured him. She straightened his tie, bent over and kissed him, said, "Let me know if you get lonesome," and then rustled out through the palm fans.

Instantly Adam jumped to his feet. He was sure something had happened to the spotlights carefully placed at the foot of the palm trees to show them at night. He looked out into the patio; everything was in good working order.

He sat down again, perspiring. He felt foolish and ridiculous, yet he couldn't down the sick feeling that had taken hold of him without warning. He didn't know how long it was that he sat there, clasping and unclasping his damp hands, until the first guests arrived. Then he sat stiffly, acutely attentive.

He was disappointed that these people said nothing he could hear. They went upstairs where the furnished apartments, including Michael's, were open for inspection, and came down again without uttering a single word when they passed Adam to give him some indication of what they thought. He swore at them under his breath.

The second batch was a little more productive, though not much. He caught one comment. "Well," a woman said in a shrill, supercilious voice, "it's certainly different!"

Adam was sure she meant this in criticism; it couldn't be anything else.

The third group made him feel at least hopeful. "I don't care what other people say," a woman declared, "I think it's beautiful."

Adam wanted to rush out and throw his arms about her. Instead, he held himself quietly to hear more. But their voices trailed off, he suspected, in argument about the woman's heresy.

The first male comment he heard was definitely bad. He caught two remarks as men passed discussing the building.

"So this is Paine architecture."

"It's a pain, all right."

He wanted to throttle them, until he thought a bit and then saw how easy and obvious a joke it was. The men had also sounded tentative, not altogether sure of themselves, as though waiting to see how others were taking it before committing themselves all the way.

He was more disturbed by two more men who stood for a moment near his hideaway discussing the building. One said:

"Of course, he isn't an architect in the true sense of the word. This is a stage setting. He used to be a scenic designer, you know."

"That's it," the second man said. "It's a stage setting, not a building people can live in."

Adam peeked through his palms to see these men and felt a lot better when he recognized them as local architects come to find fault and pick him apart; he was a threat to them. He sensed that they were afraid of him, and took courage himself.

He heard other voices. "It's one of the most attractive buildings I've ever been in, and that's all there is to it."

"Of course it is. There isn't any question about it being accepted."

Adam saw that these were Michael's friends. He recalled what Michael said about their opinion, and discounted their remarks.

He watched for the Bradburys. He knew them by sight from having seen them at the Royal Poinciana, where they stayed, the little, spindly man with his cropped white mustache, the pouter-pigeon woman with her ropes of pearls and bulldog jowls. He couldn't clearly see everybody passing his palms, but he wanted to see the Bradburys. He resolved that if her thumb went up he would join the party at Michael's table. If her fat thumb went down he would sneak out.

People were arriving fast now. The comments came rapidly.

"That ceiling is magnificent."

"Did you see the bathroom in Sumner's apartment? Those tiles—I think I'd like that."

"I haven't seen anything like these pieces of furniture since Europe. Where did he get them?"

"In Europe."

"I want to go back and see that paneling in the main lounge."

"Well, I don't know about it. I haven't made up my mind yet."

"You mean," Adam told himself bitterly, "Mrs. Bradbury hasn't made up your mind for you yet."

Eve appeared, slipping through the palms. "Tiny, they like it."

"Do they?"

"Don't you believe it yet?"

He shook his head. "Have those creatures, the Bradburys, arrived?"

"No."

"Maybe they won't come." That would be worse than their coming.

"They'll be here. She always waits until everybody else has arrived. Don't you want something to eat?"

"I'm not hungry. But I'll take a drink. Send a waiter with a drink."

"All right, Tiny." She looked at him, smiling fondly, and went away again.

The waiter stared curiously when he found Adam behind the palms, and delivered the drink. Adam scowled at him. He gulped at the drink. Just then the orchestra began to play. The noise frightened the flamingos penned in behind their chicken wire. Even though Adam couldn't see them, he knew what was happening when people cried out. Then they were looking up, and Adam, watching, too, saw six pink forms flying past the lights on the coconut palms. The flamingos were on their way back to Cuba.

A man called loudly above the music and murmuring of the people, "There goes a lot of breakfast food!"

A shout of laughter came. Adam was sure it ridiculed Michael and all they had done. Slowly, he began to realize that the laughter was good-natured, more in sophisticated sympathy with Michael than anything else. It served to bring the people together, bind the crowd in a way that you could feel rather than see. It made them more receptive, ready, and wanting, perhaps, to accept his building if it received the social leader accolade still missing.

The departure of the flamingos made him miss the Bradburys when they passed on their tour of the building. He only saw their large party go to its table set all along one side of the dance floor, and seat themselves. He leaned forward to watch the expression on bulldog face. There was none. She was busy directing the seating at her table. She did it with a sure, didactic hand which allowed of no questioning. If Mrs. Bradbury said a thing, it was.

Finally she had her party arranged as she wished. She looked about as if to say proceedings could now begin. Her effect was actually this, for people who had been watching her now turned back to their own parties with a greater animation. The talk, even though Adam could hear none of it plainly enough to make out, was rapid and continuous, and he knew it was almost altogether about his building.

He kept watching the face of Mrs. Bradbury. He could read

nothing on it. The fact made him angry. He finished his drink, and looked again. It was still only bulldog.

Adam spoke aloud to himself. "'Damn it!" he cried. "Who the hell is she—"

He realized that it was Mrs. Bradbury, more than anybody else, who had placed him behind these palms, hiding out like a timid schoolboy. All at once he felt silly and fully angry.

He pushed the palm fans aside so roughly that he tipped over one of the pots. He strode out into the patio.

His entrance, unplanned, was all the better timed for that. The orchestra was between selections. Few could help notice the near-giant of a man who appeared so suddenly among them with a severe storm on his broad florid face. A good many knew him. "That's Adam Paine," they said, or, "There's Paine." They murmured this to others. It swept about the patio. Faces turned toward him. Even waiters stopped their work and stood for a moment to look.

The attention arrested Adam. He hadn't expected this. He stood, wavering. He caught Eve's glance; she nodded at him encouragingly. Then he was staring at Mrs. Bradbury, and she was gazing back. She had been told who he was. She studied him carefully and thoroughly. Still there was no expression on her jowled face. People turned to her. Adam fully expected her to actually raise a thumb high in the air and then plunge it downward to indicate that he should be slaughtered.

Instead, Mrs. Bradbury raised her hands and began to applaud, lightly. Her husband, watching, followed suit. Then others came in on it, until the handclapping rose and swelled in volume, paying sincere tribute to the man whose imagination had created the lovely building in which they sat.

Adam gulped. He was sure he was going to cry, right out there before them. His eyes filled and he blinked rapidly to get the tears back in.

He bowed awkwardly, then whirled and strode to the empty place at Michael's table waiting for him.

"Wonderful!" said Michael, while the others spoke their congratulations.

Adam looked at Eve down and across the table from him. Her

eyes were more than glistening; tears ran tiny courses down her cheeks. She wiped them away with her handkerchief, swallowed, and asked him in a choked voice, "Are you hungry now?"

"I want a steak," he growled. "Two steaks."

"Two, sir?" asked a hovering waiter.

"Two," Michael told the man. "He has a large appetite."

THE EVENING BECAME

a gala event. People came to their table to commend Adam and to tell Michael they wanted memberships in the Club. Others inquired about the apartments. Both the men got so tired of shaking hands and getting to their feet that they simply stayed seated after a time, taking their accolades that way.

The captain of waiters appeared at Michael's elbow. "Sir," he said, "Mrs. Bradbury requests that you bring Mr. Paine to her table."

Michael arched an eyebrow at Adam, who was polishing off his second steak. "You've been commanded," Michael told him, pushing back his chair.

On the way Adam muttered out of the corner of his mouth, "What's she going to do, give me the Congressional Medal?"

"Maybe better than that," said Michael.

They arrived before the august presence. Michael presented Adam, who said, "How do you do, Mrs. Bradbury?"

She didn't notice him at once, or acknowledge the introduction. Instead, she said to Michael, "What's the matter with your waiter captain? I distinctly told him to ask all your party. Get them!" she ordered. "Join us. Have them bring chairs. Distribute yourselves down the table. Go along now, Michael, while I talk to this fascinating architect of yours."

An extra chair had been brought and squeezed in beside that of Mrs. Bradbury, who instructed Adam to sit in it. As he did so she asked, "Where did you get these fascinating chairs? Madrid? Cordoba? No, I think Granada, that was it, I'm sure it was Granada."

"Seville."

"Seville?" She regarded him for a moment as though he should not correct her even with the truth. "Seville, of course; I should have known. Now, then, young man—" She peered at him. "You aren't too young, are you? And how tall are you?"

He told her, and she said, "I should have thought even more. Are you sure you aren't keeping a couple of inches to yourself?"

He denied it.

"How much do you weigh?"

He told her that. He had come here to dislike her, but now was amused by her questions.

"Your building is good, you know," she said. "I never dreamed it would be like this. We were all against it and what it would do to Palm Beach. But now I can see it's going to be an excellent influence. Everything will be Spanish with a dash of Moorish thrown in; that's right, isn't it? Don't you tell me it isn't."

Adam didn't say anything. Out of the corner of his eye he saw Michael bringing their party to the table. Eve was given a place about midway. Mrs. Bradbury made no motion to pay any attention to her or the others; she had the lion on her lap and didn't mean to let him get away or share him, but to treat him merely as her due.

"You've done a really fascinating thing here," she went on to Adam. "Absolutely fascinating. I don't tell many people I like a thing, because there aren't many things worth really liking. There are fewer people, too, if you want to know, which you ought to." Mrs. Bradbury didn't often connect her thoughts. "Your bathrooms, now, everybody is talking about them. Whoever thought of using such beautiful tile?" She didn't lower her voice when she went on, "And that idea of yours to cover the commode with a wicker chair—why, nothing could be more delicious! I can't wait to have one."

Adam looked at her closely. He wondered if she just wanted a wicker chair over her toilet or if she wanted more. He hadn't heard anything, and when anybody wanted a house, especially anybody like Mrs. Bradbury, word got around. He searched for an opening and found one.

"Where do you want it installed?" he asked.

"In the cottage you're going to do for us," she announced.

In spite of himself, Adam's heart missed a beat. This really put the cap on it. He tried to catch Eve's eye, but she was looking the other way.

"Of course," he said to Mrs. Bradbury, "you mean a cottage here in Palm Beach?"

"Nowhere else," she assured him. "Ours shall be the first you will do, of course. We insist on that."

He nodded agreement. "What kind of a cottage do you want?"

"I think Spanish Renaissance. A Moorish entrance arch at the road end of the drive. Something like the entrance to the Club here, I think. Our property is out on North County Road. It's on the ocean, of course. We have forty acres. Oh! I forgot to tell you!"

"What?"

"It's nothing. Speaking of the property reminded me of it. We already have an architect who has drawn up plans. In the North. But he isn't fascinating. We got him in the North so people down here wouldn't hear of it and pester us. We'll dismiss him and get you."

Adam had no sympathy for the Northern architect who did not yet know his plans were to be jettisoned; it was probably somebody who had looked down on him. He was now slightly dazzled by Mrs. Bradbury. "How many rooms," he inquired, "do you want in your cottage?"

"We think about fifty. That was our plan."

Adam was staggered not by the number of rooms, but by the reference to a house that size as being a cottage. It came from the first frame houses of Palm Beach being called cottages and the people who lived in them known as the cottagers.

"A fifteen-car garage," Mrs. Bradbury went on. "And servant quarters for twenty."

Adam looked down the table. He caught Eve's eye now and winked at her. Her face shone back with happiness for him. His glance caught sight of another, of a little man with a close-cropped white mustache. He turned to the famous woman beside him and asked, "What about Mr. Bradbury?"

"Oh, he fully approves."

Adam understood that what she told him would be the thing

that went. "Would you like to see your cottage?" he inquired.

"See it?" she demanded. "How can I do that?"

"I'll draw you a picture of it."

"The way you did for Michael? We heard about that. Yes, do!"

Adam called for a piece of paper, the largest that could be found in the Club. This turned out to be a piece of butcher's wrapping paper brought from the kitchen; there were still a few bloodstains on it. He had a stub of soft-leaded pencil with him. Always he carried one in a pocket to finger and have on hand. The tablecloth was pulled back and Adam spread the paper on the table. He began to sketch.

People didn't have to be told by Mrs. Bradbury what he was doing, but she told them anyway. They came to watch with her, standing behind Adam while he drew. He wasn't bothered by them. He liked an audience. It stimulated him.

It wasn't difficult to know exactly what she wanted and would like. The house flowed out of his fingers. All his knowledge of Spain and love for it found its way from his heart and brain to his fingers and then to the lead and from the lead to the paper. Walls, towers, roofs, balconies, loggias, columned windows, and arches he had known for years were at his ready command. They sprang alive at his request. His fingers flew.

Finally he sat back and informed Mrs. Bradbury, "That's the way you'll see it, generally of course, from the road as you enter. I'll do the sea side some other time."

"Tomorrow," she said. Examining the drawing, she cried, "Fascinating! Perfectly fascinating!"

Others exclaimed at it. They came to view it, until nearly the whole party had been there, including Eve, Michael, and Mr. Bradbury, who now saw the house that was to be his. As they filed away, Adam heard a husky, slow, drawling voice say, "Hello, Adam Paine."

At first he thought it was a man's voice. He turned, to find a full-blown blonde girl in a white gown cut so low that the V nearly reached her waist. Contrary to the current style of flat-chested women, her breasts pushed themselves out so decidedly that it was evident she could have nothing on beneath her dress. She was darkly tanned, so that when she spoke and smiled, her teeth shone whitely. Her eyes were as blue as Adam's own, her lips vivid with color. They curled slightly, as if with challenging contempt, when she said in her deep voice, "I've come to ask the great architect to dance with me."

He couldn't refuse her. He didn't want to. Excusing himself from Mrs. Bradbury, he stepped out on the dance floor with the blonde girl.

"I'm Mona Otis," she told him as they glided away.

"Oh, yes," he said.

"I don't like the way you say that. What does my name mean to you?"

"Two divorces. You acquired a fortune with each."

"Do you like money, Adam?"

"I'm crazy about it."

"Do you like women, too?"

"I like my wife."

"You sound as medieval as your architecture."

"You sound as if you've stopped marrying and are free-lancing."

"I thought I'd try it for a while. After my last husband, I feel I deserve it." She snuggled close to him, putting her head on his shoulder. "You're so big."

"Don't get any ideas."

She took her head off his shoulder, made her eyes round and asked innocently, "What's the trouble, Adam? Don't I do anything to you?"

"Not a thing."

She drew back and searched him with her blue eyes. Her throaty voice rose a little with discovery. "You remind me of my last husband."

"How's that?"

"He wasn't interested enough." Her hand, which couldn't reach to get around his neck, pressed his shoulder. "I think you are, but you won't admit it. I've never met a man yet who wasn't interested at all."

"Now you're boasting."

"No," she said simply, "I'm not boasting."

"In my case," he told her, "you are."

"No," she said again, "I'm not."

99

He looked at her. Involuntarily, his eyes followed the bare expanse of her gown down her naked brown torso between her magnificent breasts.

She laughed, huskily.

He tore his eyes away.

They kept on dancing. "Adam, listen to me," she said. "I'm more than a predatory rich female who's out to take what she wants, or can get. At least I'm a little more. I don't say much more, mind you, only a little. I started out to be a decent woman, a creative person, that's what I wanted to be. I wanted to paint, be an artist, the way you are. I didn't have enough money to go on with it. When the chance came I married a rich boy. That got me into this. Society, it's called. It also killed my ambition. Talent can't stand comfort, unless it's had to fight for it."

Adam stared at her, surprised. She was talking sense.

"It killed mine, and I think I had some."

"Pick it up again," he advised.

"Not when I've come to enjoy rich living—and other things. I'm a hedonist now, Adam, completely. You know what that is because you're one yourself. Only you've got room in yourself to work, too. You've still got ambition; you want to do things—which you'll do. And you're a man. You can do both. I envy you."

"You can still try."

"After my first marriage broke up, I thought I could, too. But I'd gone soft. A creative person can't be soft. No matter how tender and sensitive he is, inside, far inside, he's got to be hard, selfish, and ruthless about his work. He can't let anything interfere with that. I found I wasn't like that. I'd come to enjoy sensation too much. I was lost. Don't think I've minded. Many people dedicate their lives to physical pleasure and I've never heard them complain. Others would like to if they could, or if they had nerve enough. Still others do it in secret—some of the very best people."

"Have you ever tried the secret method?"

"Secrecy wastes time. You only live so long. Then you're dead a lot longer."

"A nice, sweet philosophy. Why did you tell me about your artistic ambitions, even though you've buried them?"

"Because I wanted you to know that when I look at your building, or at that drawing you made, I can see what is there."

"Why do you want me to know that?"

"It might help in my going out to get you."

"Just what do you want of me?"

"Adam, don't be coy."

"Do you think, even if I wanted you—which I don't—I would take you?"

"I mean to find out."

"I'm telling you one thing: go to hell."

"How delightful, Adam!" She laughed at him huskily.

In spite of himself, Adam had to grin.

"Let's be friends," she suggested. "You're going to be the rage of Palm Beach. I must know you. And I must have you do a cottage for me. After you finish the Bradburys."

"Is this a commission?" he asked.

"Definitely."

"What kind of a cottage do you want?"

"Anything you say."

"About sixty-five rooms?"

"Not more than fifteen. I want a small place. Intimate and cozy. When I haven't house guests and am not entertaining I don't want to rattle around in it. Of course," she said, "there is one condition."

"I saw that coming."

"It's settled, then?"

"My stud services don't go with my work."

The music ended. Their hands parted from each other, Adam's first. He led her back to the Bradbury table. "It's been charming," he said.

She watched him go without saying anything.

Adam danced with Eve. "Michael told me," she said, "what she must have said to you."

"I'll bet he didn't know one thing."

Eve looked her question.

"She wants me to do a house for her if I'll sleep with her."

Eve frowned. It was no part of a joke to her. "Tiny, you're

going to be a big success here—you are, already—and with the boom they say is coming, it will be awfully big. But is it going to be good for you, for us?"

"If you're worried about that gold-plated courtesan, forget it."

"It's more than that. I mean, what are these people, or at least most of them? Look at them, eating wonderful food, drinking fine liquor, guzzling it. They're the elite, the wealthy, the socially elect—or at least they've elected themselves. Listen to them, with their affected ways of speaking and manners. All I can see, except for Michael and a few others, is a lot of pampered pigs fighting at the trough."

"An excellent description of them," Adam approved.

"I mean it seriously," she said.

"So do I. Listen, Eve, some people haven't anything except money. That's what we have here. They're a means to an end, my end. They're going to let me do something in architecture that I couldn't do any other way."

"That part is fine, Tiny. But the other part . . ."

"There isn't any other part."

"If there is," she pleaded, "don't let it make you too big for your pants."

"I'll buy a good quality cloth," he promised, "that can stand a lot of wear and tear."

THE ENTIRE TOP

floor of the wooden house had been turned into offices. Additional draftsmen were hired to work under Aubrey, whose sleeping room was moved down to the second floor. On the third Adam had a private office in one of the smaller rooms. He sat here, overflowing a protesting swivel chair in which he dared not lean back because of the certainty of toppling over.

He wore the clothes that had come to be most comfortable to him in Florida, rumpled white duck trousers and a white shirt open at the throat, sleeves rolled up. Canvas sneakers were on his feet. At night this uniform was changed to white flannel trousers and white sport shoes. He never wore socks, and a tie only on extreme provocation. The weight he had lost during the building of the Flamingo Club was regained, with a profit. Once more he needed a haircut.

He was talking with George Andrews, of whom he asked, "Well, what do you think now?"

"You did it, Michelangelo," George admitted. "You know how I didn't think you would, not even when the building shaped up and I could see it. I don't mind saying I was wrong."

"You might as well," Adam advised, "since everybody else has."

"There you go again."

"You ought to learn," Adam lectured, "the difference between boasting and a simple statement of fact."

"It's the way you make it sound," complained George.

"I'm really a modest man," Adam claimed, "the soul of humility."

"Are you also," George inquired skeptically, "the kind of a guy who keeps a bottle in his desk?"

103

Promptly Adam pulled out a half-filled bottle of whiskey and plumped it on the desk before George. They went through, in reverse, with George taking the first drink, the ritual they had practiced the day Adam first went to see him at the shack in his contractor's yard.

"George," Adam asked, "do you want to be a rich man?"

The builder eyed him. "I don't have to be. I've been up and down a couple of times, not way up and not way down. But enough to know that money alone isn't the whole answer."

Adam regarded him narrowly. "By God, George!" he swore. "Do you read my mind and tell me what I want to hear?"

"When I start trying to tell you what you want to hear," George informed him, "I'll shoot myself."

"The thing is," Adam persisted, "would you just as soon be rich?"

"Who wouldn't? But if my getting rich means sucking around you, why—"

"Listen, George," Adam interrupted, "be independent—I want you to be—but don't be too damned independent."

George examined him to see exactly how this was meant. He noticed the crinkles, in action, working themselves, about Adam's eyes. He laughed; Adam roared.

"You and I understand each other," Adam stated. "That's why you're going to do all my building for me."

"Am I?"

"Yes, damn it, you are. I don't want to have to fool around with different builders. I want one who knows what I'm after and can deliver it."

"That's me?"

"That's you."

"Any strings?"

"One."

"That's what I thought."

"Have you also thought what the string is?"

"That's easy."

"Prove that."

"Why, hell, you want me to kick back on what I get, starting with this Bradbury shack you're doing."

"And you'll kick back?"

"You know damn well I won't."

"And you know damn well that isn't it. You just wanted the point established, isn't that right?"

"That's right, Michelangelo."

"I'm not against a kickback on ethical grounds," Adam made plain. "They'll accuse us of doing it, anyway. I just don't want it because it wouldn't be good for the architecture. If I had an interest in your profits we might forget certain things about the specifications. I'm out to build buildings that are good. They'll last longer than any money I make. They'll last after me. I want them that way. When I'm dead and gone I'd like my buildings to be still alive and working."

"Then what's the condition?" asked George.

"That we work together exactly as we did on the Flamingo Club," Adam explained. "I'm the architect. You're the builder. I want you to keep me away from your men. I know I'd only antagonize them."

"I'll buy that."

"But I want you around all the time so I can tell you what to do, and you can tell them."

"I'll be around when you are if you'll let me know."

"You'll have to guess sometimes. And I warn you I'll yell and holler at you."

Unimpressed, George replied, "I've heard you yell and holler."

"And it won't bother you?"

"When you start to bother me, I'll—"

"Shoot yourself," Adam finished for him. He stuck out his hand over the desk. George took it. They shook firmly, establishing formally the bond and agreement between them.

Adam took him to the other side of the office and on a long, broad table showed him the recently completed plans for the Bradbury place. They made George whistle and say, "This will cost a million."

"That's the figure the old lady has given me to work with," Adam said coolly. "Without the furnishings, of course."

"High, wide, and handsome," George observed.

"It's that or nothing here. Now," Adam went on, unrolling other plans, "this is my own building, to go up across the road from the Flamingo Club. It's a store building."

"That?" queried George. He looked at a building that appeared to be a section of the slums of Naples, well scrubbed. On the ground floor were shops with carved stone entrances under an arched gallery. Apartments were on the second floor with open, railed loggias. The tower would contain an apartment for Adam and Eve; to one side of this were offices for Adam. A horseshoe-shaped alley, with uneven paving, went through and around the building, with shops and a space for an outdoor cafe lining it. This was labeled "Via Paine."

"What's this 'via'?" questioned George.

"That's Italian for street."

"Have it your own way."

"Think you can handle both jobs at the same time?"

"Got any more?"

"Six more little cottages ranging from eighteen to twenty-five rooms. But they'll wait until these are done. Aubrey's only started on those now."

"One thing," said George.

"What?"

"It isn't exactly my business as long as you put out the dough."

"Let's have it."

"This version of a store building of yours. You won't build that for three dollars and twenty cents. Where's—"

"That money coming from? Ever hear of Michael Sumner?"

"I eat him for breakfast every morning."

"Well, he isn't putting up the money, but he's arranging for me to be financed. If that answers the question. Let's go on to labor. That's your affair, but how about it?"

"The white men who worked on the Club are boasting of it now. No problem there. Orey asked me for work yesterday; I told him I'd think it over."

"Keep him out of my way or I'll brain him with a hollow tile."

"I'm going to keep some of the black crews."

"And I want them for two things. To lay tile roofs so they'll be irregular, and for the third thing we'll need built right away."

"Third thing?" asked George. "I thought you said the other places could wait—"

"This is something else. This is where Eve comes in." Adam went to the door and shouted down the stairs. "Eve! Hey, Tall One! Bean pole! We're ready for you."

While waiting for her to come up, Adam unrolled still other plans. "I'll let Eve tell you," he said. "It's going to be her baby."

When Eve came into the room her face was slightly flushed from her quick climb up the stairs and also because of her excitement at the project to be launched that she was to operate. "I don't know what he's told you, George," she said to the contractor, "but we're going to reproduce a lot of the things you've seen that came from Spain."

"You mean fake them?"

"No, George," Eve explained. "My friend here," she went on, indicating Adam, "at first wanted to pass off as originals the products we're going to make, but when I raised certain objections such as choosing between doing that and having me for a wife, he saw the light. We will only reproduce and sell reproductions. We think we can make beautiful ones, in some cases as good as the originals."

"Better," Adam claimed.

"One thing he means by that," Eve explained, "is that some antiques we've seen here, and even some we brought back, are falling apart in the climate. We'll make them so they won't do this."

George rubbed one hand along his hairy arm. "Well, I don't see anything the matter with that. As long as you don't—"

"If people ask how the wormholes got in the furniture," Eve went on, "we'll tell them we made the holes."

"You know how to put wormholes in furniture?"

Eve said, "It seems my pal here, along his way somewhere, learned how."

"That's only part of the process," Adam said. "Antiquing, making a new thing look a hundred years old, is an art."

"And an honorable one," said Eve, "as long as the aging is used to make a nice thing that doesn't pretend to be anything that it isn't."

A slightly pained expression came to Adam's face as he addressed George. "These are going to be so good that you won't be able to tell the difference between something made in Seventeen Fifty and something made in Nineteen Twenty."

George made a deprecating sound. "An art expert—"

"I didn't say an art expert, though I'd be willing to limit it to a dozen in the country who'll be able to tell the difference; I said you."

"Do you mean to tell me," George demanded, "that you can make an imitation—"

"A copy," Adam corrected.

"A reproduction," said Eve.

"A copy or a reproduction or whatever you want to call it," continued George, "of one of those things you brought back from Spain with you, and put them side by side, and you think I can't tell which is which?"

"I'll take any bet on it you want to name," said Adam.

"One hundred dollars."

"You got yourself a bet."

"I think he'll win it, George," Eve advised.

"Who's going to do this work?" George asked.

"A few men in the North have been persuaded to come down," said Adam, "when I described the opportunities here. Others I'll pick up around here and teach. Eve is going to do the tile and pottery herself, and oversee the whole thing."

"Clay has me worried," Eve told George. "I've tried the local kind, and had some sent to me from other places. It isn't right."

"Florida clay is no good for that," George told them. "I know a place up around Macon in Georgia where you can order what you want. I begin to get it now. Instead of importing tile, for instance, including roof tile, you're going to manufacture it but get imported prices for it."

"It takes you a while to catch on," said Adam.

"What else are you going to make?"

"Let Eve tell you."

"I can do it best," said Eve, "by showing you on the plans for buildings we'll need. Most of it can be outdoors, I mean, only sheds with the sides open, like the small ironworks here, and my tile and pottery place here." She touched the plans with a finger. "I'll need three beehive kilns. The cast and cut-stone works will be the largest, over here at one side; Adam will have to explain the technical end of the equipment needed there, or maybe it's best to wait for the stone man he has coming down from Long Island to tell you. The furniture works must be entirely enclosed. We're going to call the whole thing Artisan Arts."

"The thing we need right now, most of all," said Adam, "is land for it. It has to be over in West Palm Beach, of course. Have you got any ideas?"

George thought for a moment. "I don't want to sell you anything," he said, "and don't think I'm trying to, but since you asked me, I own property on both sides of my yard. I'll only need to expand one way. There's a couple of acres on the other side. There's a small one-story house on it; I don't know if you could use that."

"We'll have to have an office of some sort over there," said Adam. "If already built, so much the better."

"I'll have to sleep over there," said Eve, "some nights when I'm cooking."

" 'Cooking?' " asked George.

"Baking tile," Eve explained, "when the kilns go for twenty-four hours a day, or more."

"Well, you can have the property for the current market value," said George. "Whatever that is. Some people say values are up, or going up. Say, there was a guy—that friend of yours Gerry Vance who came here to work that day on the job and jitney out men— he came to see me about the land last week."

Eve, glancing at Adam, asked, "Did he think its valuation was going up?"

George shook his head. "He said I'd better get rid of it if I could. I never knew he could talk the way he did. Let him go on and you get to believe practically anything he says. He nearly talked me into letting him have the property as his without him putting down a dollar. Craziest proposition I ever heard, except it sounded good when he explained it. I understand he actually convinced a few other people."

"Is he in the real-estate business?" asked Adam.

"By carrying his office in that straw hat of his," George said. "Haven't you heard what he's really doing?"

They shook their heads.

"He got to own the whole of that flivver he has, all right, just as he said he would. But now he operates it in a different way. Since prohibition went into effect you've heard about bootleggers. Well, this Gerry is working for one. He delivers booze to your door in the Lizzie."

Interested, as if he had heard something of this new business, Adam asked, "Where does the bootlegger Gerry works for get his liquor?"

"The Bahamas, I understand. They're running a lot of stuff in from there."

Adam nodded thoughtfully.

Eve glanced at him and cried, "Adam!"

George inquired, "Did I say anything?"

"No," said Adam. "Go on, about Gerry."

"He told me that before he's through he'd own the boat this bootlegger has."

"Tell him to come and see me, will you?"

"Why, sure."

"Tiny," Eve said, "I thought a little better of Gerry Vance when he came to help you, but now I don't. Not if he's a rumrunner. And you shouldn't—"

"I told you in Spain," he said, "that there was only one way to get certain articles I want. It isn't hurting anybody, except a whole country a little, and that can't be very much or it wouldn't let the things get away from it."

"But rumrunning—"

"Who said anything about rumrunning?"

George began, "I don't get everything you're talking about—"

"You'd better not know," Adam advised.

"And I certainly don't want to," said Eve.

"Let's go over and look at where Artisan Arts is going to be located," suggested Adam.

GERRY DROPPED THE

case of liquor so hard on the kitchen floor that the bottles jarred alarmingly.

"That time you did it," Eve said.

Gerry wiped his forehead with the back of his hand. The August heat, together with his exertions, made him perspire profusely. He grinned, flashing his white teeth winningly. "Nothing broken, Mrs. Paine. That's your usual three cases, one of Scotch, one of gin, and one of rum."

"And here's your money," Eve told him. She had it ready for him, and now gave it to him. She said nothing more.

Gerry sighed and complained lightly, "I don't think you'll ever like me. I wish you would. I'm really harmless."

"No," said Eve, "you're not, Gerry. You're dangerous."

Gerry laughed. He had an attractive laugh. "Me, dangerous? I wouldn't harm a fly."

"The worst part of it," Eve told him, "is that you really believe that."

He changed the subject. "You and Adam are certainly having your boom all by yourself. That art manufacturing plant you're putting up across the lake, that's a smart idea, one of the smartest things I ever heard. If you find you need a good salesman for your products, why—"

"No thanks," Eve refused him.

Gerry laughed again. "I guess you don't need any salesmen. You've got your own arrangements with the buildings you're doing. And the business block is wonderful, absolutely wonderful with that fancy alley. I knew Adam was good, but I never dreamed he was that good. I said before he had talent, but now I know it's more than that. He's got genius, real, genuine genius."

"You sound as if you're selling something on the midway."

"Can't get out of the habit," Gerry assured her. "I could go on the same way about the Bradbury house; excuse me, cottage. Stupendous and terrific, that's all that is. This is the land of opportunity, sure enough, as the Crackers say. Why, it was less than two years ago that we met on the highway coming south, and now look at us—"

" 'Us?' " queried Eve.

"Oh, yes."

"But your boom doesn't seem to have started yet," she pointed out.

"It's started," Gerry assured her, smiling easily. "Most people just don't realize it. But it's started, oh, yes, indeed. It's bubbling in the pot."

"If it is," Eve inquired, "why are you still a bootlegger?"

"This is the easiest and quickest way to get some capital," he explained cheerfully. "I'll need that when the real time comes. Otherwise I'd be just a salesman collecting commissions. I mean to be in on the principal money this ride of the merry-go-round. I'll have to have at least a little capital for the kitty, or people like your friend Michael Sumner would never let me in on any of their deals."

"Do you think he would at all?"

Gerry laughed. "Well, maybe he wouldn't." He looked out the window into the yard. "I see you have a flivver to go with the Ghost."

"I use it to go across the lake to Artisan Arts."

"How far along with that are you—if you don't mind my asking."

"I don't mind—just as long as you don't plan to own the place." His handsome face beamed. "I never do things like that."

"The iron works is going, already producing," Eve said. "So is the furniture department. The stone casting and cutting end of it is just being set up. Tiles and pottery have been experiments so far, but soon now a professional batch will be baked. That's my department, though I'm managing the others, too, after Adam tells the men the way to do it."

"I expect your men don't mind working for a woman, at least for you. I'm not trying to flatter you, but I wouldn't mind it myself."

Eve studied him. She saw that he was sincere. Or at least he sounded sincere. It was difficult to tell.

She faced him. "Gerry, you know how I feel about you. I believe you're essentially dishonest, or at least you're right on the edge of being dishonest. You would rather do a thing the slick way than the straight way. You enjoy making a sharp deal, fooling the other fellow. You don't care what you're selling just as long as you sell it."

Still Gerry did not take offense. He waved a hand. "I'm not unique."

"All I ask," Eve pleaded, "is that you don't do anything to hurt Adam."

"What could I—?"

"You could. He won't listen to me about you. There is a little something of you in him, that's why, I guess."

"But what makes you think—"

"You're going to do business together. As soon as you get to own the boat of the rumrunner you work for. Then you're going to smuggle in furniture for Adam that's been landed in the Bahamas. I wouldn't be surprised if you're ready for that now and you've tried to have this talk with me to get me to think better of you."

Gerry shook his head with admiration. "You're a discerning woman, Mrs. Paine. The owner of the boat sold it to me this morning."

" 'Sold' it?"

"Well, he found himself in a position where it was best for me to have it."

"Adam is out at the Bradbury place. Don't get him into trouble," Eve warned. "If you do, and I can ever hurt you for doing it, I'll hurt you."

"We'll never come to anything like that," Gerry assured her. "We're all friends helping each other, a happy family that's going to work together to make everybody rich."

"All I want," Eve informed him, "is for everybody to stay happy in the process."

"There's nothing I would want myself more than that," he assured her.

She didn't say anything as he left.

Gerry found Adam in the great high Gothic drawing room of the Bradbury house, which was in the course of construction. Gerry stood in a cluttered unfinished doorway looking into the room and admiring the man who conceived it and was now bringing it into being. He listened, eavesdropping.

Adam Paine sat on a wooden box in the center of the room. His white clothes were dirty and covered with dust. The skin of his bare ankles was nearly black, as were his sneakers. In his hand he had a short stick that looked like an orchestra leader's baton. This he waved or pointed on occasion. George Andrews stood at his side, silently waiting.

Adam stared about the room. He seemed to be dreaming. He glanced at the high, long window openings, which waited to be finished with cement and stone columns. The sounds of hammering and pounding, or things sliding and being let down, or rasping, and the call of men's voices, could be heard.

Adam got up, lifting himself with effort from the box. He looked out of the far windows. He stood there, considering and pushing out his lower lip, gauging and frowning. He sat down again. The box cracked loudly. He looked at it once, saw that it would probably continue to hold him, and then regarded the windows again. He held up his stick in front of him. Moving his thumb along it, he squinted, sighting at something.

Finally he seemed satisfied. "George," he commanded.

"Yeh."

"Lower those windows eight inches."

"For God's sake—"

"I don't mean make them eight inches longer at the bottom; that would throw them out of proportion. I mean lower the whole business exactly eight inches and no more. And no less."

"Do you know what that means?"

"I know you can't see the ocean sitting here where I am unless that's done."

"Let them stand up to see it."

"Stop sounding as if it's going to cost you anything."

"Couldn't you see that before this—"

"No, I couldn't see it before this, damn it! Get your men on it right away."

"I can't get to that until tomorrow."

"I want it done now, for tomorrow!" Adam yelled. "So I can see how it's going to work."

George bellowed, "What if it doesn't work?"

"Then the windows will be moved up again!" Adam hollered.

George subsided, not backing down, but becoming resigned. He shrugged his thick shoulders and said, "Okay, Michelangelo." He moved off, out of the room, calling outside, "Hey, you, Tom! Orey, and you, all the rest of this gang. Drop that and come with me."

Gerry walked up to Adam, his feet making loose boards creak, so that the big man turned and demanded, "What are you doing here? Have you come to snoop like the Palm Beach architects so they can steal from me? You going to be an architect now?"

"Only a humble bootlegger," said Gerry, "on the high seas."

Adam beamed. "You got the boat? It's yours?"

Gerry nodded.

"Let's go see it."

They left the growing mansion, picking their way down the roughly graded driveway through the long grounds and between massive piles of building materials, to the road. Here the Rolls-Royce stood. Adam pulled the silver Lady out of his pocket and screwed it on the radiator. They got in and drove off, heading for West Palm Beach across the lake. "Tell me how you did it," Adam instructed.

"He didn't want to sell," Gerry explained. "None of the usual kind of persuasion would make him, not even enough money."

"That's bad."

"Bad."

They laughed.

"We'd been taking alternate trips to the Bahamas," Gerry explained, "where they're running most of the stuff in from. Well, the revenue boys are getting pretty active. They're chasing us now, when they see us. Depending on which ones catch us, we get confiscated and pulled in, or we simply buy them off. Usually it's a buy-off. But some of them are getting a little tough. On my boss's last trip, somebody took a shot at him."

"Revenue agents?"

"No."

"You?"

"Not exactly."

"Friend of yours?"

"Well, my man's got a wife and kids. He got scared. He sold out then—at a slightly lower figure than he'd been offered before."

"He's better off at home with his family."

"I figured there was a good deed done."

"And so there was. How is it out there running the stuff?"

"The trip isn't so bad. It's arriving here that isn't good. You can rarely come right in the inlet to the lake, only on dark, stormy nights when you can't see your hand before your face. Even then it's risky. Mostly we've got to land on the beach. When there's a heavy surf, you work for your living. Once I had to ditch the load, sinking it off the beach. I only found about half of it later."

The boat, when Adam saw it, disappointed him. "It won't do at all," he said. "Maybe you can bring in a good load of booze in a twenty-five-foot boat, but you sure can't bring in any furniture, or enough to amount to anything. You've got to have something bigger."

"There isn't any bigger, there isn't anything at all," Gerry said. "Other bootleggers have bought up everything."

"What's that over there on the other side of the dock?" Adam wanted to know.

A fifty-foot flat-bottomed sharpie lay there. It was a battered, old schooner that had long since seen its best days. A superstructure, obviously added to a former small cabin, seemed too large for the boat. On the stern, in faded letters, was painted, "Margaret D."

"That got in a couple of days ago," said Gerry. "I don't know a thing about it."

"Let's find out," suggested Adam.

They went aboard the schooner and a slim young man, hardly more than a boy, stuck half of himself up out of the oversize cabin. He looked to be about eighteen, and he was blond, with blue eyes. He didn't say or ask anything, but merely looked quizzically at the strangers.

"Want to sell your boat?" asked Adam.

"How did you know?" The young man spoke softly and precisely, with a slight British accent.

"We didn't," said Gerry, "but now that we do, let's talk about it, shall we?"

The young man emerged all the way from the cabin, and then sat on its roof, indicating that the other two should do the same. They waited for him to talk.

"My name's Bethune," he said. He spoke gravely. "Jim Bethune. I'm the son of Captain James Bethune, one of the early settlers of this place. My Daddy and his brother, my uncle, who was called Doc Bethune, once ran the general store and post office right across there." He pointed a brown finger across the lake. "They had something to do with calling it Palm Beach, along with a man named Steven Pierton, who was their ward and who used to walk the beach with the mail between here and Miami; that was before the rails or any road was put in. I been talking today with friends of my Daddy, including Jenny and Tip Totten, and the Doolittles —he used to be the mayor."

Adam showed signs of impatience, but Gerry indicated that they were very interested in Jim Bethune's story, and that he was to continue it.

"My Daddy," he said, "left here a few years after the turn of the century because he thought it was getting too crowded. He didn't tell anybody where he was going, but just disappeared in the Margaret D. He went to a far island in the Bahamas and married a Conch woman there; that was my mother. Well, they were both drowned in a hurricane a few years ago. I was left with the sharpie. I built on some more cabin and tried running the islands with passengers. It didn't work out very good. Then I decided to come over here; I'm an American citizen because my Daddy was one."

He revealed that he had looked up Steven Pierton, the former barefoot mailman, who was now living in West Palm Beach. Pierton had inherited his Daddy's and uncle's property, a valuable one consisting of quite a bit of land and the largest department store in West Palm Beach. Pierton was agreeable to giving him a share in this, if he could prove who he was. This was going to take a few hundred dollars, to get records from the Bahamas, and go there at least once.

Gerry looked at Adam, who nodded.

"Well, son," Gerry told Jim paternally, "I think we can help you out. In fact, we're just about made for each other. We'll buy your boat from you and we'll also let you use it to go to the islands. We even want to hire you to make a number of trips. That is, if you don't mind carrying some cargo."

"Don't mind at all."

"Want to know what kind of cargo?"

"Don't see where it matters."

"That's fine, because it's liquor."

"Furniture to start with," said Adam.

"Either one's all right," said Jim. "Especially since the boat will be in your name."

"Well, now, about that, son," Gerry began, "maybe it will save time, in order to get going right away, if we just left it in your—"

"No, sir; you got to pay me the money and have it in your name." The blue eyes had narrowed; Jim, by looking, knew with whom he was dealing.

"Hah!" Adam exclaimed, with his glance challenging Gerry to talk Jim into it.

"We'll pay you the money, all right," Gerry assured him confidentially, "right now, if you want, but after you hear the reasons you'll see there won't be any harm in letting the boat stay in—"

"Mister," Jim said politely but very firmly, "you got to pay the money and have it in your name, or the Margaret D ain't for sale."

"I can see your point absolutely," Gerry went on, dropping his voice to a whisper, as if imparting valuable secrets, "and I agree with you in principle because you're doing the right thing, but—"

"You better get off the Margaret D," said Jim, "if you got to argue it more."

Adam roared with laughter. "He's on to you!" he cried to Gerry. "No pitchman is going to twist his tongue around him."

Showing no sign of chagrin, Gerry asked Adam, "Will this do for what you want?"

Adam stuck his head into the companionway leading to the cabin. He surveyed the deck space and small cockpit. "It will do, though it will take quite a few trips. I'm going on the first one. I've always wanted to ride the Spanish Main."

EVE SAW THEM

off at the dock. She didn't want Adam to go. She saw no purpose in it. He said he had to see the shipment from Don Fadrique and supervise its first handling on the schooner, particularly Queen Isabella's bed, their bed. Eve declared that she was going along, not because she wanted to, but to protect them from landing in jail. Adam wouldn't hear of it.

As Gerry climbed aboard, Eve said to him from the dock, "Remember what I told you."

"Nothing to worry about, Mrs. Paine," he assured her blandly.

"What did you tell him?" Adam asked.

"That I'd tear his eyes out if he got you into trouble."

"We won't get in any trouble," Adam assured her.

"You may not get in too much," she corrected, "if you keep your promise not to bring any liquor in with the furniture."

"Not a drop," Gerry said.

"Let's hear you say it again," Eve requested Adam.

"Do you think I'd risk that furniture in any way?"

"You aren't saying it."

His eyes were steady when they looked straight at her. "Absolutely not a drop."

"Of course, it's just as bad that you're bringing in the furniture without declaring it and paying duty."

"It's worse, because bootlegging has become almost patriotic."

She couldn't argue further with him. She held out her arms. He enveloped her in his. "Take care of yourself," she urged. "You're all I've got."

"You're all I have, too."

"I wish I were."

"What else have I got?"

"Your stub pencil and a piece of drawing paper. Right now this crazy trip."

"It's only for a few days."

They parted. "You've got your coat?" she asked. "And wear your socks."

He advised, as he stepped aboard, "Don't let George go an inch beyond what I showed him. And I expect to see the stone castings for the Bradbury entrance arch when I get back."

Eve looked at the Margaret D. "You ought to be flying the skull and crossbones," she observed.

Adam said, "I wish I'd thought of it."

Eve looked at young Jim Bethune. "Watch out for my husband," she asked him.

"Yes, ma'm," he promised.

"Somehow," she said to him, "I think you're the only one of the three who has any sense."

"Yes, ma'm." In confusion, Jim glanced at his companions and tried to amend his statement. "That is, I mean—"

Adam laughed. "You got it right the first time."

The Margaret D was slowly warped away from the dock. Her sails were raised, and she sailed up the lake to the inlet over the sparkling water, pushed by the brisk southeast breeze.

Four days later she was tied fast to the quayside in the Bahamas. The low-lying, horseshoe-shaped island was like an atoll. The Margaret D was loaded to the gunwales with furniture. Spanish antiques, including Queen Isabella's bed knocked down, filled every inch of her cabin. Other pieces, wrapped in tarpaulins, were lashed on the decks. They even filled most of the cockpit. A corrugated tin shed near the dock contained the remainder of Don Fadrique's final shipment.

In what room there remained in the cockpit, Adam half lay, dozing in the heat beneath a sail that had been raised flat over the waist and stern of the boat for shade in the hot morning sun. Perspiration oozed from him, running over his unshaved face, dripping down into the open collar of his shirt. He stirred, as someone came up out of the cabin. He saw Gerry, and murmured, still partially asleep, "You're going to let me know when we're ready to sail."

"That's now," Gerry said. "Or almost now. Jim's seeing about his paternity papers and will be back any time."

Adam sat up. He was fully awake. "Nothing more to come aboard?"

"We're loaded to leave." Gerry cast an eye on the laden deck. "I hope we aren't top-heavy."

Adam asked casually, "What were you doing in the cabin?"

"Oh, just giving a last look."

"I'll give one myself."

Gerry lowered his voice. "Everything's all right there, Adam."

"I'll just take a peek anyway."

Adam dropped into the cabin. He was there for some time. Gerry sat on the edge of the cockpit. At first he looked worried. Then he raised his eyebrows and shrugged his shoulders. He tried to appear hopeful but didn't quite succeed.

Adam came up. He let himself down in the same place he had been before. A note of weary admiration was in his voice when he asked, "How did you do it?"

Innocently, Gerry inquired, "Do what?"

"A better question," said Adam, "is when did you do it? Last night, I expect. The men you had do it must move like cats. And know how not to clink bottles together."

Gerry spoke with rapid persuasion. "Just a few, Adam, hardly more than samples, probably no more than we'll need to have a nip for ourselves on the way back, and absolutely not enough to do any harm—"

"I figure," said Adam, "you've got about twenty cases in individual bottles stashed in the furniture in the cabin, in drawers, and between things. I suppose you've got as much up here on deck."

"Nothing like that, not a real load at all."

"You go play slick with other people, not with me," Adam informed him. "Our arrangement is no booze."

"I didn't think you were taking Mrs. Paine seriously—"

"I'm taking myself seriously," Adam told him. "This is furniture moving, at least this time, and furniture moving alone. The

121

things I'm taking in are worth forty times that booze you've got hidden in it. I'm not taking any chances."

"Well, the amount on board, as I say, isn't enough to call it taking any chances."

"Get it off," Adam ordered. "Every bottle."

"I still can't believe you're serious—"

"I'm serious as hell, so get it off. If the agents catch us they'll look in every cranny, so don't let them find as much as a cork."

"Adam, now that it's here, there won't be any harm—"

"Get it off. Now. And I want to see every drawer opened so I know it's empty."

"But that means—"

"Now," said Adam. "While we're waiting for Jim."

"The work—"

"When we sail," Adam said, "I want one bottle of Scotch aboard. We'll drink that before we get to the three-mile limit. If there's another bottle on board, so help me, Gerry, I'll break it over your pretty head."

Gerry smiled as he finally acquiesced. He was always agreeable, even in defeat. For several hours he and three black men struggled with the removal of the liquor aboard the Margaret D. A grunting, hot, and sweaty Adam followed them, being shown that without question crannies and drawers were empty. At last he was satisfied.

The Margaret D sailed in the afternoon on a smooth sea. Jim Bethune, at the tiller, said the run back would be fast, virtually riding the wind straight to the Palm Beach inlet. That dark night he sat, humming at the prospect of his identity papers being arranged for successfully, as he guided the sharpie. Adam, sitting near him, pulled at the bottle of Scotch, handed it to Gerry, and asked Jim, "How do you know where you're going?"

"I know."

"You haven't got any compass."

"I just know."

"How?"

"Mostly by the wind."

"That isn't enough."

"I can feel it, too."

"What do you feel?"

"The right way."

"How can you figure the pull of the Gulf Stream?"

"I can feel that, too."

"Say some more."

"You got a place to go," Jim informed him, "you can get there. My Daddy came from there. I know how to get back because he told me how. And I already been there once."

"Do you think he'll make it?" Gerry questioned.

"There's no question of it," Adam said. "Some people have a little extra something over others. That's why you've got millionaires and why you've got valets who hold their pants for them to step in. Jim here is the millionaire in what he's doing tonight. We're the valets. He'll hit the inlet right on the nose in the morning."

As if for reward, Adam held up the bottle to Jim.

"My Daddy," said Jim, "taught me when to drink and when not to. This is a not-drinking time."

By two o'clock that night Adam and Gerry had finished the bottle and tossed it overboard. They weren't drunk, yet not entirely sober. They were merely interested when Jim lifted his head, as if smelling the air, and made a sound. "Boat ahead," he announced.

"Duck it," advised Gerry.

"Let's see what it is," said Adam.

"We couldn't run if we wanted to," Jim said. "They see our sails by now. And they got power, lots of it."

They listened, straining for a sight or sound. Neither Adam nor Gerry could hear or see a thing.

"Right straight ahead," Jim told them.

In a few more minutes they first heard the sound of its motor, and then saw it, a low hulk a little darker than the night. The boat swung around and followed them, running alongside not far off. The three men on the Margaret D said nothing to each other. They knew what it was before a voice, obviously shouting through a megaphone, identified it.

"Revenue agents!" they were informed. "What are you?"

123

"Say what I told you," Adam instructed Gerry.

Gerry cupped his hands and called back their identity and destination.

"What are you carrying?" they were asked.

"Furniture!" Gerry called back. He enjoyed making this announcement.

"Furniture?" The voice sounded shocked at the word. "Haul up!"

Adam called out then. His voice boomed across the water through the night. "We aren't in the three-mile limit!"

"It'll do! Haul up!"

"You haven't got any right—"

"Haul up or we'll fire!"

"Will they?" Adam wanted to know of Gerry.

"They will," said Gerry.

"They ain't got the right to stop us here," offered Jim.

"Then keep on," said Adam.

They sailed their course for a moment more.

The megaphone voice came again. "This is a last warning! Haul up so we can board you! We'll fire if you don't."

"They're going to shoot," said Gerry. He wasn't excited, but highly interested.

"You want—" began Jim.

He was interrupted by the crack of a high-powered rifle. The three men in the Margaret D instinctively ducked, and ducked again, and then a third time, as the rifle crashed out. Nothing happened on board. They were firing across the bows.

"That's enough!" cried Adam. He was sobered. "Heave to," he instructed Jim, who swung the tiller instantly, bringing the sharpie about into the wind, where her sails flapped.

The Margaret D, barely making way, waited while the revenue boat, nearly as long as the sharpie, came alongside. On its deck half a dozen armed men stood. Their boat, with Jim's help, was made fast to the side of the Margaret D. Three men jumped aboard. Each had a weapon in one hand and in the other a flashlight, which he played on the sharpie and its occupants.

One of the three men demanded, "What is this? Why didn't you haul up at once?"

Adam answered him. "I wanted to see what you would do."

"You what?" The man's flashlight shone in Adam's face. "Who are you?"

Adam told him. It didn't mean anything to the man. Adam didn't want it to. He named his companions.

The revenue man looked about the sharpie. "Furniture," he said skeptically. "That's a new name for it."

"Look for yourself," Adam advised.

"That we will do," the agent promised. "Strip the tarpaulin off that stuff," he ordered his men.

They pulled off the coverings, using their flashlights to look it over, then probing the beams into drawers and cabinets, and emitting sounds of disgust at finding them empty. They went down into the cabin and worked there for some time, now cursing at their failure to locate what they wanted.

They were angry when they came up.

"I'm sorry," Adam told them, "that you didn't find what you were looking for." He held up a fifty-dollar bill. "Would this help?"

One of the men snatched it, crying in scorn, "Chicken feed!"

"There'll be fifty more, " Adam promised, "when my men come through with another load of furniture next week."

"Don't bother us," a second man snarled, "with your damn worm-eaten junk. Just keep out of our way."

"But if you see us—"

"We won't see you."

The men climbed back on their boat. The lines were cast away, and they roared off into the night seeking more profitable game.

Jim pulled on the tiller of the Margaret D. The sharpie heeled slowly about. Her sails filled again, and she got under brisk way once more.

"Now," said Adam to Gerry, "you can bring in a double cargo." Judiciously, he decided, "I think you could even load the drawers of the chests right up here on deck."

"Wonderful," said Gerry. "No worries about landing on the beach. We go in to the lake, comfortable and nice, right to the boathouse where you want the furniture. Neat, very neat. I'll hire somebody to run the motorboat while I ride the Margaret D."

"Did you know that Morgan, Lafitte, Black Caesar, Teach, the whole kit and caboodle of those old buccaneers rode these waters?" Adam mused. "With the revenue boys and us, it hasn't changed much."

"I don't see how it's changed at all," said Gerry. "The buccaneers raided Spanish ships for treasure. You've raided Spain for treasure, too, and we've got it aboard."

"By God!" Adam yelled. He hit Gerry a clap on the back that sent him coughing for breath and finally, when he had it back again, laughing, to join Adam's boom, so great that soon it had young Jim Bethune chuckling as he steered the sharpie through the night to the Florida shore.

THE VIA PAINE

building was completed before Casa Sol, as the Bradbury house was to be called. Nearly all the shops on the street and alley were rented before the plaster had dried. Several establishments that had long been located in the Fashion Beaux Arts moved to the Via Paine.

Eve marveled at their own triplex quarters in the building. An enclosed arched bridge led from the first story of their tower apartment to Adam's now extensive offices and drafting rooms. On this floor of the apartment were the kitchen, servants' quarters, and dining room. The second floor was entirely taken up with a living room furnished with all the best pieces they had found in Spain. The third story contained bedrooms, especially their own.

Adam had redesigned the original room he had planned for them, and drawn another built around Queen Isabella's bed. It was an enormous chamber. One end was devoted exclusively to the bed, which was set on a raised platform. It seemed even larger here than it had in Don Fadrique's warehouse. Four could have slept in it with entire comfort.

Lying in it with Eve, Adam declared, "It's the first bed I've ever had with absolutely enough room." He groped for her. "The only thing I don't like about it is that it's so big I can't locate my queen."

"We're going to get in here some night," Eve predicted, "and never find our way out." She was pleased with the beautifully furnished comfortable chamber and its two fireplaces, one large, the other a kidney warmer set in the wall waist-high from the floor.

Eve thought she could still get along without servants while running both the apartment and Artisan Arts. Adam let her try for a week and didn't say anything when she gave up. It took two to make the Isabella bed with its oversize sheets and bedclothes. Eve hired a wiry little Filipino houseman named Manuel and a broad-beamed Irish cook called Martha. Adam promptly invited twenty people to dinner without giving anybody warning. Manuel and Martha were more equal to this than Eve, who retired at midnight while the party was still in progress.

Eve spent most of her time across the lake at Artisan Arts. She directed the enterprise from a small office installed in the little white frame house that had come with the property. Here she went every morning in the flivver and remained the day. Several times she hadn't come home for three days at a time, when the kilns were going and she had to be sure that the man she had feeding the fires kept them at exactly the right temperature.

Adam went often, too. She would not allow him to get in the light Model T, for his weight sank it nearly to the axle. They went over in separate cars, the flivver leading the Rolls-Royce like an advance guard for royalty. Adam interfered little with her pottery and tile work. He told her what he wanted in tile and the various shapes he required; when she delivered his orders he only grunted. He mixed a green glaze for the pottery that came out of the kiln so successfully that she adopted it and named it Paine Green.

The decorative iron work was turned over to the man brought down from Long Island to take care of it. He was given the samples brought from Spain to copy. Soon he was turning them out in a manner that made Eve hesitate before saying which was the original and which the copy. Here, at the forges and ringing anvils, were fashioned by hand heavy iron gates, railings, grills, door latches, hinges, candelabra, lamps, and all the accessories needed for Adam's style of house.

The noisy stone department handled both natural and cast stone. The natural stone came from the Florida Keys and was cut, with tremendous racket, by a great, whirring blade with inch-long steel teeth that had to be sharpened frequently. The cast stone was treated by an expert to make it look old. The man could manufacture, right before your eyes, imitation granite, limestone, or marble. He machined the surface to simulate hand chiseling and then aged it by sand-blast and stain.

Outside of her own department, Eve liked best the manufacture and antiquing of furniture. She was amazed at what Adam knew of this, exhibited when he discussed it with the men doing the work. When she learned their secrets she didn't blame them for letting no one else witness the processes. They kept out even the men from the other departments. George Andrews was the only outsider ever allowed in the furniture building and then only for a few minutes one day when Adam decided, "It's time I won that bet from him."

George was brought in from his shack next door at his builder's yard. He looked about, wide-eyed, at the sight of men working at cabinetmaking which started with fresh, clean lumber at one end of the building and ended up at the other in the form of pieces of furniture that looked not only old, but actually ancient with wear. He stared at a man flaying a beautifully carved chest of drawers with a length of heavy, rusty chain. "What's the idea of doing that?" George asked.

"That's part of antiquing the same kind of chests you see over there," Adam told him. He pointed to two chests that stood side by side.

"One of those," Eve said, "was made over a century ago in Spain. The other was made here last week."

"Which is which, George?" Adam demanded. "For the hundred dollars we've got on it."

George gave him a look, and then strode over to the chests. He glanced from one to the other. After a moment of indecision he said, "I admit it's a good job, but I'll tell the difference in a minute."

He kept looking at the chests. He walked all around them. He bent down and examined them closely. He straightened, puzzled.

"Well?" asked Adam.

"I don't suppose you'd let me look inside," George said.

"You can," said Eve.

George was shaken by Eve's confidence more than he was by Adam's as he lifted the lid and looked inside. He peered for some time and then dropped the lid.

"I don't care what you say now," Adam told him. "Not even if you win the bet by a lucky guess. You don't know."

"I'm damned if I do," George admitted.

"Want to try the guess?"

"I figure I owe you the hundred without making it."

"Call it off," suggested Eve.

The men agreed, though George added, "I'll pay it if you show me how those wormholes are made."

"Nothing doing," Adam told him.

Eve asked George, as they left the building, "We'll see you tonight at the Bradbury housewarming dinner?"

The contractor shook his head. "I'm not going, Eve. The old lady only asked me because Michelangelo here is her fairhaired boy of the moment and he asked her to ask me."

"Don't tell me you've got tender feelings," said Adam.

George shook his head. "It isn't that. A roughneck like me doesn't belong there. I know my side of the lake. I'll build houses for them over there, but I don't want to be a part of the life that goes on in them."

Eve looked at him approvingly.

"You sound like my wife," Adam accused.

"What's the matter with your wife?" George demanded.

"She doesn't like Palm Beach people."

"Maybe she can see they're one thing," George said, "and regular human beings are another."

"I can see that, too," Adam claimed, "and go on beyond it."

"Is there some place beyond it?" asked George.

Adam growled, "A roughneck like you wouldn't know."

Eve's gown for that evening was made of Spanish lace she had bought in Madrid. It had an overskirt of French blue taffeta with pink rosebuds. The upper part of the bodice was French blue tulle veiled with rose pink tulle. It had full elbow sleeves and a high girdle with a butterfly bow. Over her gown she wore an evening wrap of rose pink taffeta trimmed with ostrich feather bands of the same shade and lined with French blue georgette.

She knew she had never looked more stylish. She saw this reflected in Adam's eyes when he approved, "Anybody can see you're the wife of the most successful architect in Palm Beach."

Adam drove the Rolls through the Moorish archway of Casa Sol. They had to wait in line along the curved driveway leading to the covered, arched car entrance. The many cars, people, chauffeurs, servants, and lights made a bright, smart scene.

"Now it's a house," said Adam. "It doesn't come alive until this happens."

Liveried footmen appeared at either side of the car and opened the doors. They got out. One man slid into the driver's seat. Adam, after only a second of hesitation, went to the hood of the car and unscrewed the Lady. The footman waited, saying and expressing nothing. Eve bit her lip to keep from laughing as Adam slipped the figure in his pocket and joined her.

Inside, they passed through the high, groined entrance hall which they saw was lighted only by giant candelabra. Passing into the vast drawing room they were attended by an elderly butler clad in green tails with gold buttons on his jacket. While they waited for him to announce other guests lined up, the butler gazed frostily at Adam.

"What's he got against you?" Eve asked.

"He doesn't like the size rooms I gave him."

When they were announced, heads turned. Here was the man who had designed the fifty-room cottage in which select people gathered tonight. Mrs. Bradbury's gloved hand, held out in front of nearly a solid bosom wall of pearls, touched that of Eve. The two women murmured polite greetings. Eve passed on to bow to little Mr. Bradbury, who stood straight and correct and making the proper remarks of welcome.

Eve stood alone, with no one coming up to her, until Adam joined her. Then people came up to Adam rather than her. Not all of the women even spoke to her, but ignoring her, attended Adam, looking up at him and saying:

"I'm mad about it, I promise you."

"It's frightfully amusing."

"It's too miraculous!"

Footmen passed about with trays of cocktails, small thin sandwiches, and an endless variety of fancy canapes. Carrying their drinks, and followed by servants offering more, people strolled through the house. They examined the magnificent fireplace in the drawing room made with a carved stone lintel supported by engaged columns and lined with firebrick in a herring bone pattern. They admired ornamental, multiple-paneled doors.

They strolled down dimly lighted vista cloisters overlooking an expanse of green lawn and the star-lighted sea beyond. They trod on tiles Eve had manufactured, and passed through a belvedere leading to a patio in which grew royal palms illuminated with blue spotlights. Beyond this was the immense swimming pool in whose azure depths lights burned. At either end of the pool were large perches occupied by great blue macaws dripping a yard of tail and screaming for attention.

Adam and Eve, after their own tour, held court in the flagged campo, with people introducing themselves and offering congratulations. A man nearly as tall and heavy as Adam came up brusquely. "I'm John Durst," he said. They knew him for being the owner of a large railroad system. "This is all very well," he told Adam, waving an arm at the Bradbury house. "All very well indeed. And not bad, not bad at all. But I'll tell you what I want you to do for me," he informed Adam. "I want you to build me a place here that will make this look like a backhouse."

Even Adam, Eve saw, watching him, gave a slight gulp. "A little difficult," he said, "but I'll see what I can do."

"When can I look at plans?" Durst wanted to know.

"In a few weeks. I've got—"

"I'll only be here another five days," Durst said. "Make me one of those sketches of yours so I can see it tomorrow."

"Have you got any land?" inquired Adam.

"I'll get some. What has this place got? Forty acres, I think that little Jack-in-the-Box Bradbury told me. I'll get eighty. What time tomorrow?"

"Noon."

"Ten o'clock, my apartment at the Flamingo Club."

"That early," Adam said, "it will have to be my office across the street."

Eve glanced at Adam. It was all very well not to salaam before one of the richest men in the country, but she thought this was carrying the refusal too far, and bordered on the high-handed.

Durst, however, acceded. He seemed even to admire Adam's attitude. "All right, damn it, your office." He indicated the Bradbury mansion. "And don't forget—like a backhouse."

As Durst strode away, Michael came up to tell Eve, "I'm taking you in to dinner. You, great man," he said to Adam, "are taking Mrs. Bradbury, and your services are now required."

Adam began, "What does she think—"

"Don't say it," advised Michael, "because you won't mean it. You know you love every minute of tonight."

Adam glowered at him and turned and left. Michael held out his arm to Eve, who took it. As they joined the line of people entering the vaulted dining room, they stopped at intervals as the procession halted. Once they overheard a group discussing the house and the Paines.

The Bradbury place reminded one man of Grand Central. Another said, "I'll admit this bastard Spanish does fit the country." A third predicted, "Paine will live as the architect who put a wicker chair over the john." A woman approved of Adam Paine, but held that his wife couldn't do anything for him. "Not that bean pole," she said. "She's wrong."

Michael glanced at Eve. He ran a hand over his closely cropped fair hair. "Are you bothered by that?"

"Not much," she answered. "Only as far as Adam is concerned. Michael, do you think, for his sake, I should play up to them?"

"You know you shouldn't," he told her, "and you know it wouldn't do any good in the first place. I don't have to tell you to be yourself, Eve; you've got too much sense to be anything else."

"Still—"

"We're everything you think we are," he assured her. "At least most of us. Too many have inherited their wealth and subconsciously realize they could never make it themselves. So they hang on to it with a death grip and offer a snooty crust to the world to hide their basic inferiority. Others got their money too quickly and feel so unsure of themselves they do much the same thing. The result is a shallow and selfish life, sometimes vicious. It also becomes jaded and weak, and a good deal meaningless."

Eve looked at him. "You aren't like that, Michael."

"And a few others aren't. There are excellent people among the rich, too, fine people. They're the ones you rarely hear about. They are more like you." He was gazing at her now, and to Eve's surprise, she sensed in his glance more than the admiration he had previously shown toward her.

She dropped her own gaze, confused, because she wanted nothing like that from him. Suddenly she felt her height alongside Michael, and she tried to shrink down to his size. Accustomed to Adam, she hadn't experienced that in a long time.

The glittering company, with the men in gleaming white shirt fronts and the women ablaze with jewels, seated itself at the tremendous refectory table Adam had provided. Eve and Michael were placed about halfway down the table, and as they seated themselves, they saw and waved to Adam who sat on Mrs. Bradbury's right at one end. With a start, Eve saw who sat next to Adam on his other side.

Above the table Mona Otis was nearly naked, and Eve saw one of her brown hands steal out and place itself on Adam's arm as she leaned toward him and spoke and smiled, flashing her white teeth.

Michael followed Eve's glance and observed, "She didn't get there on her social standing, which is dropping. She must have contributed at least five thousand to the old lady's favorite charity."

"Michael, it scares me a little that she would do that."

"The money part of it," he assured her, "doesn't mean as much as you think. It would only be about fifty dollars to most people."

"Is she that rich?"

"She hit the jackpot twice in a row. Her lawyers really made deals for her. She owns stock in my breakfast foods. I'm working for her a small part of the time."

A footman reached over Eve's shoulder and placed before her a tall silver goblet filled with shaved ice and sliced fruit topped by blood red cherries. "Do you think," Eve began, and hesitated, "Michael, do you think she'd listen to me?"

He glanced at her sharply this time. "Now you're not being your sensible self."

"I've got to try."

"I wish I could help you." He suggested, "I expect there is only one person who could do that."

"I know," Eve admitted, "I shouldn't question Adam. But any man, if that is thrown in his face often enough . . ."

"There you have an age-old state of affairs," said Michael. "So go after the starting point, Eve; it won't do any harm."

It was quite late that evening before Eve had an opportunity to speak alone with Mona Otis. She had to wait for her outside the powder room and felt on the defensive for doing it, when she said, "Mrs. Otis."

Mona looked her up and down, coolly, appraisingly. "You're Adam Paine's wife," she stated.

"You know that," said Eve. "Just as I know what you're trying to do with him."

Mona's beautiful lips flowed and curled. "Did he tell you—? How naive and delightful."

"Leave him alone," Eve warned.

"That's rather a frontal attack, isn't it?"

"I mean it to be. Just as you mean yours."

"I'm sure you must be mistaken."

"Stop it."

Mona sighed, her prominent breasts lifting and then slightly dropping. "What is it you want to say to me?"

"I've already said it. Leave him alone."

Mona placed her hand on Eve's sleeve. Eve brushed it off with a flick of her arm. Mona said, "I'm sure there's nothing to worry about."

"I'm not worrying," said Eve.

Mona looked innocent, widening her blue eyes. "No?"

"I'm just telling you."

"I was going to say," Mona repeated, "I'm sure there's nothing for you to worry about because when I asked Adam again tonight to build me a cottage he refused—under any circumstances. If you know what I mean."

"I'm not sure I know what you mean."

"There were no conditions. All I wanted was a cottage."

"And he wouldn't take the commission?"

"A pity, because I really want him to do a house for me. And he's become so much the rage that no one else will do. Perhaps you can persuade him."

Eve didn't answer. She turned from Mona and left her.

GERRY GOT OUT

of his new Buick and strode jauntily up the walk of the little house on the outskirts of West Palm Beach. He had discarded his stiff straw hat for a shining smooth white Panama that set off his handsome face. He wore plus fours and neat ribbed golf stockings down to smart two-toned black-and-white sport shoes. His light jacket was thrown open.

On the walk a small boy played with toys. Gerry addressed him warmly. "Hello, sonny."

"My name isn't sonny," the boy replied equitably.

Indulgently, Gerry inquired, "What is your name?"

"Fred is my name. It's what my father's name was, too."

"Fred Pollock?"

"That's what my name is."

Gerry glanced toward the house. "Is your mama home?"

"She's in there." Fred pointed to the screen door.

Gerry thanked the boy and mounted the two wooden steps to the porch. His rap was firm and precise.

A pretty woman in her late twenties appeared behind the screen. She was slim and trim in a print dress whose waistline was at her hips and which was so short it showed most of her shapely legs below the knee. She looked even prettier when she opened the door and could be seen without the screen intervening.

Gerry, at the sight of her, doffed his Panama with a little more sweep than usual. "Mrs. Mary Pollock?" he asked.

"Oh," the woman said, "I thought you were a boy—I mean, with your knickers . . ." Her face flushed and she stared, in confusion, at her mistake about the good-looking man she confronted.

He smiled and confided, "This is Nineteen Twenty-three, you

know, and men's clothes are getting to be quite gay. My name is Gerry Vance," he told her, paying no more attention to her embarrassment. "I've come to see you about the property, the thirty acres, you own in the north end of town."

"Won't you come in, Mr.—? Oh, I'm so awful on names; you just told me yours and I've forgotten it already."

"Think nothing of it. Vance. Gerry Vance."

"Please come in, Mr. Vance."

As he entered the little house and took a seat on the sofa after Mrs. Pollock chose an overstuffed armchair, Gerry said, "Fine boy you've got out there. Nothing like having children, absolutely nothing like it; they're more than fame and fortune. And I can see where little Fred gets his good looks."

Mrs. Pollock lowered her eyes. She murmured, "From his father, too . . ." When she looked up, it wasn't directly at Gerry.

Sympathetically, he said, "It was seven months ago, wasn't it?"

She nodded. "I suppose I should have worn black. But somehow —it didn't seem right down here, mourning in the bright sun and all—and it's going out of style, too. I don't think Fred would have minded."

"I'm sure he wouldn't," Gerry informed her.

"They tell me—Mr. Parsons does—he's the man Fred told me to ask advice of if anything happened to him, that some day I might even want to marry again. But I—well, I don't think I ever could. . . ."

Gently, Gerry advised, "Your faith and love for your husband are certainly wonderful, Mrs. Pollock, but time, perhaps, will have something to say. You're still young—"

"Yes," she interrupted, "that's the trouble. I'm—" She stopped, in deeper confusion at having started to speak so involuntarily. "I mean, what was it you said you wanted to see me about, Mr. Vance?"

He studied her for an instant before he replied, "About your property—your undeveloped property—in the north end of town. I might be interested in helping you to dispose of it, Mrs. Pollock— if the price happened to be right."

"You mean buy it?"

"If it is attractively priced."

"Well, I was thinking of asking—"

"I believe you have a price of one hundred dollars per acre on it, Mrs. Pollock."

"I did have that price, but I thought it might bring a little more—"

Gerry laughed with light deprecation. "More, Mrs. Pollock? Oh, no. Less, if anything."

"But prices have been going up, haven't they? Some people even talk of a boom."

"Well," said Gerry, "some people talk of anything, I guess. They don't know the boom has been here and gone. Yes, there has been, there *was*, a certain little rise in the price of property. But it reached it's peak some time ago. There's only one place to go now, and that's down."

"Is that right, Mr. Vance?"

"That's right, Mrs. Pollock, absolutely right. Why, just last week I handled a large piece of property right out near yours—making both pieces valued at about the same price—for a client of mine. He had paid one hundred and twenty-five dollars an acre and he was glad, very glad, I'm at liberty to say, when I managed—with some hard persuasion—to get him eighty dollars per acre for it."

"You don't say?"

"You're a sensible woman, Mrs. Pollock, I can see that, and I'm sure you can see the intelligence of my client to take a good price when he could get it. If he'd waited another twenty-four hours I doubt if I could have gotten seventy for him."

"Yes, I know," she said doubtfully, "but I thought I ought to get—"

"You want to sell the property, don't you, Mrs. Pollock?"

"Well, I do. I need the money, but—"

Gerry leaned forward and almost whispered, "Then I advise you to get in on a sale while you can. If you wait too long, you might not even get as much as fifty dollars an acre."

"Oh, I wouldn't ever accept—"

"Mrs. Pollock," Gerry announced sternly, "you can never tell about real estate. Before you know it sometimes, things get to the point where it isn't a question of what you'll take, but what you can get."

138

Impressed, and a little frightened, she asked, "Do you think that's the case with me?"

"Not quite," he conceded, "but you're getting close to it, perilously close. If you wait much longer, you will be there."

"But," she stammered, "but how much are you offering for the property?"

"Oh," said Gerry easily, "I'm not offering anything for it." He let that sink in while he studied his manicured fingernails.

"You aren't?"

"What I mean to say," he then told her, "is that I am representing another party. Sort of a syndicate."

She was clearly impressed. "A syndicate?"

"Sometimes," he explained, "this syndicate doesn't offer quite as much as certain private individuals. Almost as much, however, so close there is barely a difference. And the thing about a syndicate is that its money is as good as gold, Mrs. Pollock. It's a thing you can count on. You can't say that of everybody's money."

"No," she said, "I guess you can't."

"I was told," he said, "not to go above sixty-five dollars per acre for your property. But I think," he stopped her move to interrupt, "I think, in consideration of your being such a pretty little lady, and being a new widow, and having such a fine boy out there, that I could persuade them to offer you a full seventy."

"Seventy dollars an acre? Oh, I'm sure Mr. Parsons would think—"

"I'm sure he would, too. And looking at it from the viewpoint of Mr. Parsons, he would be absolutely correct, Mrs. Pollock. He would tell you never to accept such a price, and I say again, he would be correct. From his viewpoint. But there are other viewpoints. There is the viewpoint of reality. That is to be found in today's real-estate prices, not those of yesterday. By the way, how old is Mr. Parsons?"

"Oh, he isn't young. He's seventy-two."

"You see?" Gerry asked, and then hastily went on, "A wonderful age to reach. I hope I may live to be more than three score and ten myself some day. At that age of retirement you can look back on a full life and think about your successes—and your failures, too, of course. Is Mr. Parsons a rich man?"

"No, but—"

Gerry lifted his nose and sniffed. "Do I smell chicken?"

"Baked," she said.

"With bread-crumb dressing?"

She nodded, worried at what had been said about real-estate prices, and her faith in Mr. Parsons subtly shaken, but smiling at Gerry's mention of the chicken.

"Nothing I like better," he declared. "And it's been a good many years since I've tasted any real home-baked chicken as I'm sure you know how to cook it." He waved a hand to express regret. "But that is something else, your personal life in which I have no right to intrude. I am here to ask if you are prepared to consider the offer of the syndicate for your property."

She looked startled at this abrupt change of subject. "Why—"

"If you are," he said, "and I hope you are, I will take the risk of definitely keeping to the higher figure of seventy dollars per acre that I quoted to you. I will do this even if I have to make it up out of my own pocket."

"I wouldn't want you to do anything like that—"

"I would be glad to do it. Then we are agreed?"

"Agreed? Oh, I would have to ask Mr. Parsons first if—"

Gerry shook his head. "Unfortunately, Mrs. Pollock, there won't be time for that. You see, the syndicate men are buying a good deal of property. They have many tracts under consideration. But they intend to buy just so much, and no more. I'm afraid if you wait, if you delay any time at all, they may have purchased their quota and would not be interested in your property at any price."

"But seventy dollars an acre—"

"Have you any other offers for it, Mrs. Pollock?"

"Well, no, but—"

"One reason the syndicate can offer even that amount is that it is composed of wealthy men who can wait many years before realizing anything on their investment. They have the capital to do this. That's why they can pay cash, too. I told you they would pay cash, didn't I?"

"Why, no, you didn't—"

"I thought that was understood. Yes, Mrs. Pollock, unlike private interests—who might not be able to keep up payments at all—the syndicate will pay you cash—twenty-one hundred dollars in cash; that's over two thousand dollars."

"Two thousand . . ."

"Over. And I am empowered to advance you, as a down payment to clinch the bargain, one hundred dollars in cash immediately."

From the pocket of his coat Gerry took a thick wallet. Holding it slightly aside, he took out ten crisp new ten-dollar bills. He spread them in a fan to exhibit. He ruffled them like cards. He counted them expertly, flashing them. He held them on exhibition while he reached in his pocket and took out a piece of paper. "All you have to do is to sign this agreement. I'll make it out for the amount I mentioned, Mrs. Pollock."

She wavered while he wrote. There was a sizzling sound from the kitchen. She started to get up. The sound stopped. She sat back again.

"I really don't know—"

He held out the paper and pen to her. "You will never regret it, Mrs. Pollock." He leaned closer to her, smiling intimately, showing his fine teeth, his eyes lighting, his glance running with frank admiration over her face and then down her body, to come up again, and look her straight in the eye. "You're doing the right thing. I promise you."

She swallowed. His glance held her. She could not keep from her expression the attraction he held for her. She flushed as she reached for the pen and their hands touched. She trembled a little as he held the paper for her and she signed it. She gave it back to him as if getting rid of it, almost afraid to have anything more to do with it.

She didn't make any move to take the hundred dollars until he proffered it to her. Then, as if ashamed to be receiving money from him, she snatched it and thrust it into the bosom of her dress. Just then the sizzling sound came again from the kitchen. She jumped up and ran out as though escaping.

After a moment, when she didn't return, Gerry picked up his Panama and rose. He called through the doorway. His tone was tentative. "I guess I'd better not take up any more of your time, Mrs. Pollock. I want to thank you, and say I'll be out with the papers in a few days—"

He stopped, as she appeared in the doorway. Her pretty face was almost tragically serious when she asked, "Would you—you said you liked baked chicken—would you care to stay and have some?"

They stared at each other for a moment. Gerry dropped his hat on the couch again. "I would be delighted, Mrs. Pollock. I certainly would be delighted, Mary—you don't mind if I call you by your first name, do you?"

"I—I don't mind."

GERRY SAT SLOUCHED

on a Savonarola chair in Adam's office. He sat up with a pained expression and leaned down to look at the X shape of the chair. "This thing," he said, "is the most uncomfortable chair I ever sat in."

"Chosen for exactly that purpose," said Adam, who occupied a broad, padded leather chair at an immense carved Spanish table he used for a desk. "If the person I'm doing business with is physically uncomfortable it gives me an advantage over him."

The idea tickled Gerry. "I'll have to remember that and get me a chair like it when I have an office."

Idly, Adam asked, "Haven't you got an office yet?"

"That's the next thing. I'm out of the bootlegging business and now in real estate all the time. So far I haven't really wanted an office."

"Didn't want anybody to know what you're doing, hey?"

The two men laughed.

Gerry crossed and then uncrossed his legs in their plus fours. Adam asked, "Where'd you get the short pants?"

"Ought to outfit yourself with some, Adam, and be in style."

"Can you imagine how I'd look in them? What I've got suits me." Adam indicated his rumpled duck trousers and sneakers. "Is that what you came to see me about?"

Gerry hitched in the chair, trying to get comfortable. "I've got a job for you."

"I've got enough jobs."

"I'd like you to do this, Adam."

Adam regarded him. "Are you up where you can build a Palm Beach cottage?"

"Not yet. I just want the entrance pillars so far."

Adam stared at him. "Gerry, I thought I'd already had the damnedest commission I'd ever get. Durst, the railroad man, asked me to build him a place that would make Casa Sol look like a backhouse. I gave him the general scheme of things, and I mean that was a shack I drew him. And he paid me for it. He says he'll put off building for a while, even though he got his land. Now you come along and say you want a place I know damn well you haven't got the money for, and all you want is the entrance pillars. What is this?"

"What I want," Gerry explained, "are plans for an ornate set of gates leading into a subdivision."

"Who's subdividing what?"

"I am. I've got a piece of property. Up to this time I've only dealt in lots. But now I've got a good piece that will make some real money."

"What widow did you steal it from?"

Gerry grinned. "You having me followed?"

"Is she young?"

"Just right."

"Pretty?"

"Nicest thing you ever saw."

"I hope you're paying her more than your affectionate attentions."

"That's only an extra dividend. I'm paying her, Adam. I believe in that, if only to establish a good reputation."

"Or to keep out of trouble. What's this entrance-pillar idea of yours?"

"I guess you've been building mansions so much you haven't seen what's going on down below you," said Gerry. "And when I say below you I mean also south of here, around Miami, Fort Lauderdale, and a place called Hollywood-by-the-Sea. It's happened here, too, or at least across the lake. Here's what it is: You get a good tract of land and measure it off into lots. You've got to clear it, too, so people can see what they're getting. Later on I don't think you'll even have to do that. You get a good name for it and put this up on your entrance columns. It's those I want you to design for me. They'll have class coming from you."

"When do you mention how much you pay?"

"Well, I thought I'd give you a lot—"

"Make it two."

"All right, two."

Suspiciously, Adam pointed out, "You agreed pretty fast to that."

"I'm generous with my friends."

"Hah! How big are these lots of yours?"

"Forty feet."

Adam gave him a look. "You really leave room to spread out, don't you?" He took a sheet of drawing paper from a case set beside his table. Picking up a pencil stub he said, "Here go your gates. Would you care for them Spanish, Italian, or straight Adam Paine?"

"Straight Paine would be fine."

Adam sketched. Gerry fidgeted on the Savonarola chair. "If the chair is making you squirm," Adam advised irritably, "get off it. If you just want to see what I'm doing, come around and look."

With vast relief, Gerry got off the chair, and went to look over Adam's shoulder. He began, "Do you mind—"

"Don't offer me any advice or tell me what to do or criticize," Adam directed him. "If you don't like what I'm going to give you, you can use it for toilet paper."

"I'll like what you do," Gerry assured him. "It isn't that. I was only going to ask if you mind talking while you draw?"

"I don't mind at all. Talk."

"I haven't got a name for my place yet. I want something really tony. I don't know these Spanish places. You do. How about reeling off some names?"

Adam, while he worked, began, "Seville, San Sebastian, Cordoba, Barcelona, Alicante—no? Well, then, Palma, Tarragona, Malaga —what is this? How many do you want?"

"Keep on."

"Escorial, Toledo, Burgos, Salamanca, Granada—"

"That's it!" cried Gerry. "Granada. That's a beautiful sounding thing. The name of my subdivision will be Granada Manors."

"I know some people," said Adam, "who would vomit at it, but I suppose it's fine for what you want." He held up his sketch. On the paper were pictured twin columns that looked a little like the Giralda in double miniature.

"Wonderful!" said Gerry. "On the strength of this I can raise the lot prices I had in mind."

"Take it to Aubrey," Adam told him. "He'll translate it into plans for you."

"When the time comes," Gerry predicted, "we'll go places together, Adam."

Adam raised his eyebrows. "I've been," he pointed out.

"What you've done is great," Gerry said. "But compared with what's coming, it's small potatoes to what you're going to do. This is only practice."

"Tell me when the real show is on," Adam requested dryly.

"When I sell Granada Manors," Gerry suggested, "come out and see the first act. Bring Mrs. Paine."

Adam promised to be there, and forgot it until Gerry phoned him one day some months later and said that on the following Sunday the first sale of lots at Granada Manors would take place. "If I said I'd go, I'll go," Adam growled, "and I suppose if I said I'd bring my wife, I'll bring her. Where is this swamp you're selling?"

Over the wire Gerry laughed. "'Swamp?'" he repeated. "That doesn't come until later."

"What do you mean?"

"Nothing. This is good land." He gave Adam directions about how to reach it.

On Sunday, in the Ghost, with the top of the phaeton down, they didn't need much in the line of directions when they reached West Palm Beach. Several buses packed with people, and with a huge sign strung along their side reading, "Come to Granada Manors," were leaving from a downtown corner. Gerry was offering free transportation to his subdivision. Others in cars were streaming toward the site.

The Rolls-Royce joined it, and soon arrived in the middle of a mad traffic jam. Cars were piled up long before and far beyond two ornate brown entrance columns Adam faintly remembered having designed. Eve, looking at them, asked Adam, "Did you have anything to do with them?"

"Not with the final awful result," he said. "How about you?"

She shook her head. "He didn't come to me for that atrocious

146

work. But I must say they're garish and probably more effective than things in good taste."

Adam nosed the Ghost gingerly through the crowd on the road until he reached the gates. There was no place to park. One of the buses went back for another load. The other was depositing its crowd near the gates. A man was trying to direct traffic before the gates, and he now motioned furiously to Adam to keep on going. He was interrupted by a loud voice calling, "Let the Rolls-Royce through! Let it come right in! Let the Rolls-Royce in!"

The Ghost was motioned to go between the columns. Adam steered it through. A little beyond, standing on a high platform, was Gerry. It was he who had called in his best carnival midway manner. He motioned to Adam to park right opposite the platform, and this Adam did.

They looked at Gerry's preparations. In back of him on the platform was a large, clear map of the subdivision, each lot marked off. The land it platted, cleared of scrub, was a sandy waste with a few Caribbean pines left standing because it had been too much work and expense to take them down.

Today Gerry was bareheaded. In his hand he held a light brown bamboo cane. He waved this at the Paines, who waved back. He rapped it smartly on the railing of the platform, calling for attention, his voice bellowing to make itself heard in a commanding way to all present.

The crowd quieted. An air of expectancy hung over its members. They looked up at Gerry, craning their necks. He waited a long moment before he spoke, and then it was as if in awe of what was going to take place.

"Howdy, folks," he greeted. "Friends and neighbors of the great state of Florida, which has a climate incomparable on the face of the earth, and I don't care if you include all of Europe and the world-renowned Riviera, and all of South America, and all of any place you may care to name! The sovereign state of Florida is blessed with a climate better than all of them put together, and it is now, today, here, that this great state is to come into its own and this fact be realized to the fullest extent as it should be and has the right to deserve."

He came to the front of the platform and lowered his voice, to impart confidentially, "Let me tell you that when I say that right here, today, on this spot—when I say this is going to be realized —I mean what I say. Anybody who has had the good sense to come here today and listen to what I've got to say is going to profit by it in a way he could never dream would come true. For here, and for the first time right in this particular section, are going to be offered pieces of the great state of Florida which has this climate comparable to no other, at prices that reflect only a very small part, a minute portion, a very beginning, of their true value and worth."

He waved his cane at the horizon. "Look at it!" he cried. "Look at the wonderful, fruitful, valuable land spread before you! And let any man dare to tell me he has ever in all his life, anywhere on the face of the globe, seen better!"

No one accepted his challenge. The crowd turned, following his instruction, looked at the land, and then back to Gerry, listening avidly, drinking in every word.

"I believe in Florida," he declared. "I believe in this piece of Florida. And I am going to ask you to believe in Florida. I am going to ask you to believe in this piece of Florida. It won't be difficult for you to do, for you, as I do, love this great sovereign state and can see what a future lies before it. Today we see the bare land except for the magnificent trees still left standing upon it. Tomorrow we will see house after house, home after home, green lawns before them, orange trees laden with golden fruit growing in the back yards, making a garden spot of Granada Manors. Nothing in old Spain, after which it is named, is more favored."

He stepped to the very edge of the platform. "I know I could have put the fine, big, spacious lots of Granada Manors on the market in the regular way, from an office downtown. But if I had done that it would have meant a lot of extra expense, the cost of hiring an office, the cost of a staff, many other costs. I didn't do that because it would have raised the price of this incomparable land. And I wanted it to be as cheap as possible. I wanted to pass that saving on to you. And that is the very thing I am just about to do, for the benefit of those fortunate enough to be able to take advantage of this great saving."

He paused for a moment, and then bent down to say, "Before

148

doing this I want to let you in on a secret. We have with us today a man who has become the leader in his field, a man whose name is known to all of you, a man whose name is known to all the civilized world as the foremost architect of them all. Many of you have seen, or passed by, or heard about his incomparable achievements in Palm Beach, the Flamingo Club, the great mansion he built for the Bradburys, the most unique office building in the country that carries his own name, and other houses he has built or he has now in the course of construction. I refer to my friend, my very good and close friend, Mr. Adam Paine, who sits right over there in his Rolls-Royce car with his gracious wife, Mrs. Adam Paine."

People turned, twisting their necks to catch a glimpse of the Paines.

Adam lifted a hand, waving to the crowd, while he whispered to Eve with admiration, "The cute son of a bitch."

"My close friend Adam—Mr. Adam Paine—designed the artistic entrance pillars to Granada Manors. And that is not all. Mr. Paine also named Granada Manors. And that is still not all, my friends. Mr. Paine is the first one to believe in Granada Manors. He is, I am proud to announce, the very first one to acquire lots in Granada Manors." Gerry turned and strode to the map, touching two lots on it. "These are the lots of Mr. Adam Paine, Palm Beach architect extraordinary."

Eve asked, "Did you buy—"

"They're my fee for the entrance atrocities," he told her.

"He shouldn't—"

"He hasn't told any lies so far. I 'acquired' the lots. I'm probably the first. I designed the entrance columns, or what they were supposed to be. I named the place. It's stretching a point for him to call me his close friend, but I suppose I'm his friend."

Gerry returned to the edge of the platform. "Now I don't know, exactly, why a man like Mr. Adam Paine is interested in having two lots in Granada Manors. He didn't confide in me. That's his business. But I can tell you that when a smart man like him, with all his Palm Beach connections, has two lots in Granada Manors, it must mean something. Perhaps he wants to get away from all the high life over there across the lake and come here for some peace and quiet and relaxation. At any rate, your first neighbor is one you can be proud of."

Gerry spoke more rapidly. He was at the selling point. He waved his cane briskly, as if whipping the crowd to greater interest. "Now, right now, this minute, while the chance for you smart ones to get in on the ground floor is good, I'm going to start selling this valuable land at prices that won't stay down where they are overnight. You all know what's happening in Florida, what's going to happen here. So who wants to be the first? Who wants to be Adam Paine's neighbor? Who wants this lot right next to him? Speak up, quick!"

Even Gerry wasn't quite prepared for the near roar of voices that responded. He was slightly taken back, but only for an instant. He didn't hesitate. Though it was doubtful if he could have heard any individual voice, he pointed his cane at a man who stood in the front row of the crowd. "He's the one!" he cried. "That's the lucky, lucky man! That's the smart man. Get his deposit, Jack."

Gerry's assistant went to the man with a receipt pad and contract form. Gerry himself kept up his spiel. The lots went like hotcakes. His assistant could barely keep up with the clamoring crowd.

"He's going to sell out the whole thing," Adam predicted.

"That's what is called using your friends," Eve said.

"The cute, cute son of a bitch."

ADAM'S FIRST TWO-

million-dollar house, exclusive of furnishings, was the Villa Mar,
built for an automobile manufacturer. Here he carried out his
plan to place a house virtually on high tide line and protect it
from storms. This he did by making its seaside foundation a battle-
ment, dug and anchored to the coquina rock. To break the force
of the waves a great curving lip, its flat top used as a terrace, extended
out over the beach. The breakers, running up and dashing into
this, were flung high, to dissipate their strength in trying to climb
back on themselves, and thrown then upon their own force and
routed in a form of watery suicide. It was a feat of engineering
that Adam's enemies called minor and not worth the expensive
proximity to the sea it afforded the house. The owners were less
satisfied with another thing: during great storms the maddened and
frustrated waves created a booming vibration in the house, which
sometimes shivered under the impact.

The housewarming dinner party given at Villa Mar was the first
Eve did not attend with Adam. Dutifully, she had gone to all the
rest. She had even held several formal dinner parties of her own
in return, and seen to it that Manuel and Martha were prepared
to do their best with many casual gatherings arranged by Adam on
the spur of the moment. The day before the Villa Mar dinner,
however, she told Adam, "I don't see how I can go, Tiny. I've got
all my three kilns cooking; it's chilly weather and they'll have to
burn for thirty-six hours, maybe forty-eight, and I don't dare leave
them."

"Couldn't you have waited before firing?"

"Not if you want the floor tile for La Luna by next week. This
is just the biscuit stage."

"Well, I've got to have that, but—"

"I know I should go, Tiny. I know my place is beside you there."

"Of course, you don't want to go."

"I'll admit that."

Adam studied her. "Most women would give their eyeteeth for your chance to social climb."

"I guess they would, Tiny."

"You don't care about it at all?"

"Not at all."

"That would be sour grapes in others," he said, "after the way they treat you. But you mean it."

"Yes, Tiny. I'd rather turn out a beautiful jar on my potter's wheel than be runner-up to Mrs. Bradbury, or even Mrs. Bradbury herself."

"I feel the same way."

"Do you, Tiny?"

He swung on her. "What do you mean?"

"Nothing much. Only I've had the impression that you like society life."

"I told you about that. It's a means to an end."

"I hope it doesn't get to be any more than that."

"Don't worry."

"I do, a little."

"About me? Listen——"

"About us. For instance, tomorrow night. You'll be one place, with a lot of people and some loose females thrown in. I'll be another place. It isn't good to be separated like that."

"What do you want to do about it?"

"If I thought it was really serious, or would lead to any trouble between us—Tiny, I'd ask you to pack up and we'd leave here."

He stared at her. "You know I'd do it."

She studied him. "I hope so."

During the winter of 1924 Adam reached almost god-like heights as an architect in demand. He could choose his clients, and did. If he didn't like what they wanted in a house, or if they had too many ideas of their own, he refused their commissions. One he rejected was the talk of Palm Beach for a week. Adam made one of his rare appearances on the ocean beach, at the Breakers Casino, the proper place for stylish people to be seen. He didn't go near the water, but sat on the sand with acquaintances and looked up at elaborately gowned women on the Casino terrace. They in turn closely examined everyone on the beach, particularly the women in their wool challis bathing frocks patterned with tropical flowers. Suits consisted of a blouse that reached over knickers to the knees, which were daringly bare above rolled stockings.

Adam lay on his back surrounded by a group whose members were trying to persuade him to design a house for a couple named Brace, who also added their own entreaties. "It isn't the day for a house," Adam told them.

"Oh, come on, Adam, do a house for them."

"I've got too many to do."

"They need a house; they've got to stay with all the Buckwheats coming to the Ponce now."

Mrs. Brace, a plump, middle-aged woman, made her personal plea. "There's another reason." She leaned down to Adam and whispered in his ear. "I need one of those outside staircases of yours."

That interested Adam. He glanced at Brace, a gaunt, wispy man totally unaware of what his wife might have whispered. In every house he had built lately Adam included an outside stairway leading from the gardens up to one of the master suites. Thus a lady who had an admirer was provided with a way for him to reach her without any of the rest of the household knowing about it.

Adam sat up and looked around. A woman cried, "He's going to do a house for the Braces!"

Lumbering to his feet, Adam picked up a stick of driftwood and began to sketch with it in the sand. He drew one elevation of the house while the Braces and others looked on, commenting and exclaiming. When he indicated the outside staircase a woman whispered viciously to Mrs. Brace, "I see you're provided for." Adam completed the rough sand sketch and turned to Brace, saying, "There it is."

The man studied it. A woman gasped at his effrontery when Brace asked, "Do we have to have a tower?"

Coldly, Adam informed him, "I always have a tower in my houses. You can't have a Spanish house, at least not one from me, without a tower."

153

"But does it accomplish anything?"

"If you mean," Adam said acidly, "is it utilitarian, this one isn't. It's pure decoration."

"I don't think," Brace said, "something that isn't used for anything—why, what are you doing?"

Adam kicked at the sand, destroying the sketch. He slashed it to pieces with the help of the stick, which he then flung down. "There's your house!" he cried.

He strode off, to excited comments behind him, divided equally in sentiment between him and the Braces.

He was alternately amused or enraged at other clients and their desires. To a silly quick rich woman who came to his office he said, "I'm not sure whether I'll do a French Romanesque house for you, or an Italian Romanesque. Or possibly," he said, studying her the way a cat looks at a mouse, "a French Gothic. Or would you like one of the Renaissances, Italian, French, or Spanish?"

"I don't know what you're talking about," she giggled, "but one of those sounds awfully sweet."

"Spanish Romanesque," he decided, and added, "with a little Baroque idiocy thrown in."

"That's it," she agreed, "and my husband says to keep it in a million dollars."

Shocked, Adam protested, "Not including the furnishings?"

"Well, I don't know . . ."

"I haven't done a house this year," he said, "under a million that included the furnishings. Or the landscaping."

"Maybe not including the furnishings or the landscaping, then, though I don't know what Horace will say."

"Let me know," Adam ordered.

"I will," she promised. "I will. First thing in the morning. I'll need a night—that is, after this evening. . . ."

He went to her and patted her hand. "I understand, dear," he said sympathetically.

Durst appeared again, to say, "Those plans you made for me. They were good enough. But I've decided I want a somewhat larger and more elaborate place than that. What was it, sixty rooms? Well, I want at least seventy-five. And they didn't make everything else here look enough like a backhouse. Do some new ones. And don't forget. Like a backhouse."

Solemnly, Adam made new sketches, and showed them to the railroad magnate. As gravely, Durst approved, paid for the work, and said he would give orders soon for the detailed plans and the awarding of the building contract. As before, he left Palm Beach with nothing more said about his house.

Adam put two new things in Vista del Firmamento, a two-and-one-half-million-dollar residence built for an oil man. This was his first house utilizing land running from the ocean to the lake. He solved the problem of the public Ocean Boulevard running through the grounds by digging a tunnel under the road. This led directly into the beach house. High walls, banked with seagrape, shut off the gounds on either side of the road, so that the owner could pass from sea beach to lake front without being seen.

During the pouring of the foundations for the house Adam noticed a ragged board ripped off a form. Its surface, grayed from the concrete, had long, irregular gouges in it as though made by a madman handling several chisels. "Wait a minute," he said to the workman handling it. "Let me have that."

Examining it, he became aroused, yelling, "George! Hey, George!"

George strode up to him. "What's the excitement?"

"What's this wood?" Adam demanded.

George looked at it contempuously. "Cypress, cheapest stuff there is. That's the peck part, the top section of the tree."

"What makes it like this?"

"Some say insects, others say rot. Either way it's junk wood, good only for forms."

"George," Adam informed him with portent, "you're looking at the new ceilings of my houses. And some walls, too."

He raced across the lake with lengths of pecky cypress, taking them to Eve and Artisan Arts. Here, for several days, he worked with blowtorch and wire brush to clean out the gouges. He experimented with paints and stains to color the wood. The ceilings in the main rooms of Vista del Firmamento were made of pecky cypress stained with slashes of blue and green and white as though painters had closed their eyes and used their brushes. The effect immediately became the rage, with pecky cypress ceilings demanded by all who were planning houses. From being the cheapest kind of wood it soared until it was selling for the highest price of any.

The engraved invitation to the opening-night dinner party at the oil magnate's house read only, "Mr. Adam Paine." Eve wasn't mentioned. When this had first happened, many invitations ago, Adam refused to accept. "That's a hell of a thing," he then raged.

"I understand they do it all the time," Eve had said.

"Well, they won't do it to us."

"I don't mind. I don't blame them. I haven't exactly shown them I think they're wonderful. Go, Adam."

He hadn't gone alone. But since then he had. It became an accepted thing, in most quarters, to ask Adam Paine but not his wife. In the degree of sophistication reached here this was little remarked. Adam, knowing that Eve was content with it, finally accepted.

He went to the Vista del Firmamento dinner and returned late in the night. Eve, lying in the great Queen Isabella bed, was awake when he came into their bedroom. The night was cool and she had had Manuel build a lasting coal fire in the kidney warmer. In its glow she watched Adam undress, get in his pajamas, and stand before the little fireplace, warming his middle. "How was it?" she asked.

"The usual brilliant drunkenness. When I left they were throwing each other in the pool, fully dressed. And none of them will have pneumonia tomorrow, which they deserve. That's what I build swimming pools for."

"Are you sober?"

"I am now."

"What made you?"

"You won't like it."

"What is it?"

"It's all right, you understand."

"Let's have it."

"On my way home I fully realized that I'm going to do the house for Mona Otis."

It was like a dash of cold water in Eve's face. She didn't say anything right away.

Adam told her, "I said you wouldn't like it."

156

Eve decided to give her opinion instead of dodging it. "I don't."

"I put the conditions this time."

"What are they?"

"The dining room isn't going to have any electric outlets in it. That way candles will always have to be used or there won't be any light. That's the only thing I couldn't make other people take. This is a chance to do it."

"Yes?" Eve's one word question indicated she was waiting for important considerations.

"She isn't to come near the construction. She's looking at a plan, approving it, and leaving everything else up to me until the day she moves in."

"Is she going to have an opening night?"

"I've already refused the invitation to it. She's given up about me, Evie."

"Has she?"

"Women. Do any of you believe anything good about others?"

"Not much, Tiny. Especially not about the Mona Otises."

He left the wall fireplace and came to the bed, getting in. "It's a house," he grumbled, "like any other. It's giving me a chance to do something I'd like to do. To hell with Mona Otis."

"To hell with Mona Otis," Eve repeated like a prayer.

He pulled the bedclothes over his big form, half uncovering her. She yanked her share back. He stayed on his side of Queen Isabella, far away from her. She whispered, "You don't come over here as often as you used to."

Sleepily, he murmured, "I guess I'm getting old."

"Do you feel old right now?"

"Evie, I'm too tired."

She was shocked, then suspicious. She put the suspicion out of her mind. The shock remained. It was the first time he had ever said such a thing to her invitation. It marked a changing point in their lives. She wanted to call it back, not have them reach the point. She opened her mouth to say something, to get it back, when she heard his slight snore in sleep.

In the faint light thrown by the kidney-warmer fireplace, Eve watched her husband's face. Her black eyes were flecked with concern.

THAT SUMMER ADAM

acquired for a personal pet of his own a monkey named Dottie which had been trained to perform the trick of lifting a woman's skirt, peering beneath, and shrilling, "Eee!" The first time Dottie did this to Eve, she slapped the little beast away. Aggrieved, it leaped to Adam's shoulder, where it peered at Eve and chattered objection to her.

"It's a joke," Adam said.

"It's a nasty joke," Eve told him.

"I guess it is, at that," he admitted. He patted Dottie. "I'll only let her do it to nasty people."

Through the hot, sticky months they worked together on several houses, including that of Mona's. Eve worked conscientiously on Mona's house. If she had any misgivings, she didn't show them. Artisan Arts turned out exquisite tile, filigree wrought iron, and beautifully fashioned period furniture for the house. Though a comparatively small structure of fifteen rooms, it was one of Adam's best. It was located on El Valencia Way, a secluded side street. In its flagged patio was an oval swimming pool about which towering coconut palms were planted. The pool was enclosed by a high pink wall on three sides and the house on the fourth, giving complete privacy. It was to be called Casa Mona.

Adam built a third thing during the summer. In the middle of Durst's eighty acres on the beach front on North County Road, the most expensive piece of private property in Palm Beach, he had a protesting George erect a one-holer, complete with a quarter moon in its door. The raw wooden privy could be seen from the road, and soon was the talk of the Palm Beaches. Word went further by way of the gossip newspaper columnists, so that

Durst, who was out in California, heard of it. He wrote to Adam, "I wish to thank you for my excellent Florida house. It is just what I need there. I would occupy it if it were not for the fact that I have decided to build a hundred-room place in California."

Mona kept to her word about her house. She didn't come near the construction. Eve did not express her conviction that the large reason for this was no desire to come to Florida during the hot summer. The first heard from Mona, apart from her checks during the course of building, was the appearance early in December of a manservant who introduced himself to Adam, "I am Rock, Mrs. Otis's butler. I have driven her car down with the other servants to open and prepare her house. Mrs. Otis will arrive by train before Christmas."

Adam eyed Rock. The man was tall, hardly thirty, and very presentable. He was clad in dark clothes with a stiff white collar and black tie, and he carried a derby in his hand. He looked a little insolent. Adam wondered about him, and expressed his curiosity by asking, "How long have you been a butler?"

Rock didn't give him a straight answer. "For some years—sir." Whether he added the "sir" as an afterthought, or because he wasn't sure Adam deserved it, was difficult to tell. "I am a combination butler and chauffeur."

"All right," Adam told him shortly. "Here are the keys to the house."

The day before Christmas Rock delivered a note from Mona which read:

"Dear Adam,
My house is divine except for one small detail. Could you come to see me about this, professionally, of course, on Christmas afternoon at three?"

"The bargain, " Eve said, "is off, I see."
"I suppose I've got to go," said Adam.
"Why?"
"Because it's about the house."
"Is it?"
"Maybe you'd better come along and protect me."

"Tiny, I couldn't give you any more protection than you want to give yourself."

"Then I'll take Dottie. She'll protect me."

When Adam, with the monkey on his shoulder, rang the doorbell at Casa Mona, Rock opened to him. "This way, sir." There was no hesitation this time about the "sir." "Mrs. Otis is in the pool."

They crossed the circular entrance hall and entered the living room. It was dark because the shutters on the patio side were tightly closed. Before the doorway was placed a carved linenfold screen. Rock took a stand here, indicating that Adam should go out this way. As he passed the young butler Adam saw a wise expression on his face.

Mona's head, covered with a white rubber bathing cap, bobbed in the center of the pool. She lifted a bare arm from the water and waved. She cried gaily in her deep voice, "Merry Christmas, Adam!"

"Merry Christmas," he replied.

She treaded water. "I see you brought a friend." Her hand waved again toward the other end of the pool where green-padded white iron garden furniture was placed. One piece was a wide, double couch with a raised back and a fringed canopy half over it. "Lie down. I'll be right out."

Adam went to the couch and stretched out on one side of it, half sitting up. Dottie clambered to the top of an iron chair and perched there, chattering.

Adam watched Mona come out of the pool by the steps leading down into it. In spite of himself, as she emerged, he couldn't keep his skin from prickling as though a shiver had passed over him.

She was completely naked. She was evenly bronzed from tip to toe. There wasn't a square inch of her that was not beautifully tanned. It was like a covering that accentuated the fact that she had none. Outdoors in the sun, against the background of the house, her glistening, slick, dripping body had a greater perfection than Adam had ever imagined.

She gave no sign of there being anything unusual about her

appearance. She stripped the bathing cap from her head and shook her bobbed blond curls. The action made portions of her body move on their own part. She picked up a crash towel and began to dry herself, not attempting any concealment with it. Casually she said, "It was good of you to come, Adam. I wanted to thank you for my house."

For one of the few times in his life Adam didn't trust himself to speak. Mona, if she noticed his silence, gave no evidence of it, but continued to dry herself.

Dottie climbed down from the back of the chair and went to Mona. The monkey seemed puzzled. She walked all around Mona, chattering. "What's the matter with her?" Mona asked.

Adam explained Dottie's trick. As if illustrating it, Dottie picked up a corner of Mona's towel and looked under it. "Eee!" the monkey shrilled, and then, as though running from what it had observed, Dottie leaped to a palm tree and scampered up to its top, where she sat, scolding.

Laughing, Mona asked, "Will you sell her to me?"

Adam shook his head. He was determined to play Mona's game of pretending she was not nude until she mentioned it herself. "Beautiful weather we're having," he observed.

Seriously, she answered, "Divine."

"Can't believe there was a blizzard in New York yesterday."

"The newspaper said so right on the front page."

"Down here that's where they like to tell about blizzards."

She laughed as she manipulated her towel. "Adam, you're shocked."

"You're characteristic."

"If you weren't shocked you would have said something other than talking about the weather." She discarded her towel. She stood straight in front of him, no longer glistening, but dry and unbelievably brown because she was so bare. Her nakedness was utterly stark and unashamed. It hit him like a blow. He tried to excuse himself by thinking that it would affect any man like that. He wondered, guiltily, if it didn't hit him harder than most.

She asked, "How do you like me this way, Adam?"

"How do your servants?" he countered.

"You think they peek?"

"I saw it in Rock's eyes."

She glanced toward the shuttered windows of the house, and shrugged. "Well, if they do, I'm sure they like it."

"Does Rock like anything else?"

She stared at him, blue eyes wide. "You think I—with a servant! Adam!"

"All right, maybe I take that back."

"You haven't answered my question."

"I always find you amusing, Mona."

"Come off it, Adam. I want a straight answer."

"To what?"

"How do you like looking at me this way?"

He measured his reply and then gave it to her roughly. "I'm not a nance."

"That's better," she said. "It's a risk, you know."

"Mean you might catch cold?"

"You know it isn't that. Women aren't intriguing to most men with all their clothes off. Especially in daylight. It's much better to pretend that there are mysteries. And not many men can be trusted to appreciate a woman totally bare—unless he's asked for it, of course."

"You figure me for one of those men?"

"I figured you."

"And you think it's turned out that way?"

"Hasn't it?"

He looked away from her.

She laughed, lightly.

He claimed, "I didn't ask for it."

"Not out loud," she told him. "But you did. I've seen it in your eyes. Every time you saw me you undressed me mentally."

He didn't answer.

"I really do something to you, Adam," she stated. "Otherwise you wouldn't be afraid to look at me."

He muttered.

"Come on," she challenged, "look; you know you want to."

He turned back to her.

"Don't you think I have pretty breasts?"

162

They were more magnificent in reality than in imagination. He murmured, "Beautiful."

"Slim hips?"

His eyes wandered to her bare hips. "Slim."

"Nice legs?"

"Nice."

She came to the wide lounge. Gracefully, she let herself down on it. She stretched out at his side. She lifted her arms and put her hands under her head.

He started to get up.

She inquired, throatily, "You aren't afraid, are you, Adam?"

He sat back again. He didn't dare not look at her for fear of what she might say. The impact of her naked proximity made his head sing. He had never experienced anything so exquisitely wanton. He hardly breathed. He cursed her in his mind as he tried to think of Eve, to cling to her. It was impossible. He could merely notice how the brown of Mona's wonderful breasts curved up and out.

He jerked his eyes from them, and down her body. Then he had to jerk them away again, not caring what she might say.

She didn't say anything. She had only to be there.

He demanded, "What do you want to see me about?"

"I've already seen it," she answered. "Or rather, you have."

Hoarsely, he asked, "What are you trying to do?"

"I'm trying to drive you crazy," she replied, watching him. "And it isn't as hard as I thought it was going to be."

"Why, damn you—"

"Adam," she interrupted, "you know you want me. You have from the first. Why fight against it?"

"Because I'm married and—"

"Oh, that's all right."

"It isn't all right with me. I know how people here play around, and even sometimes exchange wives, but I—"

"I don't mean that."

"What?"

"Two people can want to be respectable, you know."

"What are you talking about?"

"I've decided it's time I got married again, Adam. Too many

people are dropping me because of a reputation I don't at all deserve. Mrs. Bradbury isn't inviting me to her parties any more no matter how much I offer to give to her charities."

Adam sat up. "Wait a minute. You think I—you—?"

"Why not?"

"You're crazy!"

"You're not very flattering to my proposal, Adam."

"I sure am not!" He looked down at her. The faint, fresh feminine perfume of her body reached his nostrils. He licked his lips. "If you think I—go marry somebody else!"

"You're what I want. You'd be a wonderful catch, you know."

"I'm not interested."

She squirmed on the couch beside him. "You're interested in what goes with it."

Perspiration broke out on his forehead. It had been a long time since he felt desperation. Through his brain, uncontrollably, went the thought, "This is the first time I can understand what makes a sex maniac tick. By God, I could—"

She wriggled again, making her whole body move. She watched him from half-lowered lashes.

His palms were moist. Out of his big body was forced a grunt with which he had nothing to do consciously. He felt flushed, half strangled, and faint. He heard himself saying, "This talk—there isn't going to be any . . ."

He reached out for her.

She wasn't there.

She slipped off the couch and stood up, so that he looked at her from an angle that made his mind reel. He sprang up, and tottered for an instant on his small feet before he followed her, running, as she darted away.

She let him almost catch her before she reached the edge of the pool. Then she dove into the water, eluding him, and was gone. When her head came up, blond curls dripping, he panted, "Come out of there."

"Come and get me."

"You know I can't swim."

"That's why I'm here. I've got to protect myself."

"Protect—!"

164

"I meant what I said, Adam, if you want me—and I think you do."

He looked about. He seemed to see, for the first time, where he was. He heard Dottie's chattering in the palm tree as though it had only just begun instead of having been continual.

He turned, and strode from the pool and Casa Mona, with Dottie sliding down the palm tree and leaping after him.

Mona's throaty laugh followed them. "Merry Christmas!" she called.

THAT WINTER ADAM

worked on the plans for two large houses to be built the following summer. One was in his regulation Spanish style. When he turned over his plans to Aubrey and they were examined, Aubrey discovered that no provision for any closets in the house had been made.

Adam regarded the plans after Aubrey called this to his attention and said, "I'll be damned. I must have been thinking about something else."

The second house was an English baronial mansion. Its bar was to be a complete pub, bought intact in London and dismantled piece by piece, including frosted windows, glass swing doors, counter, beer pumps, tankards, marble-top tables, and stools. The plans for this house, when Aubrey examined them, were found to lack any provision for bathrooms. After indicating this to Adam, who promised to correct the plans, Aubrey went to Eve and asked her worriedly, "Is anything troubling him?"

"Aubrey," said Eve slowly, "I wish I could tell you."

"You know what it is?"

"I know."

His pink face flushing, his eyes contrite behind their glasses, Aubrey apologized, "I shouldn't have asked."

"It doesn't matter, Aubrey. I hope you won't ever have to know —maybe you won't."

When Adam had come home on Christmas Day and said nothing about Mona, Eve realized that something had happened. She herself broached the subject, asking, "What's the change she wants?"

"It was nothing," he said.

She searched him with a long glance. "So that's how it was."

"That's the last time I'll go there. I'm finished with her."

Eve said nothing more. There was nothing to say that would have done any good. She was afraid to ask him, as he agreed before, to drop everything in Florida and leave. She feared his refusal now.

Others must have been hearing things, or Mona was talking, for Michael, after some hesitancy, told her, "Eve, it isn't my business, and I'm putting my nose in it only to possibly save you from being hurt, but—what's this about Adam and Mona Otis?"

"I don't think it's anything—yet," she replied. "Unless . . ."

"What?"

"Unless he's seeing her. I don't think he is." She pleaded of him, "Do you know?"

Michael shook his head. "He isn't seeing her."

Anxiously, hopefully, she pressed him, "How can you tell?"

"Who's been with who is a matter of next-morning general information in Palm Beach. Servants talk and the malicious talk more. You know that yourself."

"Thank you, Michael."

"Is there anything I can do?"

"There isn't anything anybody can do."

He offered, "I'll talk to him."

"That would only be waving a flag in front of a bull. He's got to work it out for himself."

"The damn fool. I can't see how there's anything to work out about you."

"It isn't about me, Michael."

"You know what I mean."

"You're sweet, Michael."

Eve hoped that Adam would forget Mona in favor of another interest. Gerry's prediction of a Florida real-estate boom was now fast coming to realization. Gerry himself had transacted several deals of much the same nature as the one she and Adam had witnessed and been drawn into. He now rode around in a big new Packard. He had money in the bank. He was a man of means. He carried himself with an air. It was with a flourish that he told Adam he had a bigger plan than ever, one so large he couldn't handle it entirely himself. He asked if Adam, Michael, George, and Aubrey wanted to get in on it. "Though that's only five with myself; I need six."

"Let's say we'd all like to hear about it," Adam told him.

"I'm not sure I trust your plan," Eve told Gerry, "but if I do, how about letting me be a part of it?" Mainly, she wanted to remain as close as she could to Adam's activities.

"You, Mrs. Paine?" Gerry never called her by her first name.

"I have money," she assured him. "I take a salary for running Artisan Arts. And I get the profits from half ownership." Her income had been considerable, for Artisan Arts was now receiving orders from many places in Florida, branching out beyond Adam's needs.

They met in the tower apartment of Via Paine. "Here's how it works," Gerry addressed the meeting. "It may sound a little complicated, but it really isn't. And it may sound as if I'm getting more out of it than anybody else, with less investment, but with all the work I have to put in, actually I'm not. I am absolutely not."

Dottie, perched on Adam's shoulder, gave a sudden, "Eee!"

Everybody laughed, and Adam observed to the monkey, "You're absolutely right."

Grinning good-naturedly, Gerry went on, "I know where I can get two thousand acres for twelve dollars an acre; in fact, I've already taken an option on it for a week. It's pretty far out at that price, but it isn't swamp; we haven't got out to the swamp yet. It's dry—or, anyway, I haven't seen it in the rainy season, and I don't want to. Now, that means a purchase price of twenty-four thousand —cash, by the way, for that low price."

"That's where we come in," asked George, "furnishing the cash?"

"That's where you come in," Gerry corroborated. "And you, Mr. Sumner, and the rest of you. Now," he went on, "it will take about fifty thousand altogether to buy and market this property. The rest goes for entrance gates, surveying, advertising, buses to take the people out, trombone players to be at the sales, things like that. We get six thousand lots, nice big lots this time. And we sell them for a mere one hundred and fifty dollars apiece, think of that, only one hundred and fifty dollars for a generous slice of Florida, along with which you get our climate down here that no one can deny is something—"

"Mr. Vance," Michael interrupted. "You don't need to sell us on Florida. How does the rest of your proposition go?"

"I guess I got carried away with myself," admitted Gerry. "Well, as I say, a hundred and fifty dollars is about the right low price to remove money from pockets like a suction dredge. And even if the purchasers only make the first payment of fifty dollars and then default on the rest, which happens quite frequently, I must say, that means an intake of three hundred thousand dollars. With an investment of fifty thousand, that is, ten thousand by five people each, it means a profit of a quarter of a million dollars. Divided into six shares, each of us would receive nearly forty-two thousand dollars, meaning a net profit each of about thirty-two thousand."

It sounded impressive.

Aubrey cleared his throat. "Just a moment," he said. "You say five people will invest but there will be six shares. Who is the sixth?"

Eve answered him. "Mr. Gerry Vance, who puts in nothing, but gets a forty-two thousand net profit."

"That's correct, Mrs. Paine. I figure my sixth of a share is worth finding the property and carrying on the sale."

"It's worth it," said Adam.

"I agree," Michael said.

"Hold it a minute," put in George. "This sounds good. Gerry here can make anything sound good. But has this boom gone as far as this? Can this property be sold the way he says?"

Gerry sighed. "I know it's the first time it will be tried on such a scale up around here. I wouldn't want any of you to go into it unless you were sure. I'm going to ask you to do something to get sure. Tomorrow take a ride with me down to Miami and back. Then, after you see what's happening down around there, if you don't want to come in this, I'll locate the capital somewhere else. If you do want to come in, we'll get right on it. Will you go with me?"

The others looked at each other. Except for Michael, they all nodded. "I can't go," he told Gerry, "but count me in your scheme."

"Thank you for your confidence, Mr. Sumner," Gerry told him.

"I'd like to be in it," said Aubrey, "but ten thousand dollars is a little rich for me."

"The hell it is," Adam told him. "You put up what you can

and I'll cover the rest for you. If it doesn't work, you don't owe any more; if it does, you make what we do."

"Adam, I can't let you—"

"You aren't letting me; I'm doing it."

The next day the five of them, with Adam and Dottie sitting on the front seat of the Packard beside Gerry, drove to Miami. At Lake Worth, the first town south of West Palm Beach on the Dixie Highway, Gerry pointed out the building of many small houses proceeding here. "Each town we'll see," he explained, "has a wrinkle of its own. Here, if you buy a lot in town you get another one free out in the back country."

The road was crowded with cars, most of them going south. The cars were laden with both people and luggage. Household goods were piled on top and hung from the sides. The occupants had eager looks in their eyes as they watched the Florida landscape. This was the promised land. They hurried, as if to get to a destination before it was too late.

"Look at them," Gerry laughed. "The gold rush has started. And this is only the beginning. It's going to be the greatest trek since the days the covered wagons hit the Oregon Trail."

All along the way were ornate gates and arches, some with heraldic devices, each with an alluring name of a subdivision, most in the Spanish manner. Of the latter motif, Gerry told Adam, "Now you can see some of your influence on the country."

At the sight of a bilious yellow stucco Moorish castle, complete with skinny minarets, Adam observed, "I'm ashamed of myself."

At Fort Lauderdale they saw an immense subdivision, completely cleared of every bush and tree, all carefully laid out with streets, sidewalks, lights, and water, yet with not a single house on it. The place was completely deserted. Gerry said it was all sold and most of it entirely paid for. But everybody had bought for speculation, not for building. It would probably all be sold over again at a profit.

At Hollywood-by-the-Sea dredges, trucks, and steam shovels were hard at work. "Fellow named Young is doing this," Gerry said. "He started it as just another subdivision and now it's rated a twenty-million-dollar municipality. He's digging a deep-water harbor for steamships. Got Goethals, builder of the Panama Canal, to do it for him. Look at those buses!" He pointed to several large white buses. "Young sent those all the way to the Middle West to bring customers."

The nearer they approached Miami the more actual building was going on. At some places armies of carpenters rushed to complete buildings or a few sample houses on new subdivisions. Hotels and apartments were being thrown up like stage sets. In the city itself, when they reached it, the sound of riveting was heard above all else. Gaunt steel skeletons were rising from the flat Florida land, the metal beams taking the place of arching mangrove roots that once stood here.

"It's going to be a city," Eve observed.

"It is already," Gerry claimed.

"Let's see this Coral Gables I've been hearing about," Adam proposed. "The dream city Merrick is laying out."

"Here we go," said Gerry, turning the Packard west.

They came to a pinewoods section where white roads, instead of leading straight, snaked in curves. Here and there a house was to be seen. Each section was to contain houses limited to a specific style, including Dutch South African, Persian, and Chinese. In the distance a tremendous hotel was going up. The pneumatic hammers of the riveters reached them faintly.

Gerry stopped before the Venetian Pool. Here many cars were drawn up. They got out and joined the crowd clustered around three sides of the irregularly shaped pool. On a raft floating in the water a heavy-set, half-bald man with a fringe of hair running around the back of his head, was speaking. He was saying:

"Miami is the only place in the world where a man can tell a lie at breakfast and have it come true at dinner time. And it is no lie to say that here, at Coral Gables, a model community is coming into being that will outshine everything. . . ."

Eve asked, "Isn't that William Jennings Bryan?"

"It is," said Aubrey. "I read that Merrick is paying him a hundred thousand dollars a year to do this."

"Half in cash," Gerry corroborated, "and half in land."

They listened to Bryan extol the wonders of Coral Gables, then piled back into the Packard to drive on. Suddenly they heard the sound of loud explosions. The blasts came at regularly spaced intervals. "Must be digging a canal," said George. "They've got rock down here."

Gerry shook his head. "It's just a gimmick for collecting a crowd to a sale," he explained. They followed other cars going in the direction of the dynamite explosions. They arrived at a place where a huge crowd was gathered about a man clad in a white linen suit who sat under a large umbrella on a platform. The explosions, taking place a short distance away, continued for some time. "Boom!" they sounded. "Boom!" When they stopped, the man rose to his feet, surveyed the immense crowd solemnly, and intoned:

"The only man who doesn't make money in Florida real estate is the man who doesn't own any. Why is this? Because Florida is where enterprise is enthroned. Florida is where you sit and watch at twilight the fronds of the graceful palm, latticed against the fading gold of the sun-kissed sky. Where sun, moon, and stars, at eventide, stage a welcome constituting the glorious galaxy of the firmament. Where the whispering breeze springs fresh from the lap of the Caribbean and woos with elusive cadence like unto a mother's lullaby. Where the silver sickle of the moon is heaven's lavaliere, and the full orbit its glorious pendant . . ."

"Wonderful," whispered Gerry. "I'll use that, especially the part about the only man who doesn't make money in Florida real estate being the man who doesn't own any."

They crossed the long causeway to Miami Beach and on the way saw suction dredges pumping up the bottom of Biscayne Bay to form islands. "They're running out of land here," Gerry explained, "so a man named Fisher is making some."

"Floating flapjacks," scorned Adam.

"They'll be the most expensive flapjacks anybody ever knew," predicted Gerry. "Guy named Davis over on the west coast at Tampa is doing the same thing."

On Miami Beach the building and trading in real estate had reached nearly a frenzied stage. Houses, apartments, stores, and hotels were going up all over the place. One empty corner lot was advertised in a novel way, with a sign that read:

"Hush, little corner, don't you cry;
You'll be a gas station, by and by."

People stood about on corners speaking quickly, showing each other papers and maps, talking fast, exchanging checks, and signing documents. Gerry stopped the car near one group. The men paid no attention to them, but jabbered on about their business.

"I don't understand what they're saying," Eve said.

The talk went so fast, in a special jargon, that only Gerry fully understood. "The short man in the linen plus fours," he explained, "bought a piece of beach front this morning and just sold it to the guy in the white shirt for a profit of twenty thousand dollars. Maybe I should have settled down here."

"Get back home," Adam ordered, "fast, and take up that option."

Gerry laughed and started the car. The sudden acceleration made Dottie grab Adam around the neck, stare with fright, and cry, "Eee!"

On the way back they discussed what they had seen. Only Adam was silent. Eve noticed that he was more preoccupied than ever. She thought it must be over Mona. Her heart dropped, then leaped with hope when he announced suddenly, out of a clear sky:

"I'm going to build a dream city of my own along here some day. I'm going to start it from scratch. It won't be held down by a haphazard plan of early settlers. I want virgin land, without a road on it. I want it on the sea, and lots of good land going right back to the Everglades. I'll lay it out for rich men in some sections and in others for people who aren't rich, though not poor. Part of it will be like Venice, with canals and gondolas. There will be a small Spanish inn that will be the best thing I will ever do. The whole thing will make Coral Gables look like a place for squatters, a bourgeois utopia."

No one spoke for a moment, until Gerry promised, "I'll find the land for you."

"This morning," said George, "I would have said you're going nuts. But after what I've seen today, I don't know."

Eve said nothing. She thought the plan grandiose, mostly high talk. But if it would divert Adam, she had no wish to discourage it. She even hoped that it might be attempted before it was too late.

WHEN ADAM SAW

Mona early in March at the last large party of the Nineteen Twenty-five season, he turned his back and walked the other way. He had come to the party in the first place to prove to himself that he didn't want her. He told himself that it didn't matter if she was here. He hadn't come because he wanted to see her. He assured himself of that.

While he might avoid her, he could not stop her from seeking him out. She came up to him slowly. She was clad in a white dress that looked like a replica of the one in which he had first seen her, except that it was shorter, reaching only to her knees. But the deep plunging cut of the V nearly to her waist was the same. Her tan, if anything, was darker than when he saw her at Christmas.

Her voice was low and lazy when she said, "Hello, Adam."

"Hello." He gave her no enthusiasm.

"I saw you turn away from me."

"What if you did?"

"Twice."

"I should have done it three times."

"That's only making it harder for yourself, Adam."

"I want it hard."

"Why don't you give in?"

"Because I don't want to."

"Of course you do. You're just fighting Puritanism and superstitious ideals of faith. The American guilt complex about anything out of the ordinary. I'm surprised at it in you, Adam. You must have had some Colonial forebears."

"I did, and—"

"You've had a long time to get rid of them."

"I'll keep them."

She regarded him. "You don't know it, Adam, but they've slipped away from you already. What you think you've got has already left you. The only thing you have to do now is see that."

"How do you know all this?"

"It's my specialty."

Hatefully, he scowled at her. "What else do you know about me?"

"Many things, Adam. For instance, you came here tonight because you knew I'd be here."

Scornfully, he said, "If I did it was to see what you're like and get you out of my mind."

"You can't get me out of your mind, Adam. I've been there quite awhile now. I haven't been out of your mind since the Christmas present I gave you."

"You're flattering yourself."

"I never flatter myself about love, Adam."

" 'Love?' " he questioned.

"Call it what you want. It would all amount to the same thing if, for instance, you were to kiss me tonight. Or would you be afraid to do that?"

"I'm not afraid of anything you can—! All right, I am. I admit it."

"So you won't try?"

"I won't."

"You'd even be afraid to let me kiss you."

He looked about. People were watching them. "I'm damned if I want to talk to you any more."

"I want to talk to you."

"Well, I'm going." He turned, to leave her.

"I'll follow you," she warned. "Then people will really talk and look."

He stopped. "Damn you—"

"Let's go out in the grounds," she suggested. She took his arm.

His face was stony as he went with her out of the house and onto the great spread of grounds with their tropical growth dimly lighted.

"This won't do any good," he asserted angrily.

175

"I like to be with you."

"I don't like to be with you."

"You do, Adam."

He stopped them. "I want you to get out of Palm Beach. With you here—when are you leaving?"

"Tomorrow," she answered.

"Tomorrow?" His word was as much an exclamation as a question.

"You see?" she pointed out.

"Well, go! Get out! And don't come back!"

"I wouldn't think of it. Not come back to my divine house you made for me?"

"Will you sell it?"

"Of course not, Adam. I'm going to live in it with you."

Savagely, he accused, "You get pleasure out of doing this!"

"Yes."

"You like what you're doing to my wife."

"I don't mind it."

"At least you're honest about that."

"Adam, is there a place to sit down?"

"I don't want to sit down."

"Is there a place?"

"I wouldn't know."

"Of course you do. You built this house."

He looked about. He saw a stone bench set against a hedge of Turk's-cap. Jerking his arm from her hand, he strode over to it. She joined him on the bench. As soon as they sat down they smelled the night-blooming jasmine. The heady odor conspired with her. She drew it into her pretty nostrils and let it out, and the perfume seemed to come from her. Adam, as at her pool, felt his senses reel.

She stood up. She couldn't reach him otherwise. He was seated on the end of the bench. She came at him as if in a dream. Her soft cool arms went about his neck. She bent a little and put her mouth on his. Her warm, full lips were open.

She parted from him and stood up again. Deliberately she put the V of her dress against his face. Instead of pushing her away, he was pressing his lips to her body and clasping her about her slim waist and hips. "You've seen all of me," she whispered. "You remember the rest. It's all yours if you want it."

He moaned fiercely, "Now—"

"Not now." Her voice was husky. "As I said."

"You want me. God help me, but I want you, after what you've done to me. Why bother with anything else?"

"I've told you."

"You don't need it."

"I do, because I don't want to be labeled promiscuous."

"You are."

"I want to get over it."

"Can you?"

"With you I can. You're more than most men."

"Then let me—"

"Only the one way, Adam. I need a husband for another thing, too. To get invited to the Bradbury parties again. You can give me that as well as the other."

"Do you have to have all that?"

"I have to."

"It isn't—"

"There's one more reason. You made me wait, and now you've got to. Until you give me what I want. Otherwise you'll be disappointed altogether."

"You're a sadistic slut."

"Yes, darling."

"I could rape you right here. Then it would be over."

"I was raped once. I enjoyed it, even though I fought. I've never been possessed like that. But if you did it you wouldn't have any eyes afterward; I'd scratch them out. And it wouldn't be over. It would only be beginning. You'd really be lost then, Adam."

Inflamed with the touch of her, he said, "If you lived back in the ages, you would be Thais. Or Aspasia."

"That's what you'll be getting, Adam."

"You know about them?"

"Phryne and Lais, too. And others."

"Are you what they were?"

"I'm better, for knowing what they were. Not many find the full art of love, even though it's all there to learn. I'm what you've

177

always wanted. What every man dreams of. What few have the courage to take."

He had never heard her voice so deep. It stirred him anew. He swallowed. It was like tasting a part of her. "You're a snake."

"A beautiful snake in your Garden of Eden."

"There's poison in you."

"Not enough to hurt, Adam. Only enough to make it a little dangerous and interesting. We can be something to each other neither of us has known before. We were made for each other. We've got to have each other."

"But my—"

"It's always painful the first time. I felt that way at my first divorce. Then I learned it wasn't so bad. You'll get over it. She'll get over it."

"I haven't said anything about that."

She bent down again. Their mouths met once more. At the same time she took one of his hands, and then the other, inside the capacious opening in the front of her gown. The contact made his pulse leap as if it would jump out of him. It lasted but an instant, a teasing, maddening beckoning.

She parted from him abruptly and entirely. Standing before him she said softly but firmly, "You'll never touch me again until you're ready, Adam. Then this will be nothing. Let me know."

She turned, and left him. He sat there, quickened until he thought he would explode, confused, and miserable.

A WEEK AFTER

Mona went north, on an early evening when Eve was again attending her kilns at Artisan Arts, Adam walked into her office in the front room of the white cottage where she sat going over records. Outside the windows shone the glow from the three kilns, attended by a Negro who kept feeding wood to the fires.

When she looked at Adam Eve knew, before he spoke, what he was going to say. It was plainly in his stricken, troubled face. It had been there for some time. She had dreaded it, wanting him not to speak, hoping he might get over his sickness without making the break.

Now that she saw it was here, Eve trembled. Oh, no, she thought, please, don't let it be. But she knew it would be.

They looked at each other for a long time before he slumped into a chair in front of the desk. It gave a loud crack, but they paid no attention. They were still looking at each other, and with their glances expressing everything they were now going to say.

In a broken voice, he introduced it. "I don't think I have to tell you."

"No," she said, her heart hammering in her breast. She added, "I guess you don't."

"You knew all along?"

"Do you think I've been blind? That a woman can't tell?"

"I tried to keep it from you."

"The more you tried the more I could see it."

From out of his pocket he took something that glittered. At first she thought it was the Lady. Then she saw that it was a revolver. Dully, she asked, "Where did you get that?"

"I bought it."

She looked up at him then. "What for?"

"I was going to shoot myself. Then I remembered something I once told you."

"What?"

"That if I ever thought of giving you up to remind you to shoot me."

"Oh."

"You said you would. You thanked me for the chance."

"Adam—"

He pointed to the gun. "There it is. And if you don't think I'm serious, pick it up."

She made no move toward the gun, but stared at it, held by what it represented.

He made another offer. "There's one more way. You've already spoken of it. We give up everything here and go away."

She considered that. Her heart sang out for it. She wanted it. But she knew it was wrong and would do no good. "That wouldn't solve anything," she said. "It wouldn't end it and might make it worse. You would only blame me. I don't know what she's done to you, but—"

"Let's not talk about that."

"What shall we talk about?"

"I don't know. What you want, maybe."

"I don't want anything." She yearned to say she didn't want anything except him, but she couldn't. Her pride prevented her.

"I mean, after—a settlement of some sort—alimony. . . ."

She looked away. "When we came here—we didn't think we'd be doing this."

"Don't rub it in. You'll get it, of course—for any reason you want."

She didn't answer.

"You're going to do it, aren't you?"

In a low voice, trying to keep bitterness from her tone, she told him, "I don't want to hold you—if you don't want to stay."

"Do you have to say things like that?"

"I should be the one losing my temper; not you."

"Then lose it."

Suddenly, she did. All her pent-up anger, out of her love for him, piled up in her and overflowed. She flared, "Why did you have to do this to us?"

"I don't want it."

"Don't you?" she demanded.

"All right, I do."

"Why didn't you just take her?" she cried desperately. "Without letting me know anything about it? You'd have gotten over her that way! Why didn't you—"

"I tried that. It didn't work. She wouldn't have it."

"Then it isn't your idea?"

"It's hers."

"I suppose that's something."

"Eve—"

"How else do you expect me to feel? Do you think I should like it, or her, or you? Do you think I should congratulate you and wish you happiness?"

"I thought we could talk about it like two grown people—"

"I'm not that sophisticated! I'm not your corrupted Palm Beach! I'm losing my husband to another woman and I don't like it! I don't like it at all!"

"I don't blame you. I know I'm doing you dirt, the dirtiest kind of dirt. I regret that more than anything else, because you're the world's best. I tried not to do it, you don't know how I tried."

"Well, you didn't try hard enough! Or you didn't want to keep me enough, or you want that—her, more."

"I can't help myself, Evie; I can't. I'll tell you this: you're worth ten of her."

"If I am, why are you going to her?"

"Because I've gone mad."

"She's driven you mad."

They were silent for a time. Their talk had been rapid, like a staccato letting off of angry steam, whose pressure had now been temporarily relieved.

He asked, "Do you want to talk about it any more, or do you want a lawyer to do it?"

"We might as well talk about it," she said. "What do you want to say?"

"What I asked before. What do you want, Eve? You can have anything I have."

She shook her head. "I want nothing like that." She looked about. Out the windows she stared at the man feeding the fires of the kilns. As though in a nightmare, she saw that he was keeping them up properly. She thought of leaving Artisan Arts. She rebelled at the prospect. At least she had this. She clung to it.

"I want one thing," she announced.

"Name it."

"Artisan Arts."

"It's yours. Anything else?"

"Nothing."

"Even with Artisan Arts, if things didn't go well some time, you might need an income—"

"Nothing. I have enough."

"Will you still do business with me, sell me things and make things for me?"

"Your business will be as good as anyone else's."

"I'll do it through George, or Aubrey, as much as possible."

"Do it yourself if you want."

"Don't be hard."

"I feel hard." Her expression changed. "Oh, I suppose I shouldn't. I'd like to think it isn't only her you want, that it's Palm Beach and what it represents, too. No matter what you've said, you've been dazzled by it, or some of it. You haven't any respect for its people, but you have for what it stands for. You can't deny that."

"All right, I don't."

"And you aren't saying it just to make me feel better."

"I'm not, Evie."

She made a sign of resignation, lifting her hand and dropping it. "Is there anything more to say?"

"I suppose not. I'll arrange with a lawyer to see you."

"Tell Martha to pack my clothes and have Manuel bring them over. I don't want to go back there. I'll stay here from now on."

"Do you want the Ghost?"

"Thanks for offering, at least. The Ghost goes with you. I'll keep the flivver."

He rose. "I'm sorry. I'm sorry as hell."

Idly she picked up the revolver. She turned it in her hands, inserting her finger in the trigger guard, taking it out, putting it back in again. Without knowing what she did, she pointed the gun at him. "Go ahead," she said. "Do what you want. You always have. You probably always will. But don't expect to come back. Ever."

"I don't."

"Don't think I'd ever take you back. This is a one-way road you're taking."

"Yes."

"There won't ever be anything for you to come back to. You're killing that now."

"Eve, are you all right?"

"I'm all right. Why shouldn't I be?"

"I thought—"

"You'd better get out of here." She flourished the revolver. "You'd better get out before I use this."

"I still wouldn't care if you did."

"Get out! Get out, I tell you, before I do!" She pointed the gun straight at him, her finger on the trigger.

He stared at her for a long moment, then turned and left.

After he had gone, she dropped the gun. It landed on the desk with a clatter. She got to her feet and made her way blindly to her bedroom in the cottage. Here she flung herself face down on the bed and the tears, which had been held in so long, finally came, and she sobbed awfully and uncontrollably.

The next day it was Aubrey, instead of Manuel, who brought her things. "I wanted to see you," he explained. He was troubled, embarrassed, and greatly disturbed. Bound to them both, it was difficult for him to tell where his allegiance lay. "I don't know what to think," he said. "He shouldn't be doing this to you. I never thought—"

"Stay with him, Aubrey."

"But—"

"He needs you. Some day he may need you more."

He looked at her hopefully, and shyly suggested, "Maybe he won't—"

"No, Aubrey." She explained. "Adam is out of love with me.

How he was driven out I don't know, though I can guess. But I'm not out of love with him. I never will be."

On top of Aubrey came the lawyer, a bustling young man named Taylor. Certainly no time was being lost. She was glad of this. There was no use stringing it out. She spoke candidly with him, agreeing to most of his suggestions. He was sympathetic without seeming to be, and helpful about her own affairs.

Michael waited a week before he came to see her. He was still in Palm Beach. The season was getting longer each year, and the Flamingo Club stayed open until the last. Running his hand over his head in his characteristic gesture, he said, "I couldn't believe it when I heard it. And yet I shouldn't have been surprised."

"I think we all knew it was coming."

"You seem to be taking it very well."

"I'm not, Michael. Not where it counts."

"It's rough on the woman, and unfair. Why didn't you shoot the big lug?"

She smiled wryly. "I nearly did." She told him about the revolver.

"What you need," he proposed, "is to be taken out to dinner. This is the last night at the Club. How about it?"

She shook her head. "Thanks, Michael. Besides, you might be named as corespondent."

He looked at her steadily and seriously. "Eve, it's far too soon even to think about mentioning it, but I'm sure you know I wouldn't mind that."

She looked away. "I guess I do, Michael."

"Do you remember the night of the Bradbury party when Mona —do you mind?"

"It doesn't matter."

"When she bribed her way to sit near Adam. Well, I've never told you, but I did a little bribing myself that night to take Adam's wife into dinner."

"Did you, Michael?"

He studied her. "Do you want me to say anything more now?"

She turned to him. "Michael, I've never been so flattered in my life, to think that you—but I don't want you to say anything more."

"Is it really like that, Eve?"

"It's really like that."

184

"I'll shoot him myself for you."

"You'll probably go into business with him instead. He and Gerry have been talking about that dream city. They want to form a company to create it."

"Eve, if you ever change your mind—"

"The worst part of it for me," she stated, "is that I couldn't ever love anybody else."

"Maybe later—"

"If it were possible," she told him, "you'd be the first. But it isn't possible. Why don't you find somebody else? With all your wealth, Michael, you haven't got the one thing that makes you really rich, a family."

"The trouble is," he said ruefully, "the money itself prevents it. Do you know that you're the only one I could ever be sure who didn't want me for my money?"

"Michael, how awful!"

"And you've turned me down."

"At least," she said, "you've stopped me from feeling sorry for myself."

DURING THE SUMMER

and fall of 1925 it was estimated that a million and a half people came to Florida. Usually, for the summer, people went north to escape the long monotonous heat. This time the traffic was reversed; for the entire year nearly three million people came, more than twice the entire population of the state. And permanent residents didn't dare leave for fear of what they might miss.

Everybody who could ride the rails, rubber tires, or the water seemed to be coming to Florida, with the pace increasing as the summer wore on. Trains rumbled continually through the night and day bringing human cargo and building materials. Automobiles lined the road in a ceaseless stream, heading south. A fleet of windjammers, called into service to transport lumber, lined the bayfront in Miami to make it look like the old days of sailing vessels.

There wasn't nearly enough room to house the people. Every corner was jammed. Hotels that ordinarily closed during the summer months rented cots in their busy halls for fifteen dollars a night. Those who couldn't locate or afford a bed slept in their cars; if they were lucky they found a tent to buy to camp out in. All were intent on making a fortune within a few days, for this had been done, and was still being done.

Motor buses roared in every direction, taking prospects on free trips to watch steam shovels and dredges changing mangrove jungle and boggy swamp into what were to be Venetian cities. Sometimes the buses brought people from as far away as New York, Chicago, and even San Francisco. The prospects were not required to buy, but they were expected to, and it was seldom that they did not; a down payment on a few lots they could sell the next week for a profit was a good bargain. Looking around at what was

186

happening here, many of them stayed, sending the buses back half empty.

Everybody and his brother became a real-estate operator. All you had to do to qualify was to buy a piece of property and sell it, or act as an agent for two principals who agreed to the transaction. Formal offices were open-faced on the street with no front. Others were composed of rough board trestles beside the road, or simply an umbrella and a chair. Most were merely in the hats of dealers who stood on the street. All stayed open until late at night.

The talk was incessant of lots that sold a short time ago for only five hundred dollars now fetching many thousands. The frenzied subdividing, entrance-arch construction, and lot-staking reached the point where it was no longer necessary to clear the land, but simply to have land. When it couldn't be sold fast enough locally to buyers, the land was advertised in Northern papers with boasts so extravagant that it sold out on the next return mail.

It was in this manner that the Everglades, where jazz bands blarred, were sold in the dry season when the land was above water. Later it was sold when under water. Sometimes land was sold that did not exist at all, under or above water.

In the newspapers and magazines articles appeared signed by learned notables who held forth on why they believed in Florida. Their protests of belief were loud and daily, as if they were reassuring themselves. When anyone whispered a word of wonder about where the boom was heading, he was scoffed down with the hearty conviction, "This isn't a boom, it's just natural growth."

Amidst the near-tropical profusion of plants, it seemed that man's development could be as lush. Those not satisfied with this explanation became so when property on Flagler Street in Miami sold for seventy thousand dollars a front foot. Then the glitter in people's eyes brightened, and no one asked any questions for a long time.

More banks were needed to handle the tremendous increase in business, so many new ones were hastily founded. Dynamite blasts announcing land sales became louder, sounding, "Boom! Boom!" like a tom-tom stepping up its tempo. Cities doubled and tripled in size without any trouble at all. Six years before, when Eve and Adam arrived, the permanent population of the Palm Beaches was less than nine thousand; now it was over thirty thousand. Current building permits were more than ten million. Real-estate prices and rents had increased eight hundred percent. The lights in the county courthouse burned until late at night where clerks vainly tried to keep abreast of their records.

Florida wallowed in prosperity. People succeeded in business because they were here and had their doors open. Often this was at the expense of Northern banks, whose depositors drew out their money to invest in the big land bubble. People outside the state couldn't comprehend why those in Florida believed in the bubble, but they did, sincerely and passionately and completely. To them it was not a bubble, but a solid, shining globe ever expanding.

Evangelists praised Miami and God in the same breath. It was virtually impossible to get away from the sound of sand-suckers, pile-drivers, riveting, cement mixing, hammering, sawing, and orators who declaimed about the glory of Florida and its blue sky and green water and unlimited future. In the town of Sanford a few faithless raised their voices and were squelched by the Kiwanis Club which sang, to the tune of, *Yes, We Have No Bananas*:

> *"Yes, we have no old fossils,*
> *We have no old fossils today.*
> *In 1920 we had them aplenty*
> *But now they've all passed away.*
> *We have a live Chamber of Commerce,*
> *Rotary and Kiwanis,*
> *But now we have no old fossils,*
> *There are none left in Sanford today."*

Gerry had a brand-new Packard, larger than his first. He now had a chauffeur to drive it, and he sat on the back seat with his hands folded over a gold-headed cane as he gravely contemplated the bustling scene. His costume consisted of expensive white linen plus fours, cashmere gray stockings, pearl gray sack coat, white shoes, white belt, dark tie, and a forty-dollar Panama woven under water which he tilted knowingly over his right ear. He had cultivated a slight Southern accent and intimated that he came of an old Florida family dating back to the time of the Spanish grants. A newspaper interview with him stated:

188

"In Mr. Gerry Vance, a leading light of the local real estate promotion world of the more solid and big-time division, we have a type of Florida citizen of whom we can be justly proud. Mr. Vance has always believed in Florida, because he is of Florida. Mr. Vance has not been afraid to invest his capital in Florida, for he knows, with the sagacity of an intelligent, experienced, conservative, and upstanding businessman, that he has his money working in the right place. Here is a far cry from the fly-by-night person who comes to Florida with nothing in his pocket and expecting to take out gold the next day without having done anything for it. Mr. Vance does not merely trade in land; he has faith in this grand land of ours and its future. Asked to give his considered opinion about what is happening in Florida today, Mr. Vance, upon deep reflection, said, 'One good investment beats a lifetime of labor.' Hail to Mr. Gerry Vance!"

Adam, when he saw this by means of Gerry bringing it to him at his offices, roared with laughter so long that he had a fit of coughing from the effort. "Hail!" he cried, rising an arm to Gerry. "Hail!"

Gerry never minded being laughed at. He could take nothing seriously, particularly himself, for long. Grinning, he said, "I'll bet I'm worth more than you are, Adam."

"I'll bet you are and I don't even have to bet that you made it with a lot less effort and trouble than the way I've had to work for what I've got."

"I've got a million dollars, Adam."

"The hell you have? Well, you beat me, though I'm not far from it. Do you remember when I picked you up on the road that day? Eve and I—" He stopped.

Gerry nodded with sagacious understanding. "When's the divorce being granted?"

"It's expected in October. Mona will come down then because I can't leave here. She's been good about that." From the floor Dottie jumped to his lap, put her arms about his neck, and switched her long tail while she regarded Gerry. "When are you going to find the land for my dream city?"

"I'm working on it, Adam. The big trouble is that you want so much acreage along with ocean front. And the prices are so high."

"That's your fault."

"And that of others. But I've got a few sites. I'll let you know."

"I have my Spanish inn all drawn and designed. I've worked at it most of the summer. Aubrey's doing the plans now."

"How about letting me see it?"

"Not until we get the land."

"Do you have to have inland water for one side of the inn?"

"I have to have inland water."

"You won't settle for less?"

"You know I won't."

"Well, it's a tough job for an old Southern gentlemen like me."

"Find it before the top blows off this thing."

"Maybe there isn't any top, Adam. I've never seen anything like this. They're buying land not because it's good land but because it's in Florida. They're selling it over and over again to each other. They can do that forever."

"I want to build this city, Gerry. I'm interested in the profits, yes, but more than that I want to build something beautiful and perfect."

"Everything is set except for locating a site that suits you," Gerry said. "Michael is in on it and some of his friends. The company can be formed overnight as soon as the land is located."

"Well, locate it."

"It's going to cost a pile of money."

"What if it does?"

In October the divorce was issued. The newspapers, making the most of the opportunity, headlined:

ADAM AND EVE DIVORCED

Upon receiving his notification, Adam wired Mona, who was in New York. A week later Rock arrived with her maid and cook. Two days after that Adam met Mona at the train in West Palm Beach. She looked young and modest in a tailored suit. He reached to kiss her, but she drew back, telling him in her low voice, "Let's wait even for that, Adam. If you touched me now, something might happen right here."

Huskily, he replied, "I feel the same way. Well, it won't be long."

Dottie greeted Mona by jumping up into her arms. Holding her, Mona asked Adam, "You've got everything arranged?"

"Just as we planned."

"Then let's hurry."

That spurred him into driving the Ghost as fast as he could to the home of the Justice of the Peace. That was all the wedding they wanted. To them both it was a mere form that had to be gone through, a necessary delay. To the bespectacled Justice it was a solemn occasion. Looking at Mona as he conducted the ritual the Justice thought that he had never seen such an innocent, virginal, and beautiful young woman. After a glance at his own broad wife who acted as a witness, and then giving an envious look at Adam before transferring his glance to Mona again, he sighed.

Adam hurried the Rolls across the bridge and to Mona's house. Dottie, as though expressing their impatience, jumped up and down on the seat top in back of them. When they drove up and stopped and got out, the door did not open to greet them. Instead, Mona used her own key to unlock it. Adam, carrying her bags, followed her into the entrance hall. The house was silent and he looked about as he put down the luggage.

Mona turned to him. "I wired them to stock the house with food and go away for three days."

He stared with delight.

"We're finished waiting, Adam."

Dottie raced up the stairs, galloping, and disappeared. Adam proposed, "Let's go up there with her."

"Why bother?"

He stared again.

"I'm glad you put a big mirror on the wall here." She pointed to the full-length mirror reaching to the floor. "Was it for us?"

"God," he said.

"I told you I was Thais and Phryne. Now I'm going to prove it to you."

"God almighty."

"Stop swearing and do something. Or do you want me to start it?"

"Yes," he said thickly. "Start it. Go ahead. Let me see you the way you were at the pool."

She began to take off her clothes. She tore at them to get rid of them, ripping them, and threw them aside. As she stripped herself and he watched, fascinated, she spoke in her low voice that now took on a vibrancy he had never heard before.

"You may think you know, but you don't. Not until I show you."

She was coming at him, then, the vision that had been burned in his brain and which he couldn't get out. He received her like a big bear attacking and crushing a willing adversary.

Later, when Rock and the other two servants had returned, their first domestic difficulty rose over the butler. "I don't like him," Adam asserted. "I never have. I don't like the way he looks at you, and I don't like the way he looks at me."

"It's just his manner. He had a difficult childhood."

"So did I. He's too young to be a butler."

"Why must all butlers be old? I hate them. That's why I hired Rock; he isn't old."

"I wish you'd get rid of him."

"I couldn't, darling. I'm too used to him. And he knows my ways."

"I've got Manuel and Martha on my hands," he said. "I'll bring them here in place of Rock and your cook."

"I'll make a compromise, and don't say I'm not agreeable and sweet. My cook has been troublesome; she doesn't like coming to Florida. I'll send her back North and take yours. You keep Manuel at your apartment and offices; you'll need him there for lunches and business entertainments."

"That's not getting Rock out of here."

"Darling, don't tell me you're jealous of a servant. It just isn't done."

"By me it is."

"I'm keeping Rock."

"Damn it—"

"Adam, we can't quarrel. Not us. Not with what we are together." She whispered, "You know what I do to you?"

He went still with aroused recollection.

"And you've done to me what I wanted. I'm safe with you. After that," she asked, "can you question me, and about a butler?"

He gave in by telling her, "If you ever use that outside stairway I built for you, I'll strangle you."

"I'd love it as I died."

The telephone tinkled. Adam picked it up and spoke. As if coming in on their discussion, he heard Rock say discreetly, "A Mr. Vance is calling."

"Put him on," Adam ordered.

"Adam?" Gerry then said. "Listen, I think I've got it. I'm sure I've got it."

"Where?"

"About twenty miles south. Place called Roca Faro."

"What does that mean?"

"I don't know. Probably nothing. Something somebody stuck on after you started all those Spanish names. Does it matter?"

"What's it like?" Adam countered. "No, don't tell me over the phone. Come and get me and we'll go down there. You've got to meet Mona, too."

They were in the patio at the swimming pool when Rock showed Gerry out. Mona was clad in a black one-piece suit that showed off her form and contrasted with her blond hair in a way that both disturbed Adam and made him proud. He was amused at the way Gerry's eyes almost popped when he saw her.

"I've seen pictures of you in the paper, Mrs. Paine," Gerry said to her, "but Adam didn't tell me you were this beautiful."

She laughed, looking him up and down. "He didn't tell me some things like that about you, either."

Gerry regarded them. "Can I offer my congratulations to you both?"

In this way Gerry indicated how much he approved of Mona. It seemed like a reflection on Eve.

"Adam tells me," Mona said to Gerry, "that you're going to build a city."

"Will you come and live in it?"

"I might consider it."

"Then it's a success already."

Adam was impatient to see the land. "Let's go."

They drove behind Gerry's chauffeur along the teeming Dixie Highway. Adam inquired, "How much is it going to cost?"

"Wait until you see it before I tell you."

"Is it that bad?"

"It's pretty bad."

They came to a crossroads community consisting of two gasoline stations and a small general store. The road led west one way and the other to the beach. They took the latter, driving up on a sand trail that ended on top of the beach ridge. Here they got out and Gerry advised, "Look southwest in back of you."

Adam turned, and stared. Two hundred yards away he saw an irregularly shaped lake perhaps half a mile wide at its broadest. No house or building of any kind had been built on its shores. Coconut palms leaned out over the water, and Spanish bayonet lined it along with sea plum and sea grape. The place was virgin Florida.

Adam caught his breath. "This is it," he breathed.

"I knew you'd think so," Gerry said. "There's an inlet to the sea down in the southeast corner of the lake. That's what you wanted. There's about three miles of ocean beach front and, as you can see, nothing is built on it, either. The land goes back for about five miles, forming a rough oblong. It's high and dry, I mean seriously. It's without doubt the best piece of property left on the east coast, probably in the whole state."

"How and why?"

"A Chicago syndicate bought it up early. They've been holding it for a killing."

"We're the ones killed?"

"You'd better sit down before I tell you."

"Come on, come on!"

"Three million."

"That isn't as bad as I thought."

"This is. That price is for cash."

"Three million in *cash?*"

"Otherwise it's four."

"Good God—who's at the other end, Shylock?"

"Just about."

"Can't—"

"That's it, Adam. I've tried to budge them. It's take it or leave it at either price. To me, if it's to be considered at all, there's only one answer."

"The three million?"

"Sure, but—"

Adam had been watching the lake. He pointed to the far corner. "My *posada* will go right over there. That's the word for 'inn' in Spanish."

"Will Michael and the others stand for the price?"

"They will after they see my plans."

"Will we stand for our share of it?" Gerry asked. "When I said I'm worth a million, and you said you were worth about that, I don't know how much of yours is just paper, but all except about a hundred thousand of mine is paper."

"I've got a quarter of a million in cash, the rest in land."

"We can sell stock in Roca Faro and go light on it ourselves."

Adam stared at the lake and said, "I'm going all the way."

"Clean yourself mostly out of money?"

"I mean to believe in this. That way it will be good."

Gerry gave his light laugh. He didn't hesitate any longer. "I'm with you."

ADAM WAS MADE

President of the Roca Faro Development Company. His name was needed to head it, and the first announcement of the dream resort stated:

"The man responsible for the unexcelled beauty of modern Palm Beach, the man who has given architectural distinction to the whole of Florida, will now design and build a cosmopolitan community that will be the world's most beautiful playground. His buildings are so subtly adapted to this state and its warm climate that, although inspired by the art of Spain and Italy, they are an order of his own which will live in the history of American architecture when we are gone and forgotten. At Roca Faro he will reach his pinnacle."

George was made Treasurer, though he protested that he knew nothing about filling such a post. Adam and Michael assured him that he was needed as an honest man to fill the position and that the company's auditor would do all the detail work. Aubrey was made Secretary with the same assurance that he was merely a figurehead, with a paid man doing the work.

Gerry was appointed Director of Sales; Michael reported that some of his friends, who were investing in the project, questioned Gerry's connection with it. Adam pointed out that Gerry's quality was as good as the Florida average, that he had found the land, and that his selling abilities were needed to put it over. He would not be allowed to sign checks.

Both Mona and Eve were asked if they wanted to invest. "We don't need you," Adam told Mona. "We found we have more than enough capital and we won't have any trouble selling the stock, but we thought you might want to make some money."

"I've made some money," she refused. "And I don't want to mix my finances with my love life. One of them—or both—might get hurt."

Michael made the offer to Eve. "It's speculative," he explained, "perhaps highly so. But if it hits it will be the wonder of Florida."

Eve shook her head. "It's all very well for you and your friends to put money in it," she said. "It's only a small interest for you. If something happens you haven't lost much. But for me it would be a main thing. I'd have to put most of my money in it. Instead, I've been sending it North."

Michael looked at her sharply. "Are many selling Florida short like that?"

"There may be some others, but I don't know them. I just don't like what's happening here. This Roca Faro thing—it's too big, Michael."

People gasped at its size and conception. Adam let himself all out on the plans. On the ocean front would be built the world's largest hotel. On the lake would be erected Adam's Spanish Posada, a one-hundred-room inn for the most exclusive people. A business and shopping center, located on a street one hundred and fifty feet wide, and containing, besides all stores needed, a movie theater and a concert hall, was pictured in a style consistent for all buildings. Thousands of sites for houses were platted all the five miles west the property extended. And among these, ideally situated, were to be three golf courses, a polo field, a yacht basin, and several civic centers complete with pools of international swimming meet size.

Snaking through all the community were to be many miles of Venetian canals along which gondolas would wend their lazy way. And topping everything, on an island to be created in the lake connected to shore by a drawbridge, was to be Adam's own house, a high-walled Italian castle.

There would be two hundred million dollars' worth of property for sale. Looking at the grand overall plan, Gerry said enthusiastically, "Now that's what I call an opportunity I can really let loose on."

It was decided that the first two things to be built would be an administration building, to go up immediately, and the Posada, to proceed more leisurely and carefully. The two-story administration building, designed to fit into the general scheme, was erected almost overnight, and from here, in the offices and Aubrey's drafting rooms, the detailed plans were made and the property sold. Here also an advertising and publicity staff was installed by Gerry.

The publicity men, under Gerry's direction, pulled all stops in describing Roca Faro. They said it was the most impressive development ever attempted and planned anywhere on the face of the globe. It was the dream city of the Western world, the golden city of the gold coast. It was to be client chosen, perfectly plotted, divinely developed.

"All the charms of the Riviera, Biarritz, Menton, Nice, Sorrento, the Lido, and Egypt," they wrote, "will be found in Roca Faro. Mere existence here is a joy. Society that sets fashions and sanctions customs demands Roca Faro, the premier Florida resort. The silvery sea, lazy lagoons, and crystal lakes shimmer with the liquid blue of aquamarine. Endless canals wind through labyrinths of loveliness to make living here almost beyond realness in its ideality." Language went a little crazy.

The full-page, and sometimes double-page, advertisements taken in the fat Florida newspapers, and in Northern cities, played much the same extravagant tunes. One said:

"The Spanish *conquistadores* who discovered Florida and the Spanish *colanos* who followed them were overeager in their quest for gold and quickly acquired riches. They failed to realize the wealth in the soil and place they trod—in the balmy breezes that brushed their bronzed cheeks—in the beneficence of the blue dome overhead. They sought advantage but missed opportunity because they lacked vision. And it is a question whether Americans of today have even yet awakened to the tremendous powers of capital and energy at work in Florida. Roca Faro offers the test of vision to the completeness and culture of America."

Below this statement, which was illustrated with drawings in Adam's most flamboyant manner, was the advice, "Attach this statement to your contract for deed; it is a part of your transaction, a promise that all plans at Roca Faro will be carried out."

Offices, designed and furnished under Adam's direction, were opened in both the Palm Beaches, Miami, Tampa, Jacksonville, New York, Philadelphia, Boston, and Chicago, while a representative was established in London. Fleets of de luxe Pullman buses were hired to bring prospects from all over the United States to see and be told by Gerry and his salesmen about what was happening here, and carry back the word with them. To whet the appetite of the public, no actual sale was made until early in January. Only advance reservations were accepted, with no one being allowed to pay any money.

Early on the morning of the day set for the start of the sale, long lines of people formed outside the administration building while clerks pored over maps with them and took their money. Sacks were brought in containing orders that arrived by mail. The work became so pressing that the large hired staff couldn't take care of it. Gerry, George, Aubrey, and even Adam came into the offices and took a hand opening envelopes, recording sales, and toting up amounts on the adding machines. Checks were thrown in wastebaskets, filling them, after their amounts were noted. They worked feverishly through the day, their sleeves rolled to the elbows, their faces flushed, snapping at sandwiches and gulping coffee prepared in the kitchen of the building.

At six o'clock, with people still lined up outside the door, Gerry, looking rumpled and tired for the first time anyone had ever seen him, glanced up from a sheet of paper and announced triumphantly, "The first day's sales amount to a little over two million, one hundred thousand dollars." His eyes gleamed.

There were whistles and cheers and exclamations of amazement. Aubrey looked stunned and pleased. George spoke. "And they said we couldn't do it."

"We don't have to sell it any more," said Gerry. "It's being bought."

They turned, then, to the man who had conceived it. Adam blinked at them and shook his head, on which his hair was long. From his hip pocket he took a huge curved silver flask, unscrewed the cap, and took a long drink, after which he passed it about. "Now we want to build it," he told them.

While sales kept up for some time at the rate of nearly one million dollars a week, they started to construct. Contracts were let in the millions for clearing the land, and for streets, sidewalks, and lights. A water plant was installed that would supply a city of fifty thousand. A radio station was built with high steel towers by which to send to the world the news of what was coming into being here.

This work went ahead because materials for it were on hand, already delivered in the section. But in the construction of the Posada, there was trouble. The unprecedented influx to Florida of investors, speculators, workmen, gamblers, real-estate men looking for greener pastures, journalists to write of what was going on, the merely curious, grafters, prostitutes, pimps, and bootleggers, had so taxed the transportation system that it had nearly broken down.

All the means of carrying building materials were overworked to such an extent that fleets of ships loaded with cargoes awaited berths outside the harbor of the few deep-water ports available. The demand for goods was so great that some ships were unloaded at distant places and their contents shipped by rail. The importation of goods was so paramount that food supplies had been overlooked or shunted to one side in favor of more desired articles, and now a famine threatened. This was so acute that an embargo had to be declared on the shipment into Florida of everything except food.

The hollow tile and other building materials ordered for the Posada lay across the state border to the north. "And there it sits," George lamented. "A whole trainload of tile for us is on the tracks in Atlanta."

"Get it down here," Adam ordered. "We've got to have it."

"How, Michelangelo?" George inquired.

"Do I have to tell you? Label it food and tell them to send it."

"That wouldn't work. They'd find out it wasn't food and would stop it somewhere."

Adam turned to Gerry. "How are we going to get it?"

"Your food idea is the thing," Gerry decided. "Only with a slight change. With a little bribing we'll have it loaded into refrigerator cars and labeled lettuce. That way it can't be seen much. I'd better get up there and grease the hands of any trainmen along the way who might get curious."

"You'll never do it," predicted George.

"Get going," Adam told Gerry.

Six days later Gerry, riding the cab of a locomotive whose throttle he had held part of the way, and which pulled a trainload of building tile consigned as lettuce, carefully iced all the way from Atlanta, arrived on the siding at Roca Faro. This was expensive, but effective, and got things done.

George brought a second problem to Adam. "Eve won't give us credit for all the stuff we've ordered from her for the Posada."

Adam asked, "Do we need credit?"

"The auditor says we could use it. We're spending everything and more to build and promote, with costs sky-high. We've got to bribe materials, even work. The paving, sidewalks, and—"

Adam cut him off with a wave of the hand. "Does she mean she wants cash at thirty days?"

"I mean she wants it on the barrelhead. We don't get delivery without it. And it's holding us up."

"She can't get away with that."

"She sounded to me as if she could. If you don't get it from her, where are you going to locate the stuff?"

"I'm going to get it from her. I'm going to see her, right now."

The noise at Artisan Arts, when Adam walked into the yard, was nearly deafening. The big carborundum saw was working on a great ten-ton block of quarry key stone; stone planes were smoothing other cut pieces, working against time before the stone hardened too much. The anvils were going in the iron department and buzz saws ripped wood in the cabinetmaking building. Adam stood for a moment watching and listening, automatically checking to see how things sounded and were going. Men spoke to him and went on.

Eve wasn't in her office when he peeked in there. He shouted into the cottage, but she didn't appear. He went around to the back. Here were pottery and tile sections. He poked into these buildings, where mechanical mixers ground at pugs of clay and a man sliced a bat ready to be slapped on a potter's wheel. Others smoothed clay in shallow forms and then cut it in various shapes for tile. Two black men bent pieces over their thighs. Adam watched them for a moment with satisfaction. Most roof tiles were now machine cut; the thigh method was slow and expensive, but he wanted them made this way for the Posada roofs, for only with them could he get the exact irregular effect he wanted. These being made now, he knew, were for him.

Eve wasn't at the kilns, which were being filled for baking. Then he saw her under a small open shed where a potter's wheel had been set. She had a splattered green smock over her dress and she was intent at shaping a vase which whirled on her jig as she worked the pedal for turning it with one of her long legs.

She didn't look up as he approached, but she was aware of him, for she showed no surprise when he spoke, shouting to make himself heard above the noises, "What's this about your wanting cash?"

She took her turning tool from the whirring damp clay and looked up at him for a long moment. She seemed to examine him, and how he looked. "Nothing about it, Adam. I just want to be paid." She was accustomed to pitching her voice in a manner that she didn't have to shout to make herself heard through the racket.

"You'll be paid!" he yelled. "In the regular way!"

She shook her head, going back to her work. "You know what it costs to turn out these things. Your order is too big for me to take a chance."

"What chance are you taking?"

"If something happened to Roca Faro and all the things made for you weren't paid for, it would just about ruin Artisan Arts."

"Nothing is going to happen!"

"I hope nothing does. But I've got to be paid as I told George."

"You—! Can't we go some place where I don't have to yell?"

She indicated her wheel. "I don't want to leave this."

"Do you have to do that work yourself?"

"You know I have jigmen," she told him. "I just like to do some of it." She gave him a glance as if to say it helped her to work in this way.

"Well, I'm not going to stand for it!" he asserted.

Equitably, she inquired, "You aren't?"

"It's a holdup!" he accused. "You know I can't do what I want down there without the stuff from here."

"That doesn't make it a holdup."

"You want to get back at me! That's why you're doing it!"

She looked up again. "Adam, can't you realize I don't want to get back at you?"

He dropped his eyes for an instant, before she turned back to her

202

work. After a moment he said, "All right, all right, but there isn't any reason you can't give us credit."

"There's one down in Miami."

"What do you mean?"

"A man named Romfh down there, the biggest banker, won't give loans on real-estate values where they are now. I would be doing the same thing to give credit to Roca Faro."

"You're crazy and so's Romfh! Four hundred and eighty-one hotels and apartment houses were built last year in Miami."

"And a banker won't loan money on them."

"What do you know about business?"

"Look around you here."

"I built this, you didn't."

"You built most of it, yes, Tiny, though I did some. And I'm carrying it on, successfully."

"I gave you this, and now—"

The wheel began to stop as Eve's leg arrested its movement for a moment, then began again. "Wait a minute, Adam. You didn't give me anything. This was part of a bargain and it sounds as if you want to break it."

"I only think it's unreasonable, and it sounds to me as if you counted on doing something like this."

"There isn't anything unreasonable about it. And there isn't anything personal about it, against you or—or anybody else. If you want the things you've ordered you'll pay for them on my terms, which is cash on delivery. Some of them are being made up now. Do you want me to keep on with them or cancel them?"

"Damn it!" he roared. "Damn you!" He stamped on the ground with one of his small feet. He winced.

"It hurts your arches to do that," she reminded. "You're too heavy, and look as if you're getting heavier."

He glared at her, turned, and started to stomp away. He whirled, and yelled for a parting shot, "You're getting too big for your pants!"

"I don't wear them, Adam. That's you—remember?"

WHEN HE HAD

time, from staying every minute of the day with the construction of the Posada, Adam worried about what Mona was going to do when the Palm Beach season ended. He feared she would want to go back North, closing her house. If she did, he couldn't go with her.

He commuted daily between Palm Beach and Roca Faro until the trip became deadly and used up too much time. Then he had a small apartment fixed up for himself in the administration building, and brought Manuel down to look after him. He asked Mona to come there at least for a few days each week between Saturdays and Sundays for which he returned.

"I'd rather stay here," she told him. "With my pool."

"You don't swim in the nude any more?"

"I promised you I wouldn't, didn't I?"

"How will you get on when I'm not here?"

"I waited before," she told him. "I can wait again—and you'll be so much nicer when you are home."

"Mona, the season is about ended. You aren't going North, are you?"

"Have I said anything about going?"

"You'll stay here?"

"Isn't this where I belong? With you?"

"Even over the summer?"

"Why not, darling? Don't you want me?"

He was both delighted and disturbed. It decided him finally about Rock. The young butler had become polite, proper, and even obsequious to him. Adam had treated him coldly, and the man evidently now knew his place. There was no longer a knowing look in his face; he was merely the perfect servant.

Yet it wasn't altogether like Mona to be so sweetly agreeable. To keep her house open and remain in Palm Beach was against everything smart as regarded by the circle to which she belonged. She would miss things on Long Island and Bar Harbor. Adam wondered, but not for long. He shrugged, decided he had underestimated her, or himself, and turned his attention back to the Posada. Mona stayed in Palm Beach and Dottie remained with her; the two had taken a great liking to each other.

In May people began to talk about the effect of something that had happened at Miami the previous August. Early that summer, like a horde of locusts, many newcomers, usually short and stubby men from the Bronx or Brooklyn, had descended on the city. They began a new kind of real-estate activity. They would take a binder, paying a thousand dollars for it, on a piece of property priced at one hundred thousand. They pronounced "binder" to rhyme with "bin" instead of "bind."

This option usually was good for thirty days. Meanwhile they found a buyer for the property at an increased price of one hundred and ten thousand dollars. In turn, that buyer might find another at a second increase. During the month as many as eight or occasionally ten purchasers, each paying a higher price, were found for the property. The last buyer was prepared to pay the second installment, a substantial amount, and then everybody all down the line took his profit. In this way the price of certain lots was run up to half again and sometimes double the original price, already inflated.

A group of Miami businessmen found the activity of the binder boys highly distressing, and decided to teach them a lesson, at the same time driving them out of Florida. At an advantageous price they threw a stretch of beach front on the market, but offered only every alternate lot. The binder boys snapped them up gleefully. Then the group of businessmen began to advertise the lots they had retained at prices far above what the binder boys had paid. With popping eyes, the binder boys watched the resultant ascending prices of the lots on which they held binders. They threw caution to the winds and began to trade in binders among themselves, running their prices up so fast and so high they had to stay up nights to do the paper work.

At the end of the month, the group of businessmen then dropped the prices of the alternate lots to about what they were worth, hardly a third of the price now put upon the lots of the binder boys. When the options came due no one took them up, no further payments were made, and the binder boys lost not only their shirts but their linen knickerbockers as well. With their tails between their legs they retreated back to Brooklyn and the Bronx.

The pleasure that went with this route was followed by disturbance. Something happened at that point to the Florida boom. It asked a rude question, in a much louder voice than anyone had ever inquired before, about the price of real estate. Fear spread like wildfire, helped by the whipped, resentful binder boys back in the North, that all was not well in Florida. Newspapers in Northern and Middle West cities, which had belittled the boom, now pounced on this definite sign of weakness. Their attack, and the awful power of word-of-mouth gossip, had its full effect by May.

People stopped buying lots. The bottom didn't drop out of the market entirely, but it was weakened and daylight could be seen plainly between the cracks. Others did not keep up payments due on property they had purchased.

Civic leaders called it temporary, a mere catching of breath before going on to greater things. A healthy rest, they labeled it, a stabilization. But Florida waited apprehensively for what might happen now.

Adam called a meeting of the officers of the Roca Faro Development Company, including the professional auditor, a little man with a bristling mustache named Grant. "First of all," Adam asked Gerry, "what do you think about the general situation?"

"Well . . ." began Gerry, and then stopped.

It was the first time Adam had ever known him to be reluctant to speak. He demanded of Gerry, "What's the matter with you?"

Gerry stared about at the glum faces. His own was as handsome and full of good will as always. He turned back to Adam. Smiling, undisturbed about what he said, he announced, "Gentlemen, the Florida boom is over."

The others attended him, and turned then to Adam when he spoke. They took hope from his protest, "It can't be over, not this quick."

"Oh," said Gerry, "it will take a little time for most to see it. The same way it took time for people to know it was coming. Not nearly as much, though. This is going to be fast. The bigger they are, the harder they fall." He seemed slightly amused at the prospect.

Grant, who had invested his life savings in Roca Faro, went white and said, "But you must be mistaken, Mr. Vance."

Gerry shook his head. He told Adam, "You know I'm not."

Adam, though he didn't believe his own words, claimed, "I don't know a damn thing like that. What I do know is that we ought to get Michael down here."

"Mr. Sumner is in Europe," Grant reminded him. "And won't be back until later in the summer."

"Cable him and tell him to come back."

"He's on a yacht, Mr. Paine, and I doubt if he can be reached."

"Try it."

"Yes, sir."

Adam turned to George. "Where do we stand financially?"

George didn't say anything, but indicated Grant, who now spoke up. "We have something less than a hundred thousand dollars in the bank," the auditor said.

"Less than a hundred thousand?" demanded Adam. "But we took in over fourteen million!"

"And paid them out," Aubrey put in. "And owe more."

"You've been too busy with the Posada to notice," said George.

"Haven't you seen all our lovely streets and sidewalks?" Gerry inquired sardonically. "And lights and water plant and—"

Adam turned to Grant. "What about current sales?"

Grant said, "There hasn't been a lot sold for six weeks."

"Well, payments are being made—"

"Almost none. Few people have made their last payments. They are defaulting on virtually everything."

There was a deep silence.

"I forgot to say," the auditor added, "the checks for the upkeep of the outside and Northern offices should go out today."

Adam thought. "Send them, and notification to close all the offices." He looked at the others. "If that's all right with you?"

"I don't see what else there is to do," George said. "Except for one thing. We've got to stop work on the Posada."

Adam got to his feet. Slowly he walked over to George and stood close in front of him. "We aren't stopping work on the Posada," he said.

"But you can't finish it now," George protested.

"We can finish it now," Adam told him, "and we are going to finish it now. It's nearly done; a few more weeks or less and it is done. That building is my guts. I'm not going to cut them out now. Or let you stab me."

"That's madness—"

"Do you say," Adam demanded, "it can't be finished with what money there is left?"

"Maybe I don't, but do you want to finish it knowing you'll probably lose it?"

"Losing it hasn't got anything to do with it," Adam said impatiently. "Finishing it is the only thing that counts. We'll take a vote on it," he declared. "You, Aubrey, what do you say?"

Aubrey looked at him with a stricken expression. "I don't know what to say."

"Well, say something."

"I'd like to see you complete it. It's your best building."

Adam swung on Gerry. "You?"

Gerry waved a hand grandly. "Go ahead. We'll hold a dinner in it and play the fiddle while Rome burns."

Adam turned back to George. "The vote goes against you. We finish it, with or without you."

George wiped his face with a furry arm.

"Which is it?" Adam wanted to know.

The two men regarded each other for a long moment. George made his decision. "Hell, Michelangelo, we started something. We'll finish it."

Adam hadn't consulted Grant, but the auditor now spoke for himself. "You can't do it," he declared. "I'm not sure it would even be legal. That money should be used to cover outstanding bills. I know I'm not an officer of the company, but I have my own responsibility to think of. And my own investment."

"You aren't going to get back any investment," Gerry told him.

Desperately and illogically, the little auditor said, "There is this money that's left—"

"It would be eaten up by the lawyers trying to straighten it out," Gerry informed him. "It would be better used going into the Posada."

Grant shook his head stubbornly. "I can't let you do it."

Adam bore down on him. "*You* can't let us do it? Who the hell are you to say?"

"I'm a stockholder," Grant persisted, "and a responsible accountant. If you go ahead with this, I would have to go to the other stockholders. We'd get out an injunction to stop you."

"Then go get it out now!" Adam roared at him.

The man hesitated, uncertain.

"Go on!" Adam urged him. "Get out! We don't want you around here!"

The man left, glowering.

Gerry got to his feet. "You won't need me any longer. There isn't anything more to sell, or at least any market for it." He looked about at the long, doleful faces. "We had a lot of fun while it lasted," he said. "It was the biggest thing I've ever been in."

"Maybe," said Aubrey hopefully, "it really isn't over?"

Gerry laughed.

"What are you going to do?" Adam asked him.

"Oh, I'll hang around a while and watch the death throes," Gerry said. "They'll be interesting. Palm Beach ought to be a good place to see them. Do you know," he asked, "that one time during our sales I figured my share here was worth over two million? Two million . . ." Impressed with his ephemeral paper riches, he walked out, pushing his Panama jauntily toward the back of his head.

Adam regarded George and Aubrey. Of the latter he inquired, "Have you got anything left from what you put in here?"

"A few thousand dollars," said Aubrey.

"Get them out of the bank and send them North," Adam advised. "If Gerry is right, and he probably is—he's got a nose for this—the banks are going to start popping around here like firecrackers. I'm sorry I got you into this."

"It doesn't matter, Adam."

"You'd better stay in the Via Paine apartment for a while until we see what's going to happen."

"All right."

"George, how do you stand?"

"I've got everything in Florida land. I haven't got enough cash to make it worthwhile changing banks."

"You sure you want to see this thing through?"

"When I said so I meant it all the way."

"Then find men to work in two shifts and get the thing done before they stop us. Something tells me we'd better develop a good technique for ducking process servers."

"You ought to be good at showing me how."

"I've got one more thing to try."

"What—?"

"If it works, I'll tell you. To play safe we've got to get up to West Palm before the bank closes."

Adam drove them, fast, in the Ghost. They took along the Company's checkbook and wrote checks and withdrew currency in the amount of nearly the entire balance. They had the checks certified and sent to the suppliers of the material they still needed for the Posada. George took to Eve a sum of money to cover the last of the furnishings she was readying. Adam admonished him not to tell her the circumstances, in case she developed scruples about accepting the money. "I don't want her crowing, either."

George, signing checks as Treasurer along with Adam as President, observed, "I'm not sure what we're doing, exactly."

"You ever been in jail, George?"

"Can't say that I've had the pleasure."

"Something tells me this may be connected with realizing your ambition."

"At least," said George, "I'll have you along to draw pictures on the walls."

It was after a late dinner with George, following their working out in detail the plans for rushing the completion of the Posada, that Adam drove to Mona's. He found her in her bedroom draped on the chaise longue and clad in a fetching, filmy negligee. Dottie lay curled up at her feet. The monkey hardly raised its head when Adam scratched her neck.

Mona didn't seem surprised to see him, but said, "I expected you'd come."

"You did?"

"You're in trouble, Adam. Financial trouble."

"How do you know?"

"I ran across Gerry this afternoon. He told me."

"He ought to keep his mouth shut," Adam growled.

"He said it was serious. He said it was the end."

"Well, he's right about that. Unless you want to help me."

"I?" asked Mona. "Help you?"

"Isn't that what you expected me about?"

She gave her throaty laugh. "That's right, Adam."

"Well?"

"Well, what?"

"Are you going to do it?"

"Tell me what you want, Tiny."

He stared at her. "Don't call me that."

"Why not?"

"Because—"

"That was her name for you, wasn't it?"

"I never knew you'd heard it."

"I know lots of things, Adam."

"What do you mean?"

"You're still a little bit in love with her, aren't you?"

"What are you getting at?"

"Maybe a good deal in love with her. Don't try to deny it," she said. "I've been able to see it. And feel it."

He hadn't consciously thought of it himself. "Maybe," he temporized, "a man doesn't ever get over his first wife altogether. But that doesn't mean it interferes with his second. Did you get over both your former husbands?"

"Definitely," she stated with distaste. "But you haven't gotten over Eve. Even after me. That hits where it hurts, darling."

"Listen, Mona, I didn't come here to argue about love. We can go into that later. When you said I'm in trouble, you were right. You can help me, maybe save the Posada for me. Roca Faro is going into bankruptcy. You might even want to prevent that."

She shook her beautiful head. "Oh, no, Adam. That's your affair. I married you, not your business. You haven't any right to ask me."

"I suppose I haven't, but I thought you—"

"You thought I'd do it, anyway? No, darling, I worked for my money. I didn't even know you at that time. You didn't help me. Why should I risk my security now?"

"Sometimes there are more important things than security."

She looked at him from beneath lowered lashes. "There's only one thing I know of that might compete with it."

"Don't you ever think of anything else?"

"Not when I can help it. Are you going to stay tonight?"

"I can't; I've got to get back to be on the job early in the morning."

"I've been lonely."

"Then come back with me."

"I want you to stay."

"I tell you I can't."

"Would you stay if I helped you?"

"I'm damned if I want any bargains like that. You either want to help me or you don't. I gather you don't."

"You're right, darling."

He turned to go, then stopped to ask, "I'd like to know something: is it because of what you think about Eve that makes you refuse?"

"Not in the least. It's a pure business arrangement, Adam. I managed to get hold of a lot of money. I mean to keep it. That's all."

"I guess it's enough. I don't blame you for that, Mona. But I think I'm going to blame you for something else. Your husband is in trouble and your place is at his side, and you aren't going to be there."

"But Adam," she protested prettily, "I'll be here when you come back without any money. And you can live with me. Not every wife could do that for her husband, could she?"

"You haven't got any of that money of yours in Florida banks, have you?"

"I wouldn't dream of it, darling. Especially after what Gerry told me is going to happen."

"If you see him again, tell him to shut up."

"I'll tell him. Are you sure you can't stay for just a little while?" Her meaning was very clear.

"You're the damnedest thing about that I ever heard of," he growled as he left.

GRANT WORKED NEARLY

as fast as the last work on the Posada was hurried. He couldn't stop the expenditure of the remaining funds of the company, for Adam and George had acted ahead of him on that. But he organized a committee of all the local stockholders he could find. The committee hired a lawyer who proceeded to go through all the legal steps possible to stop further work on the building and to throw the Roca Faro Development Company into receivership. Applications for injunctions were filed, summonses issued to be served, and all the facts given to the newspapers, which screamed them in black headlines.

Adam and George got in three days of intense work, during which many of the furnishings of the Posada were installed, before the first process server appeared. All the many doors of the building were closed and locked, with a guard at each. The process server was simply refused admittance, but George reported that the man was waiting outside the main gate.

It was simple that night, when the second shift of the men had gone home, for them to slip out another entrance and gain their quarters in the administration building. The next morning, after an early breakfast served by Manuel, they got back into the Posada before dawn.

Half a dozen process servers appeared that day, covering all land entrances. Adam and George studied on how they would elude them. A rowboat, used during the construction, remained tethered at the steps of the cloisters on the lake. After dark they got in the boat quietly, rowed to a remote section of the lake, and sneaked back to the administration building.

In the morning they were nearly caught. A man, waving a piece of paper, ran toward them as they got in the Ghost. Adam started the Rolls with a jerk that only narrowly missed permitting the process server from jumping on the running board and thrusting the paper in his hand, which would have made it an official serving. As it was, the man leaped into his own car, and roared after them. They jumped out of the Ghost at the Posada entrance, and barely got inside before the door was slammed by the guard in the face of the process server.

For the next eight days they remained inside the building. Manuel brought them food in a hamper, trying vainly to keep it warm. They worked around the clock, until they were nearly ready to drop. On the last night, sitting on an eighteenth-century settee in the lounge, with a bottle of whiskey before them on the floor, George complained, "I'm damned if I know why I did this."

"I don't see why you did, either," Adam agreed.

George looked up at the heavy-beamed ceiling struts of the room. "I wouldn't do it for anybody else."

"I don't know what I would have done without you—from the beginning."

"Don't make me cry."

"Hell of a chance you've got to cry over anything. Or maybe you will with what's going to happen."

George said, "Tomorrow noon we're finished."

"It's good, George."

"It's more than good or I wouldn't be sitting here."

"We go outside tomorrow," said Adam.

"And we get served."

"With the book."

"Everything in the book."

"I suppose," Adam ruminated, "they've got to Gerry and Aubrey already."

"Hell, yes."

"Do you know you're going to lose everything, George?"

"I told you once money alone isn't the whole answer, and that I've been up and down."

"I wish—"

"You don't wish anything," George informed him roughly. "If I had a family, maybe I'd regret it. But if I had a family I wouldn't be in this. We've built some things. We've had a time damn few men can have together. Maybe your buildings couldn't be done in any other way. I'm damned if I know. But I'm satisfied."

"Thanks, George."

"Save it. Do you think they'll put us in jail right away?"

Adam considered that prospect solemnly. He took a pull at the bottle and handed it to George. He gave his grave opinion. "Not right away. That's why I telephoned Taylor, my lawyer, to be here when we go into the world tomorrow. He said he might be able to keep us out for a couple of weeks."

"That will be nice," said George.

Suddenly, in their exhaustion, the situation became so grave that it was funny, and they laughed together for the first time in days. Their laughter rang in the high room, reverberating against the walls, softened only a little by the priceless tapestries that surrounded them. The guard at the door heard it, and stuck his head in to look at them, puzzled, before going out again.

They made a grand exit the next day. They stood before the high, huge, studded brown doors in the arch of the main entrance of the Posada and Adam ordered them to be opened. When they were thrown back they faced a small mob of process servers, lawyers, police, the county sheriff, reporters, photographers who snapped pictures of the scene, a wildly gesticulating Grant, assorted stockholders, and a generous sprinkling of curious onlookers. Papers were thrust in their hands. Questions were shouted at them that Taylor advised not answering, yelling this advice to them. They were pushed and shoved, and called names as they shouldered their way, protected by guards, to the Ghost.

At the administration building they held a short conference with Taylor. "Go home," he told them, "and stay there until you hear from me."

"Or we hear from others?"

"I'll stave them off if I can."

Adam wanted to know, "Have you heard from Michael Sumner?"

"A cable arrived from London this morning. He's going to get here as soon as he can." The lawyer shook his head. "But I don't see much what he can do. Why you drew that money out of the bank and wrote those checks—if you had consulted me—I tell

215

you it borders on a criminal offense to have used that money, it may actually be a criminal offense."

"Make up your mind," George advised.

Adam didn't look at the Posada, rising beside the lake, as he left Roca Faro. He tried not to see the miles of paved and empty streets. In West Palm Beach he dropped George at his construction yard. The two men didn't say anything in parting, even when Adam glanced next door at Artisan Arts and knew that George would be going there to tell Eve what had happened.

On the way to Via Paine Adam told Manuel, who occupied the rear seat of the Rolls, "You'd better find yourself another place."

Manuel flashed white teeth. "No go from you."

"I won't be able to pay your salary much longer."

"Stay long time with you."

Adam gave up. He would find Manuel a place later. He went up to the apartment for a few minutes to see Aubrey. A look of relief crossed the draftsman's face when he saw him. "A lot of rumors are going about," he told Adam. "They said a mob—"

Adam told him, and then asked, "Did they serve you?"

Aubrey's eyes were frightened behind his glasses. "I've got enough summonses and papers to play cards with."

"Use them for a game of solitaire for a while, Aubrey," Adam advised. "Manuel will look after you."

He went to Mona's. By the time he reached there he was so tired he could barely get out of the Ghost. He let himself in with his key. Rock wasn't in evidence. He called Mona's name. There was no answer. Evidently she was out, too.

Catching sight of himself in the hall mirror, he saw how haggard he looked. He needed a shave and his hair hung well over his collar. His duck trousers and white shirt were rumpled and streaked with dirt.

Wearily, he climbed the stairs to the second floor. On the landing he called Mona again, to see if she might be here. There was no reply. He opened the door of her room and went in. It was empty, as well as her dressing room and bath. He stood for a moment, weaving on his feet with fatigue. He strolled to the window and looked out and down into the patio and pool.

At the far end, on the double couch, two figures lay, locked in close embrace. One, he saw at once, was Mona; the abbreviated skirt of her short dress, flung up, showed a part of one slim brown thigh. The second, he saw with a jolt, was Gerry.

While looking for Rock, he had missed Gerry.

This, then, was why she had been so agreeable about staying in Florida. She had used the outside stairway to her house.

Fury replaced his weariness. Along with it a numbness entered his brain. Both carried him as he made his way downstairs. He went almost methodically, as though a thing must be done that had been some time in the making. Quietly, he went out into the patio. In his sneakers he could walk silently. Even with his size and weight he was good at walking like a cat.

He was almost upon them before they became aware that he was there. Then they sprang apart and looked up, startled. Mona stayed where she was, a half smile coming to her face. Gerry jumped to his feet, glancing about, measuring the distance around each side of Adam, who stood directly in front of him.

Gerry didn't try to get away as Adam took the few remaining steps and grabbed him by the front of his coat. He nearly lifted him off his feet with one hand, holding him close to his face while he demanded, "I want to know one thing before I hit you."

Almost equitably, Gerry advised, "Go ahead, Adam. Hit me. I deserve it."

Adam shook him. "Did you start it? Or did she?"

"Hit me."

Adam shook him harder. "Tell me! Which was it?"

"What does it matter, Adam?"

"Tell me, damn you! Tell me how it was!" He shook Gerry until his teeth clicked.

"W-wait," Gerry pleaded.

Adam held on to him by the coat and used one hand to grab his throat. He squeezed.

"She asked me to come here," Gerry gasped. He didn't say any more.

"Go on!"

"I came. She was in swimming. She—"

217

"Tell it!"

"She came out of the water. She didn't—well, she didn't have any bathing suit on."

Adam held him for an instant longer. The impulse to choke him to death was strong. It scared him that he might do it. He flung Gerry aside and turned to Mona.

She rose from the couch as he started for her. She tried to be lofty, but at the look in him, her deep voice took on a higher note. "Adam, there isn't any reason to become physically violent. It isn't done."

He lunged for her.

She eluded him by ducking low and then running. He was after her instantly. She looked back, once, to see him right at her heels. As before, she gained the edge of the pool, and plunged in. Her brief dress, when she came up, seemed to impede her swimming not at all.

Infuriated at her escape, Adam picked up one of the iron chairs. He flung it at her. It nearly hit her. The chair landed in the water only a foot from her, and sank. Frightened, she swam frantically to the center of the pool. Adam picked up other chairs and threw them at her. He flung cushions, an ashtray, a book, anything that lay about. All his missiles fell short. Finally there were no more.

Then his full weariness touched him. He was spent of his fury. Suddenly it didn't matter. Dully, he sat on the edge of the couch. He felt dizzy.

Mona's voice reached him from the pool. "It was your own fault!" she accused. "You weren't here. You did it, not me!"

In her own bared rage she then called indecent things at him. "He was here the night you came back. He was in the dressing room. You nearly caught us."

The full implication of that came to Adam. She had wanted him to stay, with Gerry in the dressing room. There were no bounds to her depravity.

Her angry revelations went on to their dread ultimate. "I've had Rock, too! You were right. I have him when there isn't anything else. I made him be polite to you so you wouldn't know. I've had him since you've been with me."

218

Adam felt sick. He was sure he would be physically ill if he stayed and listened to any more.

He raised his head and looked about. Gerry was gone. He got to his feet. He staggered as he made his way down the side of the pool, while from the water Mona continued to call awful deprecations at him. He became conscious that Dottie was accompanying him. He hadn't noticed the monkey until now.

"Dottie!" Mona called sharply. "Dottie! Come back!"

The monkey stopped following Adam and returned. Adam didn't care. He kept on going, through the house, and out the front door.

He got in the Ghost and sat there behind the wheel for a time, recovering. He had to swallow repeatedly to get over the feeling of nausea.

Automatically he turned the switch and pressed the starter of the car. The motor sounded. He pushed the clutch, put it in gear, and took his foot off the pedal to start raggedly. He forgot to shift again until he was halfway down the block.

He didn't consciously see the walking figure of a man when he passed him. He didn't know it was Gerry until he had gone on nearly another block. Then he brought the Rolls to a stop.

Gerry caught up and stopped on the edge of the road.

They looked at each other.

"You stinking bastard," Adam told him.

"You're right," Gerry said. Even now he tried to be agreeable.

"If she wasn't like that," Adam promised, "I'd kill you."

"I wouldn't blame you."

"Where's your car?"

"It seems I've got creditors. They took it."

Adam stared at him for a long moment before he said, "Get in."

Gerry, after a second of hesitation, came around the car and got in on the left-hand side. For a moment he sat there a little stiffly, withdrawn toward the side, until he saw that Adam did not mean to attack him.

Adam drove on slowly. They didn't say anything for a time.

"You're leaving town," Adam informed him.

"I was thinking somewhat along the same lines myself," Gerry said.

"I don't want you around. I still might kill you."

"Yes, Adam."

"I'll take you north on the Dixie. You can hitchhike from there."

Gerry spread his hands in acceptance of this plan. Adam drove across the bridge and then some miles north to the edge of town, where there were few houses and the open road began. On the way Gerry made one remark. "I think I'll head for Arizona. They say things are going to happen there." He seemed happy at the prospect.

Adam stopped the car. "Get out," he ordered.

Gerry opened the door and got out. He stood in the road looking at Adam as if expecting some kind of a friendly farewell.

Adam told him, "Get going as you came."

"Okay."

Adam turned the car around. Gerry watched him. As the Ghost passed and they were within a few feet of each other, Gerry half raised his arm in a goodbye salute. He smiled tentatively.

Adam ignored him as he drove on.

A DREADFUL HIATUS,

like a poisoned cloud, hung over all of Florida. What had begun with the binder boys in Miami and then spread slowly, to hit violently at Roca Faro because it was so big and had started so late in the boom, now began to be felt generally and on an unprecedented scale. The great binge of the acquisitive spirit was coming to a close, with a Gargantuan headache to be suffered in the morning. People ready to believe anything because someone said it was so now reaped the dread fruit of their folly. The positive assurance that an investment of one hundred dollars would insure a competency for life was not coming true.

A year before, in the spring of 1925, a man pointed to a lot and said, "I bought that once for five hundred dollars; last week I bought it back for thirty-five thousand, and I wouldn't sell it today for fifty." Today he couldn't sell it for the original five hundred. People were afraid even to talk about buying at any price. They didn't know what was going to happen. Most didn't realize fully what had happened and was occurring. Many walked around in a daze. Some mumbled to themselves. A few committed suicide in the hot sun.

No more new people looking for easy riches came into the state. Thousands who wanted to go back to their original homes did not have the means, but were stuck here. Many more thousands left. The gamblers, both with land and dice, began a reverse trek. People, instead of praising the palm-studded land and the blue sky, cursed the place for having sucked away their savings. The Dixie Highway became crowded again. This time the people with washtubs and mattresses strapped to their cars went North. Beaten and whipped, their faces were glum and pinched.

"Florida! Don't talk to me about that place!"

"The sooner I get back home, the better."

"Why, do you know, at one time there I was worth something like thirty thousand dollars. Maybe it was mostly on paper, but I was worth it just the same. Then—pouf! it was gone. Huh? You don't want to talk about it?

"They let me make that deposit—of my good hard-earned money I brought down from the North. I mean good money, not Florida money. And then the next day the bank didn't open its doors. My money is still there and always will be there, I guess. They say they won't pay five cents on the dollar."

"I don't care what you say, some day I'd like to go back and build a little shack on my property there."

"It's Wall Street did it. Wall Street didn't like the money being put in Florida instead of into stocks and bonds. Wall Street did it."

"I'll miss the fishing. I figured I was fixed for life, just like being retired. Now I got to back to work again."

"What's Coolidge going to do about it I'd like to know. The President ought to do something. What's he going to do?"

"I had money in Roca Faro, and I hope they send Paine and those others up for life, and they ought to, the thieving robbers!"

The boom had come full circle. It had boomeranged back on itself. The big bubble had burst with an explosion whose force injured millions of people.

Along with everything else, Eve's business suffered. For a time no one ordered anything from Artisan Arts. She shut down the plant, telling the men she would call them back as soon as she could. She was sure orders could be obtained from places outside of Florida until things returned to some semblance of sanity here. Meanwhile they would take a vacation. The men were glad to accept after the long sessions they had put in turning out the articles for the Posada.

Eve spent her time in her office going over her accounts or working at her potter's wheel. Experimenting with new vases and jars soothed her and made her forget. She had just left her wheel one afternoon and returned to the cottage when Michael came.

"I'm a little late for Roca Faro," he said. "But I couldn't get here any sooner."

"You're going to help them?" Eve asked.

"I must. But I haven't seen them yet. I came to you first."

"Michael . . ."

"Eve, I want to know if things are any different than they were last fall."

"They can't be any different."

"I didn't think you could be sure of that then. That's why I wanted to know."

"I'm sure, Michael—and just as touched and grateful."

"The reason is the same as before?"

She looked away. "The same, Michael."

Three days later he came back to see her again. She had him to dinner after he telephoned. "I've seen them all," he told her. "Taylor, the committee of stockholders, the county and state officials, the judge, the bank or at least the remains of the bank, Adam, George, and Aubrey. Gerry has gone."

"I know."

"Do you know everything that happened?"

"Only what was in the papers and what George told me after he saw Adam. Aubrey has come a few times, and told me more."

"I hope you haven't any idea of what happened at Mona's house."

"I don't want to know all of that."

"She's gone back North. Eve, the others are in a jam, a real jam. But in a way I'm just as responsible. I should never have let them put Gerry in as sales director. Though I don't suppose it would have made any real difference. Except if he hadn't been there they might not have advertised that everything planned could be accepted as a promise to be done and part of the deed for property sold."

"They can be sued for that?"

"They are being sued. But that probably won't stick. It needs only to be stalled off, with the issue confused so much it won't get anywhere. It isn't the immediate thing. The worst is that money they used to finish the Posada. That's being called theft and some other unpretty names."

"Was it, Michael?"

"I don't know. I don't care, and it doesn't much matter. It wasn't

223

meant to be theft. It was done in a good cause—I went down to see the Posada today."

"Michael," she told him, "I received part of that money, a good chunk of it. I've been wondering if I should return it."

"Don't be quixotic. You didn't know about it, and you gave value received. I want you to understand that thoroughly, Eve, before I tell you the next thing."

"You're—?"

"I'm making it good."

She looked at him. "Why?"

"Lots of reasons. As I said, responsibility. Then perhaps I have respect for a beautiful building and the man who conceived it. I like George. I don't want to see Aubrey dragged into it, innocent Aubrey used only as a figurehead. Another reason is that I can afford it."

"Nearly a hundred thousand dollars?"

"Eve, I'm rich. Very rich."

"Still, it's a lot of money."

"Not very much. The one thing I've learned about money is that it isn't any good unless you can do what you want with it."

She stared at him over their dinner table. "Michael," she said, "you're good." She reached out and covered one of his hands with hers.

He looked down at their hands and said, "That's worth all of it."

She took her hand slowly away.

"There's one more thing," he said.

"I think I know what you're going to say, but—"

"Wait. He isn't going to be left with much. Probably without anything. He had other commitments he can't fulfill. And he won't take any more from me than what I'm doing."

"I haven't anything to do with Adam." Eve's face was as set as her voice.

"I think I know how you feel."

"No, you don't, Michael. You can't know how I feel."

He rubbed his short-cropped hair. Softly, he wanted to know, "How is it, Eve?"

"When he walked out—to her—I told him he could never come

224

back. That he was killing something. Part of the thing he killed, Michael, was making it impossible for me to feel anything about you."

He inclined his head. "That I will blame him for. To the end of my days. But the other—Eve, he needs you."

She shook her head. "I don't need him."

He didn't argue it directly. "He isn't crushed so much about being ruined financially, or not being able to finish his dream city, or even losing the Posada. It's what he did to you, and not having you now."

"Did he say that?"

"He said it."

Eve looked away, then back again. "It's too late."

"Let him come to see you, Eve."

"I can't, Michael. There isn't anything left in me for him to see."

"Perhaps you'll find something."

"I don't see how it's possible."

"He won't be any good without you."

"He wasn't very good in what he did to me."

Michael didn't pursue it further. He wanted to know, "Have you been to the Posada?"

"I've only seen what we made here for it," she answered. "I didn't want to—"

"Of course," he said. "But I want to see it again. I didn't have a chance today to spend as much time there as I wanted. I'm going down again tomorrow. Would you like to come along with me?"

She hesitated for an instant before she agreed.

The next day they drove to Roca Faro in the car Michael kept at the Flamingo Club. Eve hadn't been on the open Florida road since the boom burst. She couldn't get over how deserted it appeared. It was like a strange world in which the people had left.

Roca Faro was a desolate place. Most of the additional stores that had started up after the big development were closed. Only one gas station remained open. The place was like a devastated city begun and never completed. The only structures of all the great plans finished were the administration building and the Posada. The largest hotel in the world did not stand on the beach ridge.

No single golf course, to say nothing of three, had been laid out. There was no polo field or civic center or international meet swimming pool. One beginning of a Venetian canal was already run down, with its banks falling in. Adam's Italian castle on an island in the lake with a drawbridge leading to it was not even a mirage.

Michael drove Eve around the miles upon miles of paved streets, complete with all utilities installed, including light standards. Adam's plan, with its curved streets, had been carried out to this extent. But no one trod the sidewalks. They were empty. Creepers from the scrub had already started to reach out tendrils for them, to cover and conquer them, and take over again the place where the jungle had been temporarily driven out. In a few places between the cracks of the paving, grass had begun to grow.

Michael watched her face. "It's awful," she said. "Awful."

He took her to the Posada. Its approach was along two double rows of royal palms. With a pang, Eve remembered how Adam had planned this the first day they arrived in Palm Beach. She looked up at the building.

The structure, sometimes two stories, sometimes three, was built in the rough shape of the symbol £ for an English pound. Red tiled roofs rambled up and down, spreading casually in many directions over a collection of connected buildings so perfectly fashioned that they became one. A square, spare tower rose above all, and about several parapets were to be seen crenelated eaves that made Eve think for a moment she was back in Spain. The Posada looked not new but as though, added to at intervals, it had been built for centuries.

Michael stopped his car before the main entrance. The watchman here greeted him and opened the wicket gate in one side of the great doors. They passed into an entrance hall where Eve trod tiles from Artisan Arts. She had never known they could be laid and used so exquisitely. She gazed at the long stairway leading to the rooms on the second floor of the main housing part of the building, and the delicately decorated balcony above.

They entered, on a different level, the cathedral dining room with its high Gothic arches. Exposed rafters were in the vaulted pecky-cypress ceiling, and from it hung broad circles of lighting fixtures fashioned by the best men of Artisan Arts and so well used here that Eve, in spite of herself, felt proud. She knew enough of architecture to see how dramatically Adam here had supported his vast ceiling on masonry arches that came down to stone corbels tied to buttresses. An immense fireplace occupied one end of the room, while the big chamber, like all the rest, was completely and appropriately furnished.

They went out into an open dance terrace with its dropped terrazo floor. This led, at one side, into the lounge, which was built right out over the lake, with water surrounding it on three sides. At the south, land end of this began a cloister with such beautifully fashioned columns, capitals, and arches that Eve did not at once connect them with herself. Stone steps led down to a broad boat landing.

On the other side of the cloister was a square patio surrounded on two more sides by the buildings they had already seen. In its floor were sunken colored-tile watercourses as in the Alhambra. The fourth side of the patio was composed of an open loggia that made Eve catch her breath. Six slender stone columns nearly two stories high supported a broad sloping tile roof that covered a space imported straight from the Old World and set down here. She could do nothing except stand and take in its beauty.

Michael had said nothing on their tour. Now he told Eve, "This is a gem building of the United States, perhaps of the world. It's as good as most of the best things in Europe. It's one of the most beautiful buildings ever made by anyone in history, in any age or time."

Silently, Eve agreed.

"Maybe you can understand now," Michael went on, "why I'm keeping Adam out of the hoosegow."

She nodded.

"I want him," he continued, "to be free to do this again. Eve, the creative spirit is no excuse for license, especially if it hurts someone else. But once, perhaps, it might be excused in a man who can do this."

Eve walked away from him, still gazing at the loggia. She walked about in it, looking at its tremendous arched doorway leading into the cathedral dining room. The wide doorway blended with long Gothic windows nearby, set two by two in still other arches. She

227

gazed at the columns from the other side, within the loggia, using the patio for a background. At Artisan Arts these had been merely more columns ordered and carried out to specifications. Here they came alive and formed a part of something rare, used so well that in spite of herself it nearly made her weep.

After a time she went back to Michael, joining him again. "What will happen to it?" she asked.

"Oh, somebody will come along to buy it in. It will be seen and used."

"But without him."

"I'm afraid it will have to be that way."

"I never knew it would be like this," she told him. "I understand why you brought me here." She waited a moment before she went on. "And you're right. Not only because he can do this. But because seeing it, I can see him and what he was made for. And I know I can never get away from him."

"Then can I send him to you?"

"I'm going to him, Michael. Will you take me?"

Michael let her off at Via Paine back in Palm Beach and accepted her thanks, telling her he deserved them. Eve leaned toward him and kissed him. It left him silent. Then she was out of the car and going up the familiar steps leading to the tower apartment.

Manuel greeted her first. He grinned broadly and pointed to the second story of the tower. "Up there," he said.

Eve mounted to the living room. Here Aubrey sat, and he jumped up at the sight of her. He was glad to see her, peering through his glasses, giving no greeting, but saying, "He's upstairs."

She kept on going up, gaining the big bedroom. Here Adam lay on the Queen Isabella bed. Her first quick glance at him told her that he was thin, or at least thin for him, and she could not help but resolve, a little vindictively, that this was a good thing.

When he saw her he started up, but got only to the edge of the bed, where he sat, with his legs dangling over it. His stare was utterly and anxiously serious. There were no crinkles around his eyes or mouth. His complexion was no longer florid, but pale.

"I've just come from the Posada," she said.

"Then you've seen my epitaph."

"Are you thinking of using it right away?"

"Why shouldn't I? I've done about everything, been most places."
He looked at her. "And thrown away the best thing I ever had."

"I knew you'd be feeling sorry for yourself."

"Go on. Say the things you've got a right to say."

"I don't want to say them."

"Then why did you come?"

"Take the chip off your shoulder, Adam." She sat down in a chair near the windows.

"Listen," he said, as though he was staving off speaking of something else, "they're taking everything away from me."

"Michael told me."

"I've got to get out of here tomorrow. They're taking all this stuff. Even Queen Isabella."

"What are you going to do?"

"I don't know. Aubrey says he has room in his apartment."

She waited a moment, then said, "There's also room in the cottage at Artisan Arts."

His stare was more of a glare. "Damn it, you said you'd never take me back."

"That was then. This is now."

"You said I was killing something in you."

"You did."

"Then what—?"

"Maybe a spark is alive again, a small spark."

Irrelevantly, as though he found it difficult to keep to the subject, he said, "They're taking the Ghost away from me, too."

"You'll get another. After this is over, people will build houses again. They'll want them from you."

"It would be better to put heavy springs in the flivver."

"No. We're Rolls-Royce people."

He looked hesitant, then said, "Well, we've got a start on one. I took the Lady." He pulled the silver figure from his pocket. "I stole it from myself." He glanced at her to see how she took this. When she smiled, he chuckled. Then he became deadly serious again. He asked, as if everything hung on her answer, "Evie, what can we have now?"

"I'm not sure yet," she answered. "But I'd like to find out."

He stared at her anew. "By God!" he roared, and his voice

choked over the blasphemy that was more like a prayer. "By God!"

"You big lug," she accused.

"You bean pole," he muttered shakily, "you damn wonderful bean pole."